Murder at the Lakeside Library

Also available by Holly Danvers
(Writing as Holly Quinn)

Handcrafted Mysteries

A Crafter Quilts a Crime
A Crafter Hooks a Killer
A Crafter Knits a Clue

Murder at the Lakeside Library

A LAKESIDE LIBRARY MYSTERY

Holly Danvers

CROOKED LANE

NEW YORK

PUBLISHER'S NOTE: The recipes contained in this book are to be followed exactly as written. The publisher is not responsible for your specific health or allergy needs that may require medical supervision. The publisher is not responsible for any adverse reaction to the recipes contained in this book.

Published in the United States by Crooked Lane Books, an imprint of The Quick Brown Fox & Company LLC.

Crooked Lane Books and its logo are trademarks of The Quick Brown Fox & Company LLC.

Library of Congress Catalog-in-Publication data available upon request.

ISBN (hardcover): 978-1-64385-632-2
ISBN (ebook): 978-1-64385-633-9

Cover illustration by Jesse Reisch

Printed in the United States.

www.crookedlanebooks.com

Crooked Lane Books
34 West 27th St., 10th Floor
New York, NY 10001

First Edition: July 2021

10 9 8 7 6 5 4 3 2 1

For those who share a love of the Northwoods and can't wait for the return trip. And to those who've never had the chance to experience Midwest lake livin' at its best, my wish is that this book takes you there, and you never want to leave.

Chapter One

The road ahead spanned like an endless ribbon leading to nowhere. Despite the bone-chilling blast from the air conditioner, Rain Wilmot's hands, clammy with perspiration, slid down the steering wheel. She glanced in the rearview mirror to reassess the backseat of her Ford Explorer, stuffed to the brim with all her worldly possessions. At thirty-two years old, her belongings didn't amount to much. It was as if the ten years of full-time work trapped inside a cubical amounted to absolutely nothing.

It doesn't matter. *Things* don't matter, Rain reminded herself.

The high-rise condo in Milwaukee that she'd shared with her late husband, Max, was now an additional scar on her wounded heart. The rolling wheels of the tires propelled her forward as if she didn't have a choice. She didn't really. The finality of death certainly thrust decisions on a person. She hadn't expected the condo to sell so quickly, but a high-powered insurance broker insisted he couldn't pass up the floor to ceiling windows overlooking the Milwaukee River. She wondered if the new owner would change the pale paint colors in the half-painted nursery.

The warning from her previous boss, Philip, sounded in her head like an alarm bell. "You really ought to wait, Rain. Don't you think you're making a hasty decision? Experts say you should wait at least a year before making any life-altering changes."

Easy for him to say.

Just pulling into the parking lot at Harley Davidson sent her reeling. She didn't need daily reminders at her place of employment of what she'd lost due to twisted chrome and steel.

Rain rolled down the window, needing real air in her lungs, and quickly realized she'd made a terrible error as the humidity filled the car. The smell of musty bonfire embers blew in from a nearby campground. That was a sign that she was getting close. She was almost back to her family's summer cabin—a cabin that stood on one hundred and fifty feet of prime lake frontage on one of the purest bodies of water in the Midwest—Pine Lake. She'd spent every childhood summer swimming and boating on this lake. But she'd neglected to visit for many years now, for any number of paltry excuses. The general busyness of life, work, and love, had all gotten in the way. Besides, Max had never liked coming up north. He was more of an "ocean person" he'd said on more than one occasion. Well, that certainly wasn't an issue now.

The faded blue sign on the side of the road caught Rain's eye and caused her to loosen her grip on the steering wheel. The familiar gold letters that read: *Welcome to Lofty Pines* sent a fresh surge of comfort through her. Only a mile left to go before Rain would round the corner onto Birch Lane and exhale a sigh of relief. She removed her sunglasses and tossed them onto the passenger seat as the dense pines canopied the winding road, shading her view.

Rain's shoulders relaxed and her breath slowed when she spotted the familiar hand-hewn logs with thick white chinking that had stood the test of time. She often thought the rear side of the original cabin resembled a tree house perched high above the lake. The logs had been cut from the very forest that had once covered the clearing. After removing the bark from the towering white pines, her great-grandfather Lorenzo had leveled the timber with his own hands, using an ancient tool from the stone age called an adze. The minor imperfections in the logs were now a glaringly beautiful reminder of his legacy to the house. Of course, upgrades and additions had come with subsequent generations, and now Rain wondered if her great-grandfather would be proud of how much that had changed over the years. The first sight of the family cabin caused her lips to curl into a genuine smile for the first time in a long, long while. She'd made it.

Home.

Rain turned the SUV onto the gravel driveway, kicking stones in her wake. The campfire scent was replaced with the smell of newly cut grass and the sound of a lawnmower humming in the distance. As she stepped from the car, she rolled her neck and stretched her hands high above her head to remove the kink from the four-hour, non-stop drive, and then gathered her straight black hair into a ponytail. Relief came when she lifted the long strands away from her sweaty neck. She thought about applying suntan lotion, but thanks to her mother's Mediterranean heritage, her olive skin rarely burned. Instead, her skin would turn golden by summer's end. The kind of golden tan girls from her teen years used to envy. She dropped the thought of lotion and popped a fresh piece of mint gum into her mouth before ambling down the overgrown slope to greet the waterfront.

Rain recalled how her family had always abandoned the packed car first thing and headed down to the lake before unloading. Seeing the water was proof that making the four-hour journey north had been worth it. She wasn't accustomed to long car rides anymore. In the city, she and Max had spent weekends on their feet. They often walked to nearby eateries, outdoor markets, museums, and professional sporting events. The only car time was the commute she had shared with her husband, driving the twenty-five minutes west to Menomonee Falls and the Harley Davidson corporate office. But that was then, she reminded herself.

The grass was long on the property, and strands of overgrown weeds slapped at her bare ankles—evidence that no one had been around for a few weeks. She'd need to hop on the riding lawnmower soon. But not yet. For now, the lawn could wait. Maybe she'd even splurge and hire landscape help for the summer. But she secretly missed plunging her hands deep into the soil, which surprised her. Maybe she was ready for a change after all.

The calm lake expressed the opposite of her inner turmoil. The clear blue sky and a few puffy clouds painted a reflective picture in the placid water. Peace filled her and, in that moment, Rain knew that she'd made the right decision. She knelt to feel the coolness of the clear water and watched as a crawfish scattered from the ripple. The memory of her grandma cooking the mini-looking lobsters over an open fire sent a fresh smile to her lips. Although she had refused to eat them, it had never stopped her granddad from chasing her around the yard trying to get her to return to the firepit to join the others and taste the meat. She loved her grandfather, Luis, fiercely. He always made her feel like a princess, like she was the most special little girl in the entire world. A rare gift.

Rain's smile faded and she wiped the back of her neck with the cool water and then stood again to stretch, arching her back in an attempt to remove any remaining stiffness from her spine. She stepped onto the solid wooden pier that extended seventy-five feet into the open water and noticed the pontoon boat had been delivered and sat waiting, pulled high out of the water onto the boat lift. She couldn't wait to drop the boat into the water, feel the wind in her hair, the splash of the waves, and the warm sun on her skin. The thought of motoring over to the nearby eatery, Portside

Bar and Grill, reminded her of their tantalizing menu. She wondered if they'd be open dockside for the summer crowd yet. But before she even walked a few feet down the pier, a familiar voice sang out across the water.

"Rain? Is that you?"

Rain turned her head to her right, instantly recognizing someone she hadn't seen in several years. Julia, a long-time neighbor, whose family had also spent lazy summers up north for many generations, greeted her with a wave. Since Julia was only two years older than Rain, the two had hung out quite a bit in their youth and kept up to date on each other's lives through social media. Back in the day, the two were pretty tight.

"Hey, Julia! Are you up for the summer or just a long weekend?" Rain tented her eyes to peer at her neighbor over the sparkling water. She'd forgotten that the reflection often left her blind, and inwardly berated herself for not grabbing her sunglasses from the car.

Rain heard a splash and then the whooshing sound of Julia approaching via the water. Because the thick pines blocked the shoreline between the neighboring properties, Julia must've thought walking through the water was a better option than traipsing barefoot over the prickly, pine-needled ground. As the wind picked up, the scent of fresh pine traveled with her neighbor, transporting Rain back to their childhood.

When Julia arrived, she jutted out a hand that Rain grabbed hold of to help her up on the pier. Julia's long, lean legs were dripping wet, and she wore a white, gauzy coverup over a hot pink swimsuit. Her flaming pink, shoulder-length hair was covered with a large straw-brimmed hat, and she grasped a book tightly in one hand. The pink hair was the result of losing a bet, and Julia was nothing if not true to her word. Rain had seen her admission on Facebook.

The two leaned in for a quick hug and then Julia held her at arm's length.

"I'm so sorry, Rain." Julia's expression fell, and her voice grew thick with empathy. "Did you get my card?"

"Yes. That was very kind of you." Rain wondered if this was how it was going to be all summer. People looking at her, dripping with sympathy. She almost couldn't take it, and she'd literally just arrived. She knew she should feel grateful for the expression of kindness. But Max's death—well, it was complicated. Rain took a step back and steadied herself on the pier.

"Catchin' up on some reading?" Rain asked, nodding her head toward the book in order to dodge the current topic of conversation.

"Oh, this?" Julia lifted her hand. "It's just a mystery novel I picked up about a week ago and haven't had a minute to finish, until now," she chuckled. Julia then turned and pointed in the direction of her pier where a cherry red speedboat was anchored by a rope and bobbed idly in the water. "We just stepped off the boat so Nick could cut the grass before the day got away from us. I thought I'd sneak out to the bench at the end of my pier to read for a few minutes. Which reminds me, when is Willow arriving? Is she right behind you?" Julia craned her neck to view the driveway up toward the hill, and then her eyes returned to Rain, waiting.

"No, Mom's not coming up yet. Just me for a while, I guess." Rain lifted her shoulders in a slight shrug. "Maybe she'll visit for a weekend here or there, possibly over Labor Day weekend, but honestly, I'm not sure. A lot going on this year." She squeezed her bottom lip with her fingers at an attempt to keep it vague and to hold herself back from oversharing. She then redirected the conversation, hoping to abate more inquiry, and besides she was curious. "So, your students won the contest, huh?" Rain gestured to Julia's hot pink hair whose face instantly flushed red to match.

"Yeah, pretty much. This is how teachers motivate teenagers in the classroom nowadays. I promised pink for the entire summer, with updated photos on Instagram to prove I'll keep my word. Not sure I'll be able to go to any social events without being a real standout. It's quite a commitment to keep the promise," Julia added with an eye roll, tugging at the bottom of her shoulder-length hair. "One of my students actually colored it for me. Hashtag beauty school dropout." She grimaced.

"Nah, it's not so bad." Rain cocked her head, taking Julia in again with fresh eyes. "You look great. It suits you," she added with a smile, and meant it. Julia always had a sunny disposition and now her hair only seemed to match her outgoing personality.

"So, Willow's not coming up this year, huh? Labor Day? Wow, that's the end of summer. That's a real problem."

Rain shifted her weight, curled her lip again with her fingers, and waited.

"Well, your mother always opens the cabin library to the public by Memorial Day." Julia gestured a hand in the direction of the cabin, a look of confusion washing over her face. "She never mentioned she wouldn't be coming up this summer. That's really odd . . . our own library director a no show. Now that's definitely weird."

Rain didn't want to get into the ongoing tension within her family, so she remained tight-lipped, but of course she knew about the library Julia was referencing. Her mother's grandfather, Lorenzo, had turned the original cabin structure into a makeshift library when his son, Luis, had built the first of the cabin additions and renovations. There wasn't a library in town, and Lorenzo had always been a strong advocate for literacy. Luis, Rain's maternal grandfather, had even authored a few books in his early days.

The original cabin, built with hand-hewn logs, was considered the only "public library" in Lofty Pines. Of course, that definition of library was used loosely, as it was attached to private property and had direct access to their living quarters. For some reason, it had completely slipped Rain's mind that the library would be open to the public. Had her mother mentioned this in their last phone conversation? As always, she'd been multitasking and packing boxes while her mother was ticking off cabin instructions in her ear.

Julia must've sensed her hesitation, so she plowed forward.

"Oh Rain, I do hope you're planning on opening up the library. The entire community depends on it." Julia's confusion morphed into a frown. "Willow never said a peep. Normally, your mother handles everything, and Marge was supposed to stop by to drop off a few new books this evening. She'd mentioned that when I ran into her at the greenhouse yesterday." Julia said more to herself than to Rain. "Whatever would everyone read up here this summer without your library open? There isn't a bookstore for fifty miles!" Julia said, her voice beginning to show signs of panic as if reality was starting to sink in.

"Ah, I see your point. That's true . . . it sure is a long drive to go and purchase a book, and the internet up here is spotty at best." Rain had planned on a lot of extra reading by the lake herself and had even packed a few novels she herself was itching to dig into. She hadn't had much time to sit and read—until now. Truth be known, it was one of the activities she was most looking forward to.

Julia must've sensed Rain softening as she pushed ahead. "Well, since you haven't been around in a few years, I guess your mother just wanted to fill the time and have some company while she was up here alone. She seemed to really enjoy the visitors to the library." Julia placed her book atop her hat to keep a gust of wind from blowing the hat into the lake. "She reopened the library to the public a few years ago, and it's been pretty busy during the summer months. A real hot spot to be honest."

That was news to Rain. She'd always thought her parents came up north to the cabin and spent time in the North-woods together. Her mother spending time up here alone was something she wasn't aware of. But then again, she hadn't known about a lot of things. If she dared admit it, she'd been living in her own world, with her own problems, dealing with her own "stuff." Besides, her parents were still trying to shelter her from their issues despite her age. Since she was an only child, her parents had always been the very definition of helicopter parents and kept hidden their relationship woes, although Rain wasn't inept at sensing them.

"Oh, um . . . I don't know . . ." Rain stuttered finally.

"Oh, Rain, please? You have to open the library for the summer! There'll be a lot of sad faces otherwise." Julia made a puppy dog face looking for sympathy and then grinned. She'd always had a way of convincing Rain to do just about anything when they were kids. How quickly she'd forgotten. "Your cabin is the only place Lofty Pines Lakers like to hang out." Julia put praying hands together and held them in front of her dramatically.

Lakers . . . Rain hadn't heard that term in years. It was the term folks used for the summer crowd who filled the lakeside cottages and had direct lake access to Pine Lake. The sound of the term sent a knowing smile to her lips which was just enough encouragement for Julia to continue pleading her case.

"You don't know how many nights we sat on your family's deck and talked books and life. The library really brought the community together in a way none of us thought possible. We've really gotten to *know* each other on a deeper scale through the sharing of these books," Julia's words were filled with emotion as she gestured a hand in the direction of the cabin. "The Lakers had some of their best discussions right there. Yep, we sure did!"

Rain turned her head to follow Julia's lead and noticed the wraparound deck now held numerous wooden rocking chairs that overlooked the panoramic view of the lake. When she was a child, only a few Adirondack chairs, a small wooden table, and an outdoor grill, were kept on the wide deck. Now, the place looked like some sort of beach resort, with the additional chairs and stings of outdoor globe lights overhead. When had all this happened? Rain's eyes narrowed to take it all in.

Julia continued, "I hope you don't mind. I had Nick take the chairs out of storage. Your mother gave me a spare key so if I ever made it up here before her, I'd set up the deck. She always encouraged patrons to take a book off the shelf and hang out on the deck to read a chapter or two, to see if it was a book they'd like to continue reading. She'd often bring out lemonade or snacks too. She said she'd met a lot of interesting people that way. Yeah, Willow really got a kick out of it, I think."

Rain breathed deeply, trying to take in this information and halt the screaming thoughts that suddenly cursed through her mind. She had come to the Northwoods to escape reality and relax, not to have people traipsing through her house and her life. Although she loved to read, and had a deep appreciation for the library, sharing anything about her personal life right now was the very thing she'd come here to avoid. She swallowed hard and rubbed the back of her neck with her hand. The last thing she wanted right now was company. And here Julia was basically telling her she'd have patrons hanging out on the deck daily. People to constantly entertain. She could feel the tension rising in her shoulders. Was it too late to back out of the driveway and head back to Milwaukee?

Julia interrupted her thoughts by adding, "Like I said, Marge mentioned she was going to stop by with a few new books she ordered. Your mother put her in charge of ordering them after the fundraiser we held last summer. Now that I think of it, I guess she put Marge in charge of buying the books because she didn't think she was going to make it up here. Marge has become the library's treasurer, and I've helped your mother do most of the cataloging. I guess, I'm now the official reference librarian." Julia's brows came together in a frown. "It's the perfect little library," Julia was pleading now. Practically begging. "It'll be good for you," she encouraged, extending a hand to touch Rain's arm gently. "It's good for you to be around people right now. You know, isolating yourself is never helpful." Julia must've sensed Rain's discomfort because she added, "I'm sorry, I don't mean to push."

Why was it everyone seemed to think they had the perfect solution to my grief?

Rain wasn't happy with her mother, not one bit, for not sharing this information with her ahead of time. Although, her mother knew her well, and had probably realized that if she'd told her ahead of time that she'd have the added responsibility of the library, Rain probably wouldn't have made the trip. She desperately wanted to decline, but guilt pulled her in the opposite direction.

"What do I have to do to get the library ready? I mean, what time does it usually open in the morning?" Rain asked with trepidation. "And what hours of operation is typical— like all day?"

"I'm sure we can work through all of this. Everything is negotiable and up for discussion. Marge was planning on coming this evening to discuss the hours. And a few Laker volunteers were going to join us afterward, to see how they can be of service. That's why I'm so surprised your mother isn't here. She sent out reminders a while ago saying we'd have a quick meeting to set it all up," Julia said eagerly. "I'll go change out of my swimsuit and run to the store for a few snacks. Maybe a bottle of wine? We must have food if we're going to have a meeting. Don't worry, I'll help," Julia added with new excitement to her words. "I'll help you with absolutely *everything*!"

Rain watched as Julia plopped back into the water before she even had a chance to decline.

Chapter Two

Rain began to spin a discussion with her mother in her mind. She wished she could just make a call to voice her frustrations because she certainly didn't remember her mother mentioning opening the library as one of the "deals" they'd made before her coming up north. Luckily for her, Willow was deep in an African rainforest accessing water sources for undeveloped villages, somewhere completely void of cellphone connection. Otherwise she'd be subject to the tongue lashing of her daughter across long-distance phone lines.

Rain wrestled with this as she made her way back toward the SUV. She decided to bring in only the cooler, which was filled to the brim with everything left in her old refrigerator, and an overnight bag she'd packed with a few days' worth of clothes and toiletries, in case she hadn't been in the mood to unpack all her worldly possessions upon arrival. Now she was grateful she'd gone and done that. Maybe she could make a quick escape in the morning and find another place of solitude. But she knew that wasn't really an option—where on earth would she go?

Rain heaved the heavy red Coleman by the handles, wishing now that she'd purchased the one with the wheels, before dropping it beside the back door and wiping the sweat from her brow. She slipped the key into the lock, swung the door wide, and stepped inside.

Rain wondered again why Max had found the cabin claustrophobic as she watched the sun stream into the open concept living room from the wall of windows that reached clear to the center beam of the vaulted ceiling. Unlike the original cabin, the newest addition was built with tightly stacked ten-inch round pine logs, and the room glowed like spun gold when the light hit the oiled wood just right. Yes, no doubt the room was darker at night, devoid of lightly painted drywall. But in her opinion, being surrounded by the natural large round logs felt cozy, as if you were living in the very forest itself.

Instantly, the thought of what Rain's mother had forgotten to mention (or she'd neglected to hear) slipped away and she was transported to the comfort of her youth. As she stepped deeper into the room, she felt welcomed. Years of memories filled every nook and cranny of this space. Family meals, with everyone gathered around the long wooden table, nights of Pictionary or charades with the extended family, including cousins, aunts and uncles, and friends. Her parents dueling a game of cribbage by the floor-to-ceiling stacked stone fireplace. Rain secretly loved when her parents battled through a game of cribbage as it afforded her time to sink her head into her latest mystery novel. There was no television in the otherwise common living room—another reason why Max had hated coming here. Rain's parents insisted the cabin be a place to unplug from all technology, and to encourage reading and creativity. Now that she was older, Rain believed they'd been right. Although she did bring her laptop and a hotspot to tap into the internet when needed. Spotty at best would prove better than nothing. Her parents were wise—but completely unplugging was not exactly realistic for her current lifestyle.

Rain tugged the old worn sheets from the hand-carved wood furniture and tossed them into a ball in the corner. After opening the sliding glass door leading to the outer wrap-around deck, she was happy to see the wind picking up across the lake, sending a warm, fresh breeze into the airless room. She decided to leave the screen door open as the humidity was predicted to dissipate as the day grew long. Sparkles from the sun left a glittering path along the water, and she could hear her childlike voice say to her mother, "Mommy, look! Diamonds!" And her mother answering, "Yes, sweetheart, those are the diamonds you always want to seek." Yet somehow, she'd forgotten. Rain looked down at her left hand and slipped the ring from her finger. She set the white gold band inset with diamonds on a nearby side table and rubbed the indented skin until the ring's mark became almost invisible.

Rain retreated to the back of the house and opened the outside door that led to the library via the catwalk. Before exiting, she reached into the metal box attached to the inner door for the library key and held it in her palm. A flicker of adrenaline surged through her; it'd been years since she'd been inside. Suddenly she was transported back to her youth, daring to escape the adults, and hide in the safety of the fortress.

Rain slipped the key inside the lock. The door opened easily, and she flipped the light switch, causing the deer antler chandelier to shine on the floor-to-ceiling walls of books. An aged wooden ladder was available to help reach the top shelf. The books looked newer now, and there were many more of them than she'd remembered blocking the wide chinking and square logs that her great-grandfather, Lorenzo, had carved with his own two hands.

This part of the original cabin structure had been Rain's favorite hangout as a child. She would escape to the old nine-hundred-fifty-square-feet cabin with her sleeping bag and a flashlight and hide away for hours with her head sunk deep into Nancy Drew. Why hadn't her mother told her about this expansion of the library in any of their recent conversations? Had Rain been so busy and wrapped up in her own life that she'd completely missed something her mother had mentioned? A wash of shame cursed through her for not maintaining a closer bond with her mother.

If she were being honest, she'd have to admit the lack of communication was completely her doing—not her mother's. Their relationship had cooled in the last few years. Ever since the day her mother had seemed to side with Max, a rift had grown between them. Despite numerous apologies, Rain couldn't seem to let it go, and assurances from her mother that she'd never meant to say anything to intentionally hurt her daughter did little to solve the problem. The mere insinuation that his slipup in their marriage was due to Rain's obsession with infertility issues had put an emotional wall between mother and daughter, which had only worsened after Max's death. Shouldn't a mother always side with her hurting child? To this day, the suggestion still stung. Her mother couldn't understand why she was grieving Max and still furious at him at the same time. Rain blew out a breath of frustration. Now was not the time to be rolling this over in her mind. She walked back to the cabin door to reach and return the key to its original spot, for fear she might misplace it in her scattered state.

Although Rain was miffed with her mother for not mentioning that she'd have to open the library to the public, the truth was, having community members stop by would probably prevent her from crawling deeper into her shell and remaining hidden like a hermit. Her mother knew she was an introvert by nature, and if given a choice, she would probably choose to keep her head down, buried in a book, than share time with others. As always, mother seemed to know best. Besides, these were the responsibilities that came along with coming back to the Northwoods. She breathed deep, resolving to change her poor attitude.

Rain wished she had more time to peruse the shelves of newly stocked books and sink deep into the nearby leather chair. She wanted to sink into someone else's story, as she longed to disappear from the hauntings of her own. Her eyes caught sight of something else that was new. Burned wooden signs adorned each shelf, marking the various genres: mystery, romance, non-fiction, local authors, etc. She wondered who the artist was who'd created the signs. Had her parents picked up a new hobby since she'd seen them last? Or had someone from town crafted them and donated to the library?

Something prompted Rain to walk deeper into the room, even though she had a cooler full of food that needed to be unpacked. A nearby shelf on the inside wall held her grandfather Luis's various volumes of fiction. She'd never read his work back in her youth, and had promised herself that by summer's end, she'd read them all. Atop the stack, a letter was addressed to Rain in her mother's handwriting. She opened the envelope to find a small card showing a butterfly resting on a rose. Inside the note read:

Rain,

Don't be upset with me (I can almost sense your hesitation already). Taking on this library will be good for you. You need time with others to heal and, if it's not with me or your dad, hopefully you will meet someone with whom you can share your heart. You'd be surprised at the people who will cross your path, like earthbound angels sent just for you. Don't be afraid of vulnerability, Rain. Everyone has a story, and sometimes opening your heart can help heal others, too. You always pushed your father and I away when you were hurting, even as a child. Please don't isolate yourself this summer, honey. Enjoy your time up north. I'll call you as soon as I'm able to, but I'm sure you won't mind a few weeks' peace without hearing from your meddling mother (Haha!). Until then, take good care.

Ps. I'm sure Julia and Marjorie will help any way they can . . . don't be shy and please ask!

Much LOVE,

Mom 😊

Rain puffed out a breath, sending the hair that had fallen away from her ponytail to wisp in front of her eyes. She brushed it aside with one hand and cracked a smile at her mother's wise but deceptive plan. She set the card aside and noted the leather-bound logbook and pen attached with a ribbon. The official way patrons checked out books was completely out of date. Had her mother still been keeping records this way? The person borrowing the book merely wrote in their name, the date, and the name of the book being checked out. There was no due date, nor accountability to the system. The library was organized in such a casual fashion, Rain immediately decided she'd have to come up with a more formal plan if she was indeed taking over the responsibility of Library Director. Shouldn't there be more accountability? Perhaps not a fine or anything that drastic, but if the library was growing, certainly there needed to be rules. Rain smiled. Organizing and order were her strong suits. And her mother knew that.

The original cabin, which was now the library, did not have a bathroom. To this day, an outhouse still stood on the corner of the property and was in good working condition. Unless the place was packed with people, alcoholic beverages were involved, and all other facilities were otherwise occupied, it was rarely used. However, no one in the family wanted to remove the old relic with the carved moon on the exterior door. There was once, however, a rustic "designated-private-space" located in the far corner of the original cabin if you needed to pee in a pot. Great grandfather had the foresight when he built to know that when it was too cold to venture outdoors and traipse across the lawn to use the outhouse, one did what they had to do. That semiprivate space built with the half-hidden wall, had been transformed into a cozy reading nook within the library and comprised of a seating area plumped with blue-striped pillows embroidered with nautical anchor motifs.

A feeling of regret swept over Rain as she realized she'd missed so many changes by not coming north through her adult years. Why hadn't her parents shared these changes? Did they think she didn't care since she'd neglected visiting for far too long? She glanced at the nearby clock on the wall to see if she could phone her father to chat with him about it, but then realized he was on a plane heading to Japan for his business trip. Or maybe he'd already arrived. In any event, Rain wasn't aware of the time difference and decided she'd try and chat with him later. As usual, they were always trying to catch each other on the fly.

Thoughts of the cooler still sitting by the entrance door and the stifling heat, prompted Rain back to her duties. Reluctantly, she flicked off the light and closed the library door, wishing she had more time to linger. She promised herself, after getting a few things unpacked, that she'd hurry back and spend the evening scrutinizing the shelves. And maybe even haul a sleeping bag in there like she had when she was a child.

Rain retreated over the catwalk back to the newer cabin and stopped at the nearby half-bath. While there, she pulled out a worn bath towel from the bottom drawer beneath the sink that she knew her mother kept hidden for cleaning pur-poses. She brought the towel over to where the cooler lay just outside the door and lifted half of it onto the towel. It was an old trick Max had taught her for when he wasn't around to lift heavy furniture. "Lift smarter not harder," she could almost hear him say. She grabbed hold of the two corners of the towel and pulled until the heavy cooler easily glided across the polished four-inch-wide-plank wood floor. She smiled with gratitude as she slid it with ease toward the stainless French door refrigerator. She popped the lid and emptied the last of her Milwaukee groceries, relieved to note a half bottle of creamer for tomorrow morning's coffee. It would take a while to get used to the fact that the near-est grocery store still closed at five PM sharp. In some ways, spending time up north was like traveling back in time.

Rain wiped her hands on her cutoff jean shorts and then closed the lid with a thud. Despite the long drive and mere snacks along way she wasn't even remotely hungry. She'd lost quite a few pounds since Max's death, so much so, that friends had asked with concern if she was sick. She hoped the summer in Lofty Pines, with less stress, would help her regain her appetite.

Rain walked back to her SUV and plucked the overnight bag from the trunk and then locked it. Her original plan for a hot shower and her PJ's would have to be abandoned for the next few hours. Had Julia mentioned a time when people would arrive? If so, it had completely slipped from Rain's fragmented mind.

While in the bedroom, with clothes strewn across the queen-sized bed, Rain heard her name being called and hurried back toward the screen door, where she noticed Julia with an armful of paper bags.

"I didn't even have to run to town. After he finished cutting the grass, Nick ran the errand for me. He needed to go to town for gas anyway, so he grabbed a few extra items for us while I was in the shower. Isn't that great?" Julia said animatedly as she eagerly brushed past and set the bags atop the white quartz kitchen island.

Rain was running her hand over the smooth finish of the countertop wondering when it, too, had been replaced when she heard Julia say, "You haven't showered yet?" Her eyes traveled from Rain's head to her feet and ended with a frown.

Immediately Rain looked down at her rumpled travel clothing with a coffee stain from breakfast still evident on her tank top. She aimlessly brushed the stain with her hand. "Ah, no. I . . ." she stuttered as she was surprised by Julia's innocent yet transparent words. Then quickly remembered Julia's ability to be blunt and tell it like it is. She knew Julia hadn't meant it out of a spirit of mean heartedness. But, did she really look that bad? I mean, the coffee stain, yeah . . . but . . .? Her mind was so unfocused she hadn't even checked the mirror when she'd stopped inside the bathroom. "Do I have time? To shower and change?"

"Sure, I just thought you might want to freshen up, relax, and get on Laker time." Julia recovered quickly, clearly now embarrassed by her candid remark. "I mean, Marge will be here in less than an hour, but like I promised, Rain, I'll handle everything," she added breathlessly. "Do you want me to set up in the library or out on the deck?" Julia pulled a wine bottle out of the paper bag with one hand and then held it out like an academy award with a wide smile pasted across her sunburned face.

Rain wondered just then what she'd gotten herself into. She didn't drink alcohol very often, only on special occasions. Not because she was an alcoholic, more because it was something she chose to avoid for a healthier lifestyle. The fact that alcohol sometimes caused contention between her parents only strengthened her decision to avoid it. She didn't answer. Instead, she stood like a deer in headlights before Julia swung her in the direction of the bathroom.

"Go ahead and freshen up, and I'll set up a few snacks for us out on the deck," Julia said, making the decision for the both of them.

Rain numbly headed to the bedroom to pluck a fresh outfit off the bed and retreated to the en suite bathroom. The bathroom had been renovated when she was a young girl. A white clawfoot bathtub touched the inside wall, and a separate muted tiled shower took up the entire corner of the room. Despite the heat, she couldn't wait for an opportunity to take a soak in the deep porcelain tub. Maybe after the meeting she could take a bath to release some aching tension, she thought, as she kneaded her shoulder with her hand. But for now, she stepped into the oversized shower and was instantly struck with the memory of Max. On his first visit to the family cabin, Max had been so elated about the size of the shower attached to their room that he'd joined her, and they'd made love like ravenous teenagers. The memory was so vivid, it was as if she was transported back in time, and then just as abruptly, the bubble burst.

Despite the humidity, Rain allowed the hot water and suds to wash over her shoulders to remove the memories and relieve the fresh anxiety that was forming within. She was not in the mood for company. At least not today. If only she'd had a little more time before this all was sprung on her. A day or two to get on her feet and gain her sea legs would've been nice. Hanging out with Julia was one thing, but being re-introduced to so many of the Lakers right off the bat was another. She hadn't seen many of them in years. Part of her wanted to back out and cancel, but it was so last minute, she knew she needed to just put the mask on and deal. She stepped out from the steam-filled room, wrapped herself in an oversized towel, and padded to the bedroom, leaving a path of wet prints on the hardwood floor. She hoped her pair of wrinkled khaki shorts and navy V-neck T-shirt would suffice. She was "up north" after all. No one dressed fancy when they were hanging out in the Northwoods.

Rain combed the tangles from her hair to let it air-dry naturally, leaving wet patches on the shoulders of her clean T-shirt. She kept the hair tie on her wrist in case, once dry, she might want to refasten her hair into a ponytail. She rarely wore makeup and luckily didn't really need it. She'd inherited her mother's bronze skin, dark eyes, and long, black hair, and her father's height and sharp cheekbones. On several occasions, complete strangers had the nerve to approach her on the street to suggest she'd make the perfect model. But Rain had less than zero interest in modeling and thought the idea slightly funny and completely absurd. She decided a hint of mascara might take the focus off her wrinkled outfit, though, so she coated her lashes carefully before abandoning the make-up.

The sun was sinking in the western sky, making Rain feel that Julia's idea of meeting on the wraparound deck would be a good one. Wisconsin was known for picturesque sunsets and tonight they'd have the perfect view. The water was already turning an iridescent purple color, and the clouds a cotton candy pink. The image in front of her was stunningly beautiful.

"Hey there! Feel better?" Julia asked as she opened the screen door leading to the outer deck.

She didn't. Anxiety was growing like a mountain within her, but she replied, "Yep, just what I needed," and forced a smile.

Rain noticed a few bottles of both red and white wine had been placed inside the icebox. She remembered the standalone icebox from her youth. It was a large, carved wooden box, held up by antique table legs and lined in sheet metal that her dad had made a few years after her wedding to Max. Julia must've known where it had been stored and pulled it out. Next to the icebox, a large glass plate with a myriad of flavored cheese curds along with crackers, cookies, and a few wine glasses and plates were laid out neatly on a side table. Julia had even brought over napkins in the shape of sunflowers.

"Wow, thank you for doing all of this. I'm afraid it's going to take me a few days to get reacclimated and back on Laker time."

"Of course! I told you I'd handle it." Julia grinned.

"You certainly did. Everything looks lovely."

"It's still surprisingly warm out here!" Julia said as she fanned herself with her hand. "Or maybe it's my sunburn causing me to feel slightly overheated," she added and then reached for a cheese curd to pop into her mouth. "Nick and I were out in the boat all morning, and I guess I didn't reapply enough sunscreen. First official burn of the summer!"

It was then that Rain noticed that Julia was wearing a sundress. She subconsciously looked down at her wrinkled garb and frowned. Julia must've noticed her predicament as she reached out to embrace her and then held her arms out so their eyes would meet. "You look terrific. By the way, I'm a bit jealous—you haven't aged a bit! And thank you again for agreeing to do this on such short notice. The Lakers are really going to be happy to know that you've agreed to open the library." Julia beamed.

Had she agreed? Or had she been kinda railroaded into it?

Footsteps on the stairs leading to the deck caused them to turn in the direction of the sound. An older woman with a large-brimmed straw hat that covered her silver hair was cautiously climbing the staircase while navigating a leash attached to a cocker spaniel. Despite the heat, she was wearing a navy sweater taut at the wrists, covering her slender arms. A pale aqua silk scarf, which complimented her sapphire eyes, covered her neck.

Julia gestured to the older woman. "Here's someone special I'd like you to meet, Rain. This is Marjorie. She was a huge fan of your grandfather Luis's work. And this little cutie here is Rex." Julia bent down to greet the dog, and Rain couldn't help but follow suit. It looked as if the pup was smiling as he danced happily at their feet.

Marjorie beamed a smile. "Rain, so happy to finally see you. Look at you, you're the spitting image of your mother—you're all grown up now. I haven't set eyes on you since you were a wee little thing." She held her hand about three feet off the ground to demonstrate. The fact that Marjorie didn't have to bend down even a bit, made her short stature even more apparent. "Please call me Marge." Her eyes shone with deep warmth, and instantly Rain felt herself relax.

"Nice to meet you," Rain said as she unwrapped the hair tie from her wrist and quickly pulled her hair into a knot at the base of her neck. Just looking at the older woman, dressed in a sweater, made her feel hot.

"Do you mind if I unleash my dog? Otherwise he's going to trip me for sure."

Rain glanced at the dog circling the newcomer's legs and threating to do just that. "Not at all," she answered with a smile as she leaned to pet him once more on the head, before taking the leash and unclipping him.

"Can you two excuse me for a second? I'm going to get a bowl of water for Rex; it's so hot out here." Julia moved toward the screen door and stepped inside. Obviously, it was common for Rex to tag along. Rain added a mental note to remember to have dog treats available for the next time the pair visited.

"Tell me again the origin of your name. I just love it. Such a beautiful name . . . Rain. I've heard it before, but the dementia's kicking in, and I'm afraid I can't recall." Marge chuckled and absently rubbed the back of her hand in a circular motion, as if her translucent, liver spotted hands held the answer.

"My mother told me she gave me the name Rain because the word means "life giving," and she believed that would be my calling. And of course, as you probably know, my mother's always been a bit of an earth child." She then stopped herself and attempted to steer the conversation in a new direction. "Did you personally know my grandfather, Luis? Or are you just familiar with his writing?"

"Oh yes, dear." Marge smiled wide, showing coffee stained teeth. "I knew his father, too; your great-grandfather, Lorenzo, was a tough old bird. Started this entire community with his own two hands, that one did," she said with a sharp nod of her head. And then she reached out to touch Rain's arm with her hand. Regardless of the heat, her hand was cool to the touch.

Marge continued on, "Your grandfather, Luis, and I grew up on this here lake together. I spent every summer with Luis until he went away to university. And then well, he surpassed us all. Especially after publication," she added with a hint of wistfulness. "We were common folk you know . . ." She said it teasingly with a wink, but Rain grabbed the undercurrent.

Marge's comment made Rain wonder if her grandfather, Luis, had become a bit of a snob after the success of his writings. Or if those in the humble blue-collared community placed him on a pedestal as they found he'd grown into somewhat of a local celebrity. She'd heard that gossip but had never been privy to a firsthand account.

"So, you've been coming up here a long time. I'm surprised, and a tad embarrassed, that I don't remember you." Rain admitted.

"Oh, you were so young, dear. I can understand why you wouldn't remember." Marge swatted a hand into the air as if to dismiss the nonsense and then smiled. "I abandoned Lofty Pines for many years to retire down in Florida after my husband's passing, but a few years ago, I felt a magnetic pull to return. Now, I'm back on Pine Lake during the warm summer months. In fact, I just returned from Florida this week, it's such a comfort to be back."

"The magnetic pull . . . I totally understand; I've had the same feeling. I guess that's why I'm here, too," Rain shrugged. Instead of bringing up her loss of Max, she changed the subject. "I bet you've seen a lot of changes to Pine Lake over the years."

"Yes indeed. I certainly have, dear. I've seen the cottages popping up one by one. Row boats replaced by big engine motorboats; acreages split—except of course . . . yours." Marge gazed past her to look over the deck railing as if to count the acres still held by Rain's family. "So many changes, over the years," Marge continued wistfully. "However, it's heartwarming to know so many families have kept the tradition of coming up here alive. Unfortunately, I'm one of the last in my generation." She blinked back watery eyes. "It's been so nice of your mother to open up the library to the community again. It's been wonderful to reconnect with other Lakers that I had lost touch with when I was down in Florida. I've enjoyed helping your mother so much. Where is Willow by the way? Is she here? I've yet to see her." Her eyes darted around the deck, seeking the elusive Willow.

"Maybe later in the summer."

"Well, you're kidding! Where is she? She's never missed a summer up here. Willow's been coming up to the North-woods since she was a baby!" Marge's eyes narrowed and she held a hand to her shocked face. "Please tell me she hasn't fallen ill?"

"Oh no, it's nothing like that. She's healthy and fit as a fiddle. In fact, she's volunteering this summer, working with Projects Abroad in Africa. They help dig reliable sources of water for developing countries," Rain explained. She failed to mention that her mother was traveling worlds away from her father on their so-called mini break. That was up to them alone to share.

"And Stuart," Marge's eyes narrowed. "Where is he?"

"My father's working in Japan for a few weeks." Rain smiled. "He refuses to retire, despite his age. I'm not sure he'll make it here this summer either." She lifted her shoulders in a slight shrug.

Marge mirrored her smile regarding his refusal to retire and then her smile faded into a deep frown. "Oh dear, I had so much to catch up with them about. I'm running out of time you know. This old bird isn't getting any younger." She let the comment hang in the air without elaborating further. Rain didn't know what Marge could possibly want to discuss with her parents, but then again, she hadn't been up north in a long time. It made her feel like she really didn't know a lot of the history behind her family legacy in Lofty Pines. In her youth, she hadn't paid much attention. Not at all. She was too busy flitting around Pine Lake back then, enjoying watersports and all the summer benefits, instead of caring about family heritage.

"Is there something I can help you with? I can pass on a message to one of them if you'd like."

"No, dear. This is something Luis would have wanted me to talk to your mother about firsthand," Marge said with a firm nod of her head. "I guess it can wait," she added with a disappointed sigh.

Julia returned, and Rex immediately lapped up the water as soon as she set down the stainless bowl.

"Shall I go retrieve the new books from your car?" Julia lay a gentle hand on Marge's shoulder, and the older woman turned to her and smiled.

"I can help. I know I'm old, but I still have some strong guns." Marge lifted her arm and attempted to show her muscles, causing them all to chuckle. "I actually loaded them in the trunk myself. One by one." She lifted her chin in defiance and then wagged a finger at them. "It's good exercise, you know."

"No worries, Julia and I can go and fetch them," Rain encouraged. "Have a seat and relax. Julia has outdone herself with wine and snacks. Please help yourself. We'll be back before you know it." Rain gestured toward the sky. "Besides, it looks like we're about to view a gorgeous sunset. It looks like a painting."

The older woman acquiesced and handed Rain her car keys. Julia followed Rain toward the deck stairs, and, unfortunately, Rex followed as well. The cocker spaniel slipped past his owner and bounded down the stairs before anyone had a chance to leash him.

"Get back here, Rex!" Marge called out as she snagged the abandoned leash off a nearby chair. But the dog didn't obey. Instead he galloped off, chasing a squirrel toward the distant outhouse.

Rain and Julia continued down the stairs but then stopped at the bottom, knowing the dog had already far outrun them. Rain hoped, for his owner's sake, Rex didn't have a history of disappearing. Marge moved quickly down the stairs and passed them, shaking her head in frustration and setting out in the direction of her dog. "I'll handle this. I'll meet you back on the deck," Marge directed before hollering, "Rex. Rexy! Get back here!" The older woman slapped the leather leash against her palm, making a snapping sound.

The two agreed that Marge probably had a better chance of having the dog obey without the three of them trying to chase after him. They heeded Marge's instructions and walked over to her car. Rain was growing increasingly excited to see what kinds of books had been purchased to add to the library collection. Maybe there would be a new bestseller that she could sink into.

Julia and Rain were bent over the trunk of Marge's car, collecting armfuls of books when they heard a blood-curdling scream.

Chapter Three

At the sound of the scream, Rain knocked her head against the inside of the open trunk. She didn't feel the pain, though, which was the least of her worries. Instead, her eyes met Julia's—open as wide as her own.

"Did you hear that? Of course you did, your eyes are like saucers." Rain's heart skipped a beat. "Where did that come from? Do you think it was Marge screaming?"

"It sure sounded like it." Julia's face filled with alarm and she held her position as if afraid to move a muscle or anticipating another sound.

The two dropped their stacks of books back into the trunk. Rain immediately turned in the direction from which she thought the scream had originated. She hoped Marge hadn't tripped over a fallen branch or a rock to reach her dog. Had she broken a hip? The scream had sounded as if it had come from the direction of the outhouse, so she dashed a few feet in front of Julia and led the way across the rear yard.

Rain's stomach lurched when the two came upon the scene. The vision in front of her was unimaginable. Marge was standing over a body that lay lifeless on the ground in a contorted position. Rex was sniffing around the unidentified man's head. The victim's skin held a bluish tint, and his long fingers were stretched out in an odd stiff position.

Rain's hands rose to her cheeks in horror and she let out a high-pitched squeal and Julia mirrored the sound before clutching her hands to her own heart.

"Oh, noooo!" Rain finally stuttered. "Who . . . who . . . who . . . is this man?" Her mouth felt suddenly dry as if had been stuffed with a hundred white cotton balls. She struggled to catch her breath, and her hand rose to her throat and rubbed it vigorously.

"Thornton Hughes," Julia answered with a sad shake of her head. She then let out a long slow whistling noise.

"Thornton Hughes?" Rain repeated the name but it had no effect on her. She'd never heard the name before. Who was he? And what on earth was he doing lying lifeless on her property?

"What is he doing here?" Rain finally voiced her thoughts aloud as she flung a finger in the direction of the body.

Marge plucked an old-fashioned flip phone from her khaki slacks pocket. "I don't know, dear, but you'd better call the police. It may be a little late for an ambulance," she added with a somber voice. Her shaky fingers almost dropped the phone before Rain reached out and caught it with one hand.

Rain mechanically dialed the number and then numbly shared the horrific news with the 911 dispatch operator and gave the address. "No," she said absently to the operator. She didn't think she needed directions on how to administer CPR. Marge was right. It was much too late for that. She flipped the phone closed before handing it back to Marge.

"Don't touch a thing. We don't want to disrupt anything in this area." Julia motioned them to back away from the man and assembled them to wait patiently as if she was handling children at a school fire drill. Only this wasn't a drill, it was a dead body.

Rain looked at her neighbor wide-eyed. "How are you so composed? Personally, I think I'm in complete shock." Rain could feel her eyes grow even wider. Her heart thumped so hard and erratically in her chest she felt as if she'd just run the Boston Marathon. "Shouldn't we at least check for a pulse or something? Maybe I shouldn't have hung up with 911 so quickly." She chewed at her lip nervously.

"No, dear. It's certainly too late for that. This man is headed for the bone yard sooner than this old yoke." Marge flung a hand in the direction of the victim and then her face contorted as if she'd been sucking something sour in her mouth. Rain wondered if the older woman might soon be sick. She could definitely relate.

"My brother Jace is a police officer, and he recently transferred up here," Julia said. "Hopefully, he'll be one of the first ones on the scene." It didn't go unnoticed that she was nervously wringing her hands, then began pacing back and forth as if to shield them from sight of the victim.

The three huddled around each other, each lost in their own thoughts, unable to speak of the tragedy. They stood rooted, like a copse of trees, devoid of wind. They darted nervous glances between themselves as if they didn't know what to do next.

Before long, the sound of wailing sirens interrupted the deafening silence. Rain centered herself between Julia and Marge, looped both by the arm, and led the three to greet the emergency personnel. Marge's dog was still not attached to his leash but seemed to sense the severity of the situation and followed closely on their heels.

A police cruiser and an ambulance drove in hot, kicking up a cloud of dirt and dust before coming to an immediate halt.

"Julia!"

"Oh, what a relief, your brother's here," Marge sighed heavily and patted Julia on the arm.

Julia's brother had leapt from the patrol car and ran toward them, his eyes eager and expectant. "You okay?" He touched his sister's arm tenderly and it struck Rain suddenly what it would have been like to grow up with a sibling's concern. She'd forgotten Julia's older brother was a police officer. She'd also not heard the news that he'd transferred up to the Northwoods until Julia had mentioned it. She understood why he would make that choice, though. Those raised with idyllic summers on Pine Lake, often fantasized about living in Lofty Pines year-round. As kids, they'd all believed it would be like year-round summer vacation.

"Yeah, yeah, we're holding it together," Julia said. Her eyes rushed nervously between them for confirmation.

Jace tipped his police cap toward Marge as a sign of greeting and respect. Although Marge's pallor was turning somewhat green, she kept quiet.

"Jace, you remember Rain?" Julia turned her attention toward Rain, who looked up at Julia's brother. He towered over her, which was saying something, because she stood five foot nine. His blond hair was cut short beneath his police cap, as if he had just started military training. His hazel eyes looked down on her with concern and then morphed to surprise after he'd looked her over.

"You've grown up."

Rain shrugged and smiled weakly. "I guess I have." She gestured a hand toward him. "As have you. Despite the circumstances, it's really good to see you, Jace."

"You too, Rain."

Soon after their reacquaintance, the officer's demeanor switched back to the business at hand. "So, you three are the only ones here that witnessed this?" Jace's eyes darted toward his sister, but Rain was the one to answer.

"No, we didn't witness *anything*. Marge's the one who actually . . ." Rain looked over her shoulder to prompt Marge to explain but noticed beads of sweat forming on the older woman's forehead. It looked as if she might vomit.

Rain grabbed ahold of Marge's elbow to steady her. "We need to get you to the ambulance."

"I'll only go . . . if you . . . leash my dog," Marge said, her words now coming out in short pants.

Rain removed the leash from Marge's grasp and clicked it onto Rex. A female officer who must've accompanied Jace rushed over to join them. Her blond hair was cut short in a blunt haircut that hugged the base of her neck. She wore the uniform well, and her tan arms were solid, as if she could carry Marge over her shoulder, if need be.

"Wyatt." Jace nodded in the officer's direction. "Please escort Marge over to the ambulance. Make sure she's okay before we barrage her with questions and take a formal statement." Jace pointed toward the older woman and the young female officer took the cue.

"You got it." The young officer untucked her thumbs from her thick police belt and accepted the leash from Rain.

"You're gonna be okay, Marjorie, the paramedics will take good care of you." Jace regarded the older woman before Wyatt escorted Marge away from them.

Jace turned his attention back to Rain and Julia. "All right, you two, take me to the scene," he commanded.

"This way," Rain summoned as she took the lead and turned to sprint back toward the direction of the outhouse. Julia and her brother followed close behind, until they reached the body. "There," Rain said, "wedged between the outhouse and the tree."

Jace placed his hands on his hips seemingly to take it all in. Rain noted by his demeanor that the officer wouldn't need a medical examiner to tell him that Thornton Hughes had been the victim of a brutal murder.

Rain hadn't seen a corpse since the day she'd gone to the morgue to identified Max. Maybe this wasn't such a good idea, seeing Thornton again. Her mind almost couldn't comprehend the scene. It was like an out-of-body experience. This time she noticed more details, though, such as the blood pooled around the man's head. His narrow nose seemed too small for his slender face, and Rain immediately felt remorse for thinking that at a time like this. He was wearing a dark suit, which was an unusual attire for the Northwoods, and the top of his dress shirt was popped open. She wondered where he was going all dressed to the nines in this neighborhood. Especially given the heat. Not a common attire for *Lakers*. Not at all.

Jace bent down to take a closer look. "Rigor mortis hasn't fully set in." Rain watched in horror as he reached to touch the body. "His arm is cool, but torso warm. This had to be recent, at least within the last few hours. Have you been here all day?" Jace turned to face her.

"No, I just got in a few hours ago. But Julia and I were down by the water . . . and then I was inside getting ready for the library meeting . . ." Her thoughts flip flopped as she tried to recall and calculate how the events of the afternoon had unfolded. If this was recent, it could've happened after she'd arrived. She possibly could've saved him!

43

At the very least, called for help sooner! Rain shuddered at the thought.

Jace stood for a moment, then walked around to the other side of the body where the victim's legs were wedged between the tree and the outhouse. "I'll be anxious to hear from the coroner what the postmortem report states about the exact time of death. I'm not sure if this guy actually collapsed here or his body was dumped here." Jace mumbled under his breath. "Otherwise, why would he be located on the far side of the yard?" He placed his hands back on his hips. "I'm going to have to call the chief to come join us."

"Don't you have a detective you can call?" Rain asked.

"In Lofty Pines?" he looked at her and smirked in amusement. "We're a small unit up here. So, to answer your question, no, we don't have a local detective. It's going to take me a bit." Jace then radioed in and asked dispatch to send out the chief.

Jace turned his attention back to Rain. "Do you know the victim?"

"No," Rain vigorously shook her head and then turned to Julia. "I've never seen him in my life. Do you know anything about who this guy Thornton is? He's not a Laker, is he?" Rain asked as she pointed a shaky finger to the body.

"No. But your mother does—and pretty well I might add."

Chapter Four

My mother knew *him??*

Rain's face grew hot, and it wasn't from the stifling heat of the afternoon. She barely felt the upswing of the recent breeze tickling her arms. She did, however, notice the flutter of the leaves in the nearby maple trees. She looked above, searching for answers to her life, which suddenly evaded her. Nothing was making a hill of beans' worth of sense. Her mind was barely able to comprehend it all, as thoughts shot through her brain rapid-fire.

Jace encouraged them to step away from the body of Thornton Hughes, shooing them with his hands. "I'm gonna need you two to back up here a bit. I need to get the crime tape up before we contaminate the scene. Can you give me a hand, and back up please?" Julia's brother encouraged them to continue to move farther back. "Why don't you two head out by the ambulance with Marjorie. I'll come and grab you when the chief arrives or if we have any further questions. And thank you," he added with a curt nod.

But it was as if neither of them could take their eyes off the scene. As if what was in front of them still wasn't real. Julia finally looped her arm through Rain's and turned them to face the opposite direction. She led Rain beneath a nearby shade tree, which was far enough from the crime scene tape but not close enough to any of the growing gathering of emergency personnel to overhear their conversation. Rain assumed Julia wanted to catch her bearings before rejoining Marge. They needed to be strong for the older woman. But Rain was relieved because it also gave her a private chance to ask a question that was burning in her mind.

"Can you explain what you meant back there? About my mother knowing that man, *pretty well*?" Rain was curious and afraid at the same time, as she jutted a thumb in the direction of the crime scene. She turned her head and noticed Jace had already surrounded a large portion of the area with yellow crime scene tape. She closed her eyes for a brief second and took a deep breath to settle herself. She could feel sweat beading across her forehead and down her temples, as she wiped it away with the back of her left forearm.

Julia lowered her voice to a whisper and leaned in before speaking. "I think they were awfully close . . . your mother . . . and Thornton."

"What?" Rain's heart began to beat erratically. Nothing had prepared her for what Julia's tone might be implying. Despite her fears, she needed to push for confirmation. "Can you define . . . *awfully close.*"

Julia lay a comforting hand on her arm as if to sooth a small child. "Oh, Rain. I don't want to hurt you. With everything you've been going through lately, I hate to be the one to pile this on you, too."

"Julia, I need to know . . . I have to know . . ." Rain's voice trailed off.

Julia's brow furrowed before she sucked in a breath, and then the words tumbled like loose pebbles from her mouth. "Word on the street is that your mother and Thornton were maybe . . . having a fling. I'm so sorry, I really didn't want to be the one to tell you." Concern riddled Julia's face and she paused and searched Rain's face for a reaction.

She had none.

Rain refused to share with Julia the conflict and undercurrents rippling through her parents' marriage; it wasn't her place to share. But her mind pinballed back and forth with the realization that this man . . . this *victim* . . . could have something to do with her parents' relationship issues. And now his dead body had been found on the family compound. Rain inhaled and let the air out slowly, as if blowing up a balloon. She kept her face as stoic as possible because it looked as though Julia was waiting for her to explode or totally flip out. Honestly, if she wasn't in complete shock from everything that was unfolding, she probably would've completely lost it.

Was this the real reason why her mother had made alternative plans for the summer? Was she miles away, avoiding Thornton Hughes?

"You okay?" Julia asked hesitantly.

"It's a lot to take in," Rain admitted, moistening her lips.

"I imagine."

After a few moments of silence between them Rain asked, "Have you ever seen them together? I mean *to-geth-er* . . . together?" Rain clasped her hands and intertwined her fingers as if to animate how close they'd possibly been, and then dropped her hands awkwardly to her lap. The mere thought of her mother with another man sickened her.

Julia bit at her thumbnail and seemed to weigh her words before saying anything. "Only once. Out on the deck." She nodded in the direction of the wraparound deck and Rain's eyes followed, as if she was witnessing for herself this sordid affair before her very eyes. She shuddered.

Rain turned back to face Julia. She had to know. "And what exactly did you witness? I mean . . . specifically." She cleared her throat, suddenly desperate for a drink of water. "Did you actually *see* anything physical happen between them?"

"Oh God, no!" Julia's face contorted as if she'd seen something even more horrific than the body of Thornton Hughes behind the outhouse. "No, nothing like that. Just a lot of laughter between them. And to be honest, it was nice hearing Willow's laughter floating all the way to our door," Julia admitted. "Refreshing actually. Honestly, I didn't observe anything physical between them. It was more the chatter around town—people have nothing better to do than to talk. His car was parked in your driveway on numerous occasions. And apparently, Thornton wasn't much of a reader, so his visits weren't for the library, if you know what I mean. Unfortunately, people talk," she shrugged and held up her hands defensively.

Well, at least that was a relief. The idea that a next-door neighbor could have personally witnessed her mother tangled up in some physical intimacy almost made her gag. Although the comment about her mother's laughter sounding refreshing made her wonder if Julia, too, had overheard her parents arguing at one time. She dared not ask.

Rain looked up to see Wyatt talking intently with Marge outside the ambulance. She wondered how old the young officer was, and if she'd ever handled a murder scene before. In Rain's opinion, Wyatt looked fresh out of the police academy. And to her knowledge, not much happened around Pine Lake. Perhaps a minor break in of a vacant property . . . but an actual *murder*? Was this even murder? Had the victim injured his head in some other way and, without anyone near to help, passed away? Now she wished she'd looked more closely at his injured head.

Meanwhile, Marge was running her hands up and down her arms as if she was cold, which Rain thought impossible as the sweat was trickling down her own spine.

"We'd better go," Rain said, turning her attention back to Julia, who was now studying her hands and then picking at a hangnail on her finger.

"Yeah." Julia dropped her hands to her lap. "You're probably right." After a pause she added, "I'm really sorry, Rain.

I want you to know in defense of your mother, I never said a thing to anyone. It wasn't me who spread that kind of gossip around town."

"I know."

Rain stood and wiped the soil from her seat and remained silent. She knew why Julia was expressing sympathy, but she didn't want to talk about it anymore. Besides it wasn't Julia's fault; Julia was only the messenger.

Rain walked back to join those gathered around the ambulance with Julia following closely at her heels. She was grateful for a chance to break out of the current conversation. She felt cornered and needed time to process—let this new reality sink in. Her mother *knew* the damage it had caused Rain's marriage when she'd discovered that Max had been unfaithful. Her mother was there when Rain had wept! Was it possible for her mother to have had an affair, too? Did her father know? Had he met Thornton on his visits up north?

When they reached the back of the ambulance, Rain noticed Marge leaning against the automobile with Rex standing next to her. The older woman bent to stroke her hand down the back of the dog's head. She looked up when they approached and smiled weakly.

"Feeling better?" Rain asked.

The older woman nodded. "Yes. I'm fine. The old ticker's not ready to give out just yet," she added with a chuckle. "What a shock though, eh?" She shook her downcast head. "I just can't believe a man died out there."

"It sure is a shock," Rain agreed.

"Where's the paramedic?" Julia asked, glancing over each shoulder, seeking out the elusive emergency personnel.

"I sent him away." Marge brushed their concern aside. "Truly, I'm fine. I sent him over with the other one to check on Thornton. Although I think we all know it's much too late . . ." The older woman's words hung in the air like a dark cloud. The reality of death settling in on all of them.

"Rain!"

She heard her name being called from the far distance and excused herself before locking eyes with Jace, who was summoning her with his hand. When she finally arrived at the officer's side, a look of confusion fluttered across her face.

"Rain, I think I may have found something. I need you to come and take a look."

Chapter Five

Jace led Rain by the elbow back in the direction of the crime scene. The officer must've sensed her slight apprehension because he said, "I hope you don't mind walking back here for a sec. Honestly, if it wasn't important, I'd let it slide, but I need to show you something. I'm not sure if it means anything, but I can't leave the scene until I confirm."

"I understand," Rain said as she tentatively followed.

His pace was swift, and Rain hurried to keep up with his stride.

The paramedics passed them on their way and asked, "Did you call the coroner?"

Jace confirmed with a decisive nod of his head.

Upon arrival, Jace lifted the crime scene tape and they both ducked beneath it. He turned to Rain and asked, "Does that look familiar?" He then pointed to a row of bushes against the stacked rock wall that defined property lines.

Rain looked down at the ground a few feet from Thornton's lifeless body to see what Jace was referring to but didn't initially understand what she was looking at.

In order to make it perfectly clear, Jace reached out and held back the limbs from a forsythia bush. A book lay fanned out, the pages slightly flipping in the soft breeze. A navy- and- white-striped necktie was tucked between the pages. The necktie looked expensive, like it had been purchased at an exclusive boutique. She couldn't fathom anyone purchasing it in Lofty Pines, as no such shops existed.

"No clue." Rain shrugged. "I have no idea what a book is doing there. Or whose necktie is hanging out of it. I've heard of strange bookmarks in the past, but never a tie. It's a little big for the job; a slip of paper would've done better," she rolled her eyes and a disbelieving laugh nervously fell from her mouth. She realized the seriousness of the situation was anything but funny, but after the initial shock of finding a body on her property, she didn't know quite how to handle herself. It was as if to handle the gravity of the situation, her mind made it feel as though she wasn't witnessing anything real. Rather, it was as if a movie was playing out in front of them. A movie she'd be happy to switch off.

"So, you're confirming you didn't take a book along for a visit to the outhouse today? Or you don't know anyone else who had been out here recently to use the facilities?"

This question made her laugh aloud. The nervous tension was finally getting the best of her. "No. Despite the outhouse still being in working order, I prefer to stick with indoor plumbing." Rain said, flinging a hand toward the log cabin. "Besides, I would have no reason to walk behind the structure. Nor, in my opinion, would anyone else— including your victim." She nodded her head in the direction of Thornton and shuddered at the thought of this sickening act happening so close to home. It was unimaginable.

Jace pulled a set of rubber gloves from a compartment on his thick police belt. He reached for the book and held it in his hands. The minute he flipped open the front cover, Rain recognized the familiar stamp of her family emblem, which caused her to gasp aloud. One thing she knew about the generational library; every book was coded with a stamp of two crossed American Eagle feathers inside the cover. And the stamp was now glaring back at her.

Rain stumbled backward, unable to comprehend this new revelation. The library hadn't been open for months. So how did the book get there? After Jace closed the book, she noticed the author's name stamped on the front cover: Luis Russo. The book he'd found beneath the bush, a few feet away from Thornton Hughes's lifeless body, wasn't just any random novel; it had been written by her own grandfather.

This was one novel that didn't belong outdoors—never mind behind the outhouse. It belonged on the special shelf in the local author section of the library. Rain didn't think her mother would even consider loaning out her grandfather's book. Especially after he'd passed away two years ago. Grandpa Luis's written words were always considered sacred in their home. As the novels and poetry books were long out of print, the library owned only a few precious copies of each of his works. Rain was *sure* her mother would only allow patrons to read her grandfather's work on site and not remove it from the safety of the hand-hewn logs or the library grounds. So, how had it gotten out here? Out beneath the forsythia bush?

Unless . . .

The lack of dust and dirt proved that it must've, at one time, been in the victim's hand. It was too clean to have been lying beneath the bush for very long. The book hadn't been under the forsythia overnight—not a chance. Rain had checked the forecast before her ride up north, and Lofty Pines had been expecting heavy storms the previous night, and the bush wouldn't have provided ample coverage for the book not to have gotten soaked. Especially since the spent yellow flowers of the forsythia now littered the ground. It had been a delayed spring with snow showers clear up until the end of April, and the bush had already finished its late blooming glory. Plus, it was obvious the necktie must have belonged to the victim, as his well-dressed attire was only missing that one piece of the ensemble. Anyone could clearly fill in the blanks and conclude that the tie was his.

"That's my grandfather's work. The book he wrote . . . this family heirloom barely leaves the library . . ." she stuttered. "The book . . . it's . . . precious to our family's collection . . ." Rain's voice trailed off as she tried to make sense of it.

Could her mother really have let Thornton borrow the book? Something this sacred to the family? They *must've* been having an affair. There was no other explanation, was there? Rain could feel her blood run cold and her body begin to sway. Jace reached out a strong arm to catch her.

"Hey, you okay? You look a little pale. Should I go and grab a paramedic?" Jace placed the family heirloom into a plastic bag that he also retrieved from his police belt and placed the book on a nearby rock. He then guided her a few feet away to the front side of the outhouse and encouraged Rain to rest on a nearby fallen log, with her head between her legs. "I'm going to have to hold on to your book for a bit, maybe forensics can tell us something. I'll make sure they take good care of it, though. Don't worry, it won't be returned damaged." He nodded his head in the direction of the new evidence.

Rain inhaled deeply, trying to catch the breath that seemed to be evading her.

"Are you sure you don't need medical assistance?"

"No, really. Please don't bother them. I'll be okay, I think I just need a minute," Rain said. Her words were spoken into her arms and she felt herself begin to tremble. Tears came now, her body shook, and she could feel a strong hand rubbing her back to soothe her. She was a little embarrassed, but by this point, she couldn't hold back. It'd been one heck of a summer homecoming.

"Hey . . . I'm just going to leave you for a brief second. See if I can get Julia to grab you a bottle of water. Okay? It's so warm out here today." Rain felt the rubbing subside and a pat on her sweaty shoulder. Rain didn't answer, she just lifted her head numbly and blinked back the tears in her eyes.

"Will you be all right if I leave you for a minute?" he prompted again.

Jace's tenderness sent fresh tears to her eyes and she nodded slowly.

"Okay, hang on. I'll be just a minute, I promise." Jace said and then quickly turned away from her. Rain watched him sprint with athletic ease toward his sister. She inhaled deeply and tried desperately to even her breathing. She wiped her eyes with her arm, leaving a wet patch and streaks of mascara on the sleeve of her navy T-shirt. Yes. She was officially a hot mess.

Rain heard a car door slam off in the distance, but she couldn't see the latest arrival in her driveway. She assumed it was the chief of police or the coroner, as the ambulance crew refused to move Thornton's body until both had gotten a good, thorough look at the scene. Standard protocol, she thought—just not standard in her world.

Julia and her brother came running, each carrying water. Rain was thirsty, but the amount of water they were bringing to her aid might be overkill. She attempted to stand, but her legs still felt a bit rubbery. Still, not wanting to appear as weak as she felt, she forced herself to stand and greet them with a timid smile.

"You okay?" Julia reached out and handed her a bottle of water dripping with condensation. "Here, take this."

Rain uncapped the bottle immediately and took a drink before answering. "Yeah. Thanks so much for this. I am super thirsty. It's hotter than a sack out here." She wiped her mouth with the back of her hand and then raised the bottle back up to her lips in gratitude.

"Do you think there's a chance you might be dehydrated?" Jace leaned in closer to make direct eye contact and check her eyes. "Are you sure I shouldn't flag a paramedic to come take a quick look at you? It would only take them a sec." He waved a hand in the direction of the driveway to wave down a paramedic, as if he was at a restaurant calling on a waitress. "You might be suffering from heat stroke. It's pretty hot out here this afternoon."

"No," Rain reached to deflect his call of the paramedic and then took another long sip of water. "I appreciate your kindness, really . . . seriously, I'll be okay. I haven't had much to eat today, and I had a long day of packing up from Milwaukee, traveling up here, and now all this . . ." She sucked the air into her lungs and then blew it out slowly. "I'm probably just a bit tired, too." She blinked her gritty eyes and held back a yawn before displaying a weak smile.

Julia looked crestfallen. "I'm so sorry I pushed the meeting on you tonight. How rude of me. Can you forgive me, Rain? This is all my fault." She ran her hand aimlessly up and down a second water bottle to remove the condensation, as if there was something she might be able to fix, before uncapping it and taking a sip herself.

"Oh, Julia, please don't even think such a thing." Rain reached for her hand and gave a tight squeeze. "Please, friend, no worries."

Julia looked defeated; her eyes downcast.

Rain then pleaded, "Please don't take all this on yourself. This was definitely not your fault . . . none of it." Rain's eyes then traveled in the direction of the crime scene tape. She took another long swig of water and nearly emptied the bottle. Water had never tasted so good.

"Julia, do you have any idea why a library book might have been out there behind the outhouse?" Jace's eyes narrowed on his sister.

"No idea. Why?"

"Not just any book. Grandfather Luis's book," Rain chimed in quietly. So quietly, she doubted either one of them heard her grumblings.

"The library hasn't been open recently?" Jace pressed.

"No, Willow usually waits until Memorial Day to open. And she hasn't been up here. Why do you ask?" Julia asked. Her brows furrowed in question as her eyes traveled between Rain and her brother.

"Never mind, looks like we have company," Jace said as he nodded his head in the direction of a newcomer. The chief of police joined them, and after a few introductions, he and Jace moved off in the direction of the crime scene tape.

Julia steadied Rain by the arm and they turned in the opposite direction and headed toward the wraparound deck.

"What was that about?" Julia's look of confusion did not go unnoticed as she looked back toward her brother and the chief of police and then back to Rain.

Rain was not at all ready to discuss why her grandfather's book was found at the scene of the crime. She wasn't yet comfortable openly discussing her mother's relationship with this victim, and suddenly the book made their so-called relationship all too real. Otherwise, why would Thornton have it? Instead she deflected by changing the subject.

"Where's Nick? I'm surprised with all the commotion he didn't head next door to check on you," Rain asked. "There's no way he didn't hear all the hoopla going on over here."

"I called him on my cell and instructed him to stay put. No sense muddying the investigation by adding more people to the mix. I'll fill him in when I get home. I also phoned the other Lakers that might happen to stop by tonight knowing we were having a meeting. Jace would've been so pissed if more people showed up for him to sift through."

"Ah, good point, thanks for handling that. Well, hopefully, the officers will wrap up here and you'll be able to get back to Nick. I'm sure after they take our statements, we'll be free to go. And besides, now that the chief is here, it shouldn't be much longer. You think?"

Rain couldn't wait to get a little food in her stomach and a good night's sleep. The adrenaline was starting to wane, and suddenly she felt very weary.

"Yeah, I wouldn't think it'll be much longer. But Rain, I'll stay with you if you need me to. You don't have to be alone tonight." Julia laid a gentle hand upon her arm and she instantly felt a rush of genuine encouragement.

Rain appreciated her friend's empathy but alone was something she'd grown accustomed to as of late. "Thanks, Julia, but I'll be okay. Just knowing you guys are right next door helps. I suppose they'll want to get Thornton's body off to the morgue real soon, for a proper autopsy. I can't believe these words are even coming out of my mouth." Rain emptied her water bottle and Julia offered the rest of hers, which Rain accepted willingly.

"I hear you. Nothing like this has ever happened around this lake. I can't believe it either." Julia held a hand to her heart and tapped lightly, her usual friendly smile now downcast.

Rain turned her attention back to the area of the crime scene. "Your brother is pretty amazing, taking on this kind of work. It sure is different than reading something like this in a crime novel. He's taken up quite the noble cause, and right here in Lofty Pines." She kept her musings to herself that Julia's brother had grown into a handsome man, too. The timing of stating such a thing was very much off, but she'd have to be brain dead not to notice.

"Yeah, I agree, Jace is pretty amazing. My brother has always had a way of putting others before himself. He'd storm a burning building for a friend . . . I've always admired that about him. To be honest, I hated how overprotective he was when I was younger, but now that I've grown up and look back at it, I see him in a whole new light. It's too bad Abby didn't feel the same." She added under her breath.

"Abby?"

"Yeah, Jace proposed a year ago to a gal named Abigail, we all called her gabby Abby." Julia chuckled. "Holy Maloney, that girl could talk!" Julia slapped a hand to her thigh in jest.

"What happened to her?"

Julia kicked a stone and toyed with it on the grass. "She's a photographer, who did a lot of traveling, and Lofty Pines was too small for her. She wanted out of the Northwoods. Broke my brother's heart."

"Oh."

"I realize it's nowhere near what you had to deal with last year, but Jace really took it hard."

Rain looked back at him with fresh eyes and Julia followed her lead by turning her head, too. They watched as Jace took control of the situation pointing out things to his boss.

"What do you think happened to Thornton anyway? What would be the motive?" Rain asked as the two watched the body now being covered with a tarp.

"I have no clue." Julia said. "I'm really sorry, Rain. I should've taken into consideration your move up here before suggesting we have the meeting tonight. And now all of this on top of everything else . . . I feel awful." Julia lifted a hand to her flushed cheek.

Rain turned to Julia, "It's okay." You're not responsible for this. Any of it. Please, don't keep putting this on yourself." But Rain knew someone was responsible.

The question was . . . who?

Chapter Six

Rain woke to only one thing pressing heavily on her mind. Why was a dead man found on her family compound and what was the truth behind her mother's so-called affiliation with Thornton Hughes? Had he been expecting to meet Willow for a tryst, and instead wound up dead? Or had he been placed there? To send a strong message. Or worse, was his body dumped there to frame someone in her family?

What was he doing *there* of all places? Out behind the outhouse?

These musings had resulted in a fitful slumber of tossing and turning throughout the night. Uncomfortable thoughts seared through Rain's mind, causing a dull ache to land behind her eyes. She had a hunch that, despite ibuprofen, this kind of pain would linger. Unless she got to the root of the problem.

Rain tossed the cotton sheet aside and decided a cup of strong coffee might help clear the cobwebs as she pressed her fingers deeper into her throbbing forehead.

Sun streamed through the floor-to-ceiling windows, filling the open concept living room, and causing Rain to blink and readjust as she entered. She tented her eyes and awkwardly stumbled her way blindly with an outstretched arm, toward the kitchen sink to fill a tall glass with water. She dumped the water into the coffee machine and popped in a full caffeinated pod before hitting the start button. The buzz of the machine filled her with aching anticipation.

An uncorked wine bottle atop the quartz kitchen island reminded her of the other reason she might have woken with a pounding headache. Unable to unwind from the day, she'd popped a bottle of red, long after Julia had returned home. At the time, she hadn't realized how much wine she'd consumed, but now looking at the half-empty bottle, she recognized what she'd done and remembered the room spinning before she'd fallen into bed. Unusual behavior on her part but well warranted under the circumstances. She didn't feel remorse for her behavior but more for the aftermath of alcohol consumption. She squeezed her eyes shut again, hoping to relieve the pain behind her eyes.

Tried as she might, Rain couldn't shake the image of Thornton Hughes from her mind. No amount of wine could erase it. His distorted limbs, stiff and awkward, lying on the soiled ground. The blood that had pooled around his head. She shuddered, knowing his last moments on earth must have been disturbing and painful. Her thoughts were interrupted by a knock coming from the rear entrance. Thinking it might be Julia, she rushed through the house to greet her friend. Instead, she was met by a man of equal height to her own. Rain stumbled backward in surprise.

"Hi, I was wondering why the library wasn't open? I was told I'd be able to borrow a book. Do I have the right place?" the man asked, pointing in the direction of the catwalk leading to the library.

"Oh." Rain shook her head to redirect her thoughts. "Yes, of course. I'm sorry, not yet. We will be opening, however, I'm not quite sure when. I can take your phone number and give you a call when we open. How does that sound?"

"No, that's okay. I rent a cottage about a mile down the road, I thought I'd pop in on my morning walk. I can check back again. What happened out there?" He turned away from her looking at the blaring yellow police tape.

"An accident."

"Accident?" The man winced at the comment. "What kind of accident?"

Rain swallowed. "A murder actually."

"A murder?" The man's eyes doubled in size. "Who killed him? Was it someone he knew?"

Rain hadn't mentioned the sex of the victim. It was then she realized the library patron wasn't here to pick up a book, instead, she surmised, he was here to pick up gossip. "I'm sorry, how about you check back again on one of your walks. I'm sure the library will be opening soon. Thanks for stopping by." Rain managed a weak smile.

The man took her cue and said, "I certainly will, have a good day," before turning on his heel.

Rain closed the door, but the man's comment lingered.

Was it someone Thornton knew? Someone in whom he'd once placed his trust?

The thought hit her then that the horrible incident must've taken place on her property. Otherwise, wouldn't blood be evident on other parts of his body? Wouldn't there be defensive wounds? If there was a sharp blow to the back of the head, and he was rendered unconscious, he wouldn't have been able to react as he wouldn't have seen his assailant coming. He couldn't have been dumped there. Wouldn't there be scuff marks where he'd been dragged? Or blood splatter or drips in other areas? The evidence seemed to point that the incident had taken place exactly where the victim had been found.

Didn't it?

This new realization sent a shiver down her spine. Because it meant someone had committed this heinous act close to home. But she hadn't heard a scream. Nor had Julia. Had she been in the shower when it happened? Wouldn't Julia have heard *something*? Unless the poor man hadn't seen it coming. As the indications suggested, he must've sustained blunt force trauma to the back of his head. He might not have seen his attacker. What a cowardly move that would be, hitting a man from behind. She thought about this as she made her way back into the kitchen.

But why here? On her family's property?

Why *now*?

Clearly, these thoughts would consume Rain's mind again today. She decided she had no other choice than to dig deeper into issues that were bound to prove uncomfortable. Things that Julia had inferred that she alone couldn't help but think, could provide a potential motive. She'd much rather live in a place of bliss, where her parents' issues didn't exist. And now she'd have no other choice than to confront all of them, including *that* uncomfortable issue, head on. She longed to hide in that childlike fantasyland where parents didn't have issues or, whatever issues they did have, were hidden far from view. She'd been mostly sheltered, up until this point. No doubt about it.

Now that she was confronted with the fact that Willow's so-called "lover" had been literally murdered within a few hundred yards of the cabin, what choice did Rain have *but* to seek out the truth? Had their relationship prompted this heinous act? Rain was so relieved her father was away in Japan on business. At least his trip far from Lofty Pines provided ample relief that he wouldn't be privy to all the upcoming town gossip that was sure to ensue when word of the murder broke loose. News would travel through the Lakers faster than a flame in a dry field. The thought of this sent bile to rise in her throat. How could she *think* about her mother ever doing such a thing with another man? Her father would be so devastated. And so would she.

Rain reached for the mug beneath the Keurig machine and topped the coffee off with the leftover creamer from Milwaukee, forever grateful that she hadn't tossed away the bottle. She instantly breathed in the heady scent of caffeinated goodness and took her first sip. She then set the mug aside and flipped through every cabinet door until she came upon the medicine basket where her mother kept all the outdated antibiotic lotions, allergy salves, and pills. Rain sighed with relief when she noticed the bottle of ibuprofen was not yet expired—but close. After popping two, she washed them down with hot coffee which burned the back of her throat then reached for a tall glass of water to soothe the burn. Inwardly chastising herself, knowing it would take a few days for her throat to recover.

What was Thornton's body doing here of all places? Why was he found by the outhouse?

The answer hit so hard and swift, it almost knocked her off her feet. She reached for the counter to steady herself.

Rain's family kept a spare house key hidden inside the outhouse. What if her mother had shared that information with the victim? What if Thornton was searching for the key so that he could enter the cabin? Perhaps to return the precious book either inside the cabin or back to the safety of the library? He'd have to enter the cabin in order to retrieve the library key if that was indeed his mission.

Suddenly Rain had to know the answer to this question. She took another sip of coffee so the mug wouldn't be too full to carry back to the bedroom.

Clothes from the opened suitcase were tossed in the air like confetti until she found an army green tank top and a pair of sweat shorts that could match. She quickly dressed and took another sip of coffee before slipping her feet into a pair of flip-flops. Using her hands instead of a brush or comb, she swept her hair up into a ponytail and tied it with the elastic she'd left on her wrist from the previous day. She took another sip of coffee before abandoning it on the kitchen island and heading out the back door into the humid morning air.

The dew from the grass stuck to Rain's feet, and she tried not to lose her footing as she rushed quickly toward the outhouse. Yellow police tape still blocked the entire area, and she hesitated a moment before lifting the tape aside and stepping beneath it.

"Hey! Stop!"

Rain put her hands above her head like a hardened criminal before slowly turning around to see Jace Lowe galloping with athletic ease in her direction.

She dropped her hands by her sides and stood sheepishly waiting for him.

"What are you doing? This is a crime scene, Rain! You can't just go behind the tape. What's so important that you couldn't wait? Or at the very least call me?"

"I . . . I . . ." Rain stuttered, stunned by the hostile tone in Jace's voice. She couldn't remember a time she'd ever seen his face so red, or his voice so disturbingly angry. Of course, this was long before she knew him as officer Lowe.

When Jace noticed her body go rigid, he softened. "Rain, I know this is all very hard for you, but you can't be here." He summoned her with one hand. "You can't step behind the crime scene tape. We'll have it down soon enough, I promise, and you can get back to some sort of normalcy."

When Rain didn't move a muscle, and her legs remained planted to their spot, Jace lifted the tape to join her and then placed a comforting hand on her shoulder to extend a peace offering.

Rain wasn't sure what to say but attempted to explain, "I wasn't trying to disturb anything." She held her hands out in defense. "I really wasn't . . . it wasn't my intention at all . . . I'm sorry."

"I know, I'm sorry if it felt like I was overreacting. But you have to understand it's imperative you don't touch anything and contaminate the scene. Do you understand the magnitude of the situation? We can't get the person who did this, and convict, without hard evidence. And not muddied evidence," he added with a frustrated tone, readjusting his police cap upon his head.

Rain hung her head sullenly.

"Something wrong with the indoor plumbing today? Do I need to call a plumber for you?" Jace lifted her chin so their eyes could meet. His eyebrow rose and he cracked a smile, easing the growing tension between them.

Rain returned his gaze with a wry smile and shook her head vigorously. "No, Jace, no. There's no problem with the indoor plumbing."

"Then what, may I ask, *are* you doing out here?" Jace laced his hands across his broad chest and his smile widened as he stood stoically. One eyebrow lifted as he patiently waited.

"Actually, you make a good point. What are you doing out here already today?" Rain smirked, flicking a finger in his direction, attempting to turn the tables on him. "I haven't even finished a full cup of coffee yet," she added amused. "I'd say you're at it pretty early."

Jace uncrossed his arms and gripped his hands firmly to his hips. "My job. The sooner we get to the bottom of this, the sooner I can remove this tape and you can go on about your life. I think we can both agree about that. No?"

"I don't see how that's going to happen anytime soon. I mean, the going on about my life part." Rain blew a breath of frustration and Jace nodded with understanding.

"Honestly? Do you really want to know what I'm doing out here?" Rain studied the outhouse, noticing for the first time it could use a fresh coat of paint, and then turned her attention back to Jace.

"Yep, I'm still waiting." He said rocking back and forth on his heels, his arms laced across his chest.

"My parents keep a spare key inside the outhouse and, with everything going on, I thought it is best to remove it and keep it safely inside the house with me until things settle down out here."

It wasn't entirely true, but Rain thought, as she watched the light flicker in Jace's eyes, that he, too, thought it was an acceptable answer. She wasn't at all ready to peck at him about the town gossip swirling about the victim and her mother. No. She wasn't in the mood to discuss it. Especially when she hadn't yet made peace about it in her own mind. She didn't even know if it was valid, but things weren't exactly leaning in her mother's favor. During the last visit with her psychologist, the doctor had noted her inability to trust. Now it was blaringly obvious that the professional had been right. She immediately thought the worst of people—including those closest to her.

Jace's body language changed from teasing, to instantly serious as he asked, "where's the key kept?" He removed rubber gloves from his police belt and quickly slid his long fingers into them.

"There's a roll of toilet paper hanging on a nail on the inside wall. It's usually hidden behind there," Rain said with a pointed finger. "Can you grab it for me?"

Jace turned to her before opening the outhouse door and shook his head in dismay. "Seriously, this is where your family hides a house key? I've heard of under the flowerpot, or out under a fake rock somewhere . . . but . . . this is a new one . . . even for me." He grinned.

Rain shrugged her shoulders in defense of her family. From the time she was a child, it was common knowledge to her immediate family members that they'd always hidden a spare key inside the outhouse.

Jace opened the door wider and turned his head to the right wall after looking back to verify where Rain's extended hand was directing him. He removed a roll of toilet paper and tossed it to her.

"Nothing here." Jace confirmed as he craned his neck for a closer look. "Are you sure your parents left it out here? Perhaps one of them took it out and left it inside the cabin?"

An uncomfortable feeling washed over Rain. "We *always* keep a key in there. Just in case . . ." Her eyes traveled around his shoulder, looking to verify with her own two eyes. When she couldn't, she stepped back and gripped the toilet paper roll to her heart.

A silence fell between them. And then Jace removed the roll of toilet paper from her death grip and replaced it back where he'd found it.

It was a long shot, but Rain had to ask. "By any chance did Thornton have anything in his pockets?" She was hoping, despite the key being under strict orders never to be removed from the outhouse, maybe the victim had snatched it before he was bludgeoned to death, with plans to put it back when he was finished. She really hoped not, though, because if he'd had it in his possession, it would only solidify a serious relationship. The location of the key was private to immediate family members only. The family had a very strict rule about that.

The strained look on Jace's face did not bring comfort. "I'm sorry, Rain. There was nothing found inside the victim's pockets. No cell phone, no personal identification. And certainly not a key, if that's what you were hoping for."

Rain's heart sank as she let the implication of the missing key sink deep within her.

Chapter Seven

Who on earth had the missing key?

Rain recalled that soon after she'd arrived in Lofty Pines, Julia had mentioned removing the outdoor furniture and assembling it atop the wraparound deck to ready for the library meeting, and that Willow had given her a key. However, *that* key was to the shed—not to the cabin. Besides, the key to the shed was kept in the boathouse, in an entirely different location.

Had her mother given Julia the key to the log cabin as well? Rain highly doubted it, but she had to find out. "Maybe your sister has the key to the cabin." Rain finally unloaded what was on her mind as she glanced over at Jace who seemed to take in all this new information like a sponge. His eyes then darted to the ground as if searching for something he'd missed prior. Or the key would miraculously be found beneath them, hidden in the dirt.

"It's the only viable explanation." Rain shrugged.

Jace then cocked his head in confusion. "Why would Julia have the key? If she did, wouldn't she have mentioned it yesterday, especially under the circumstances? I mean we were literally standing right here. In this very spot. I kinda think she would've mentioned that important fact, knowing I'm conducting a full-blown investigation." Jace removed his right glove and rubbed his jawline hard. His hand then traveled to the back of his neck. "That doesn't really fit, she knows how this works."

Rain supposed he was right. But it still wouldn't hurt to ask.

The two moved outside the protection of the yellow police tape, while still considering an answer to where the cabin key could possibly be located.

"Well, it certainly wouldn't hurt to ask Julia, but if it isn't in her possession, I think you should call a locksmith, or better yet, head to the hardware store immediately and see if Hank's working today. You're gonna need to have your locks changed. Like, right now. Do you understand, young lady?" Jace's tone grew more and more concerned with each passing statement, sending a trickle of unease down Rain's spine.

"I hear you," she answered. The idea that a deranged lunatic or the murder suspect potentially having the spare key in his or her possession wasn't exactly sitting well with her either.

"Yeah." Jace tapped his long index finger to his leg. "Why don't you go over and ask my sister. If she has no idea where the key is, then you need to head over to the hardware store right away. You could be in danger, Rain. I'll hang around here until your locks are changed. I have more canvassing to do anyhow. I'll be around for another hour or more." He put a hand up to silence any protestations before she could even begin to utter them. "Trust me, it's not an imposition. It's my job." He removed the other glove that was still on his left hand and tucked them both deep into his uniform pocket.

She was growing more and more uncomfortable with everything, and Jace could clearly sense that. Since the moment she'd stepped onto the property, it seemed she hadn't had a moment's peace. This was not what she'd expected when she'd left Milwaukee. She'd been looking forward to quiet time, to be alone in her own thoughts, to snuggle up with a good book. But now the idea of being alone and isolated didn't feel nearly as enticing, because her fear was escalating. Rain wasn't sure she was happy with the idea of staying in the cabin alone anymore. Despite having just arrived in Lofty Pines, it felt like she'd been there forever. As if her life had suddenly taken a one-hundred-and-eighty-degree turn. In fact, she'd also realized it was the longest time she hadn't thought of Max, which was completely foreign to her.

"You okay?"

Jace interrupted her thoughts and Rain reached out and lightly touched the officer on the arm to let him know she was fine before dropping her hands to her sides. "Yeah, thanks. I appreciate you hanging around until the locks are changed." She smiled faintly.

"It's no problem." Jace jutted a thumb over his shoulder. "I'm headed off to chat with a few of the other neighbors to see if they heard or saw anything. Catch you later?"

"Okay." Rain turned and started to walk in the direction of Julia's house when she spun back to face him. "Hey, Jace?"

Jace turned around at her call but kept walking backwards.

"Any news on when I'll get my grandfather's book back? I understand you have a job to do, and I'm in no way trying to rush the process, I'm just curious. It's really an important item to my family." Rain bit at her thumbnail nervously.

"A tech was dusting it for prints this morning. I'm sure you could pick it up at the station later this afternoon. I doubt that there would be any other reason to hold onto it. On second thought, I can drop it by this evening after my shift, if that works for you?"

"That would be great." Rain nodded. "I can make dinner, too . . . if you'd like? I kinda feel like I owe you one after disrupting your crime scene. Let me make it up to you?"

Was it her? Or did Jace blush a bit at the invite?

Rain hadn't issued the invitation as a "date" and quickly recovered by adding, "I had planned on inviting Julia and Nick for a barbeque tonight, and I hoped you could join us, too. The weather is supposed to shift and be a bit cooler, perfect for dining lakeside." She looked up at the cloudless sky and was happy to notice the humidity was already dropping with a welcome cool breeze off the water.

"Okay, then." Jace nodded slowly and then smiled appreciatively. "I'd be happy to join you guys, thanks for the invite."

Rain had hoped the invitation would be a chance to dig deeper into the investigation and to see if the police had any leads by day's end. She had NOT meant it as a date. In fact, she wasn't sure if she'd ever date again after losing Max. Dating was not at all on her radar—even if Jace *did* look like a young Brad Pitt.

"What time can you make it, you think?"

"I should clock out about five or five thirtyish tonight since I got an early start." And then reminded her with a wave of his hand that he had additional work to do canvassing or they'd never share dinner.

Rain turned back in the direction of her neighbor's house and said over her shoulder, "Sounds good. I'll go check with Julia and Nick to see if the time works for them, too."

Rain decided, instead of trying to maneuver her way through the thick pine trees by the lakeshore, she'd squeeze between the bushes and climb the stacked rock wall dividing the two properties. The wall was short enough, so she didn't find the climb much of an issue. She removed her dewy wet flip-flops and looped them through her fingers before attempting the ascent.

The memory of hopping these rocks as a child sent a smile to her lips, as she and Julia would use this path to each other's houses all summer long. So much so, in those days, the path had been well worn. Not so much anymore. When she jumped off the rock wall, she had to push aside a few prickly bushes on the other side that she didn't remember being there as a child, and she wondered if she'd indeed taken the right route. The overgrown brush certainly proved evidence that many years had gone by in a flash.

"Ouch!" She looked down to see blood oozing from her arm from where a nasty thorn had torn through her flesh.

"Rain? Is that you? What are on earth are you doing?" A strong arm reached to hold the thick brush back, and she was now staring smack dab into Nick's forehead, currently rippled in worry. "You know, you could've walked over via the road?" he chuckled. "But I suppose the police have that barricaded off, too, do they? I saw Jace out early this morning scouting out the ditches." His dark eyes held empathy and concern. "You doin' okay?"

"Yeah, I'm okay."

Rain made her way through the bush with her neighbor's assistance and then the two stood looking eye to eye. Nick wore a Milwaukee Brewers baseball hat turned backwards and sweat was beading down the side of his tan face. He removed a navy bandana from the back of his jeans pocket and mopped his sweat with it. "I'm guessing you're looking for Julia. She's inside making breakfast. I'm sure we have more than enough if you'd like to join us." Rain could smell bacon wafting from the open kitchen window and her stomach rumbled in response.

"I might have to take you up on that," she said with a grin.

"Oh gosh, you're bleeding!" Nick's eyes darted to the ground looking for something and then he reached again for his sweat filled bandana. "Here, take this. Sorry, it's all I got."

"I'm all right." Rain said but looked down to notice she was indeed dripping blood. She dropped the flip-flops from her hand to land beside her on the ground, and then took Nick's bandana to soak up the blood. "Thanks," she grimaced. "It's deeper than I thought. Sorry to stain your rag here." She handed the bandana back more soiled than when she'd accepted it.

"That old thing?" he waved a hand of dismissal. "Don't worry about it. I've got a slew of them." Nick smiled, showing just how tan his skin had browned as his teeth were shimmering white.

Rain looked down at the dug-up earth and clumps of soil beneath their feet and then reached to retrieve her flip-flops. "Whatcha up to?"

"Well, I was thinking of planting some ground cover along the base of these bushes but seeing as how you like to trek through, I'm not sure it's a wise idea. Julia told me that you two used to have a well-worn path here back in the day." Nick laughed, and his eyes danced teasingly.

"Oh, I'm so sorry!" Rain looked down at her soiled bare feet. The warm earth squished beneath her toes. "Look what I've gone and done." She threw up her hands, sending the flip-flops to shoot up in the air. "How rude of me."

"I'm totally kidding, Rain. Bad joke." Nick bent to one side, stretching an arm muscle, and laughed. "I'm just trimming some of these bushes back. Julia said after what happened yesterday, she wanted to be able to see through to your property better. You know, she's like a big sister. In her mind, she's officially your protector now. I had to hold her back from not taking watch and sleeping out on your deck all night like a guard dog. We settled on this." He spread his hands wide over the ground where branches lay strewn across the grass.

Rain hadn't felt that cared for in a very long time and was deeply touched. "You both are doing this for me?"

Nick held his arms out wide. "I'd hug you, but I don't think you want to touch this sweaty body." He grinned as he brushed dirt across his already soiled white tank top.

"You're right, I'll pass." Rain winked and the two shared a laugh.

"Go ahead over and see Julia." He pointed toward the house. "She was probably planning on bringing you breakfast and checking up on you this morning anyway. She'll be glad to see you. Besides, you should probably wash your arm there before it gets infected." His face twisted as if he could feel the cut himself.

"Thanks, Nick. And I really appreciate what you're doing here to make me feel safe. You're so incredibly kind, busting your butt out here for me."

"No problem." He swatted a hand of disregard. "You'd do the same for us, I'm sure. Now go fill your stomach," he ordered with a smile.

"Speaking of that, I just invited Jace over for a barbeque tonight and was hoping you and Julia would come, too. It's the least I can do to repay you for all of this."

"If beer's involved, I'm in!" Nick grinned. "I'm sure Julia would love it, too."

Rain turned her attention to the dried blood caked across her arm and agreed it would need some antibiotic ointment. She was pretty sure what she'd seen in the cabin earlier, though, was probably long expired. "Great Nick, I'll catch ya later!" Rain said before heading off in the direction of where the smell of breakfast was still trailing across the backyard.

Rain knocked once and then opened the side door of Julia's house. "Knock, knock," she yelled as she entered. Like riding a bike, she entered the house just the way they had when they were kids and Julia's parents owned the property.

"Rain! Good morning." Julia rushed toward her after slipping off an apron and tossing it to the kitchen chair.

"You got a good guy out there." Rain smiled, jutting a thumb behind her. "Hang onto that one, he's pretty special."

"Yeah, he sure is," Julia sighed. "Wasn't sure some days we'd make it this long, but here we are." She lifted her shoulders and her eyebrows rose in a stance of surprise.

Rain wasn't sure what her friend meant by that comment. The look of confusion upon her face must've given it away, and Julia quickly explained.

"If you hadn't noticed, I'm still a bit of a free spirit. Adulthood hasn't changed that about me. I can be a bit of a handful, a spitfire when prompted," she explained. "Just look at the hair!" she added as she brushed the sides of her head with her hands and then shook it loose.

"I know I said this before, but I actually like the pink color on you. I can't picture you any other way now." Rain reached to give her friend a hug of encouragement. "I think that guy out there loves you just the way you are, and that's a beautiful thing. Pretty rare to find that kind of love."

"Ah well, sometime when we have the time, I'll share our story and explain to you what it took to get us here. It wasn't always this pretty," Julia admitted.

"Well, from what I see, you guys are a couple to aspire to."

"How'd you sleep?" Julia asked and Rain thought her friend seemed eager to change the subject.

"Honestly? Not great, you?"

"Yeah, me either, I tossed like a salad," Julia said with a nod. "I couldn't get certain images out of my mind, if you know what I mean?"

Rain chuckled at her comparison, then grew serious. "I know *exactly* what you mean." Rain breathed deep, taking in the scent of breakfast cooking. "My oh my, it smells great in here!"

Julia grinned at the compliment. "I roasted some potatoes; I've got a ton of bacon and eggs here. You hungry? Why don't you grab a chair? I was just about to call Nick in for breakfast."

"I hope you don't mind, but I asked Nick if you guys would like to join me for a barbeque tonight. Jace confirmed he's in, and I was hoping you two would come, too."

"Sounds terrific. Just let me know what I can bring."

"Just yourselves. I've got it." Rain smiled.

Julia reached out a hand in concern. "Oh goodness, what'd you do to your arm?"

"Battle wound. I didn't realize how much brush had grown in between us!" Rain laughed. "Can I use your sink?"

"Absolutely! And there's paper towel there, too, if you need to dab your arm. Band-Aids and Neosporin are in the drawer to your right."

Rain moved over to the sink and said over her shoulder, "Nick told me that you're thinning the bushes between our properties so you can watch over me. That's incredibly sweet, Julia, but totally unnecessary for you to re-landscape on my behalf."

"Hey, maybe I just missed our old path." Julia smiled at her before she hung out the side door and gave a strong whistle for her husband, apparently letting him know breakfast was soon to be on the table.

"You know, Jace and a few other officers are back out there this morning. I wonder if they'll find anything more to help with the investigation," Rain said pensively.

"Yeah, Nick told me. I was gonna give them a bit of time to work, and then go and offer them breakfast, too. I doubt they'll stop for it, but I can still offer." Julia turned and reached into a cabinet for paper plates and placed a stack on the kitchen table along with napkins. She then turned toward the cabinet to unload a few glasses and topped them off with orange juice.

"You mind if I ask you something pressing?" Rain asked.

Julia must've caught the undercurrent in her tone because her friend immediately stopped what she was doing and spun around to face her.

"Yeah, what's up?" Her eyebrows narrowed in concern, and she led Rain by the arm to a nearby chair. "Sit," Julia encouraged, as she, too, pulled out a neighboring chair and took a seat to face her.

"Did Mom give you the key to the cabin by any chance?"

Julia looked confused. "No. Why? Was she supposed to?"

"No, it's not that. I know she showed you where the key was for the shed, so I just assumed . . ." Rain's voice trailed off.

"No, I'm sorry, Rain, she didn't. You didn't lock yourself out already, did you?" Julia's eyes widened.

Rain chuckled. "No, I still have my own key. So, just to be clear, you weren't aware? The outhouse . . ."

Julia shook her head confused. "What exactly are you asking? Sorry, I think I'm missing something here?"

"Actually, *I'm* missing something," Rain confirmed. "The spare key that my family *always* kept hidden in the outhouse is missing. And to be honest, it's got me a bit creeped out."

Julia's face fell. "Oh. I didn't even know your family kept one out there. No, Willow never told me."

Rain could see Julia's wheels turning almost as fast as her own. "So, you slept in a cabin that someone potentially could've easily broken into last night?"

"Yep, I sure did." Rain blew out a frustrated breath.

Chapter Eight

After sharing a hearty breakfast that immensely helped ease her hangover, Rain and Julia departed from Nick and headed into town. Julia had insisted she'd drive her husband's old green pickup truck, as she needed to load a few bags of topsoil into the back. The two bounced along amiably, both heavy in their own thoughts, as the truck bumped along the road.

"Are you sure Willow didn't leave the key inside the cabin somewhere? And maybe just didn't have time to return it to the outhouse? Is it possible she just plain forgot?"

"I'm one hundred percent positive," Rain said. "Any person in my family who used the key from the outhouse knew to return it as soon as the door was unlocked. It was kept there for emergencies, in case one of the family members drove hours to get here, then forgot a key. I know for a fact my mother wouldn't put it anywhere else."

Julia reached across the front console to squeeze Rain's hand as a sign of reassurance. "Don't worry. We'll get to the bottom of this and get it taken care of. I'm sure there's a perfectly good explanation to why it's missing, but in the meantime, Jace's right, it's better to be safe than sorry."

Rain returned her friend's smile and squeezed her hand before letting it go to let her know she was okay. But inside, if Rain was being honest with herself, she was a bit shaken up over the misplaced key.

As they drove through downtown Main Street, Rain noted how much had stayed the same in Lofty Pines over the years. The familiarity of the town brought a sense of renewed comfort and a flashback of fond memories. The penny candy store remained unchanged on the left side of the street, flanked by a real estate agency on one side and Bubba's sub shop on the other. Rain's mouth watered at the memory of Sunday afternoons when hot ham and buttered rolls were served at Bubba's all summer long. A family favorite for sure, as her father was often the first in line, waiting patiently to pick up an order and deliver lunch for a boatside family picnic back out on Pine Lake.

Flowering hayrack baskets spilled red and white petunias from each light pole, and blue Lofty Pines flags adorned with the outline of a boat, fluttered in the breeze. The decorations made the lakeside community feel warm and welcoming. Rain wondered how many people out walking along Main Street were aware of the recent murder in their sleepy getaway town.

Julia guided the pickup to a stop on the right side of the road, directly in front of Lakeside Hardware, and the two hopped out of the truck. The Brewin' Time coffee shop was located directly next door, and Julia flung a finger toward it.

"You mind if I pop in to get a Chai tea with almond milk before we head to the other stops?"

"Not at all. Honestly, I didn't get enough caffeine this morning. I could use another coffee, too," Rain agreed as she dug through her purse looking for cash. "My treat, I insist."

A colorful maritime buoy hung on each side of the coffee shop, and Rain touched one fondly and smiled, before entering through the glass door. She loved anything nautical, as it reminded her of her younger years, spent growing up around Pine lake.

The smell of coffee and chocolate greeted them, and the two breathed in the scent, and then looked at each other and laughed quietly among themselves.

"It smells amazing in here. Is this place new? I don't remember a coffee shop on Main Street?" Rain asked.

"It's been here about five years, give or take." Julia answered as she stepped toward the counter and gave her order to the barista.

Rain ordered a large hazelnut coffee with cream, then handed over enough cash to cover both drinks.

"Maybe I should order a dozen of those brownies for dessert tonight?" Rain said pointing to a tray with a pyramid of brownies atop the counter. "I can't fit one in right now after you fed me that amazing breakfast, but I'd be hard pressed to pass one up." Rain tapped her stomach with both hands.

"For after the barbeque? What'ya say? They smell so good!" Rain said leaning closer to the counter to take in more of the heady chocolate fragrance.

"Hey, I'm not going to argue." Julia laughed. "They're definitely smart to bake these in the morning, as I'm sure the alluring scent helps tremendously with sales. Just wait until you try their doughnuts," she added. "Plus, it'd be good for you to gain a few pounds." Julia looked down at her own stomach and sighed dramatically. "Me, on the other hand? I could probably stand to lose a few." She frowned.

The barista overheard them and, with a smile, assembled a box of a dozen brownies to add to the order.

As they waited, Julia looked at Rain intently. "How you holding up? This hasn't been the best Laker's welcome, has it?" She leaned in empathetically, then tucked her pink hair behind one ear.

Rain shook her head in disbelief. "If you told me this would be my homecoming, I'd never have believed it." She rolled her eyes and they shared a chuckle. "I was kinda hoping for a summer of reflective solitude—not a crime scene," she added under her breath.

"I get that," Julia agreed with a firm nod.

"As hard as it's been, I'm glad you're here with me and walking me through this. I've really missed you, Julia, and I'm sorry it's taken this for me to realize just how much I've allowed our friendship to take a back seat."

Julia wrapped her arm around Rain's shoulder and gave a gentle squeeze. "The Lakers have missed you, too."

She winked. "Me especially. It's really nice to have you home."

The barista brought their order, and after they accepted their hot drinks, Julia suggested they take a seat outdoors, away from the growing crowd inside the coffee shop. Rain tucked the brownie box onto the front passenger seat of the pickup truck before joining Julia on the bench.

After a welcome first sip of caffeine, Rain turned toward Julia. "I still can't believe everything you and Nick are doing to make me feel safe. Having your husband thin out the bushes and all . . . it's really going above and beyond. I just have to say it again; it really means a lot to me. You guys are too kind."

Julia's eyes softened. "Of course, Rain. I'm sure this can't be easy for you to go through alone. But please know, you're not alone. Anything else we can do . . . you just say the word okay?" Julia reached to pat her gently on the leg, before dropping her hand to her lap. The gesture only renewed Rain's comfort that both her neighbors most certainly had her back, and despite her knee jerk reaction to initially push others away, it felt good to know they weren't going anywhere.

"What do you think the motive is? Have you thought more about it? I mean, what do you know about this Thornton Hughes guy. Besides the fact that he's a bit over friendly with my mother, is there anything else you can share about him? Like is he trying to get in with the Laker crowd or is he just a renter? Care to fill me in?" Rain knew those who rented property around Pine Lake or in town were scoffed at and considered "outsiders." Unlike the property owners, who paid yearly taxes, most Lakers didn't give renters the time of day.

"Actually, I can't stop thinking about it. Nick and I talked long into the night about Thornton before we finally got some shut eye. Great pillow talk, eh? A murder investigation?" Julia shuddered and then leaned in closer to whisper. "My husband did share a pretty big something about him that I wasn't aware of."

"What's that?" Rain leaned in closer and lowered her voice, too.

"He'd heard that Thornton had bid in to buy the campground and was planning to tear it down to put up condos or time-shares or some damn thing." Julia's hand flitted in the air as if totally annoyed.

"And the town would allow that? That kinda surprises me." Rain took a sip of her coffee and, noting how hot the liquid was, rested the cup upon her leg. "The campground has been part of Pine Lake forever. People come from all over the state with their families, year after year. It's quite a tradition for some people. So much so that some of the campers are also considered Lakers. No?"

"Trust me, I wasn't happy to hear about the expansion plan either. I don't want some tall ugly condo complex going up with a slew of piers filling the lakefront with it. Can you imagine the added boat traffic? As it is, the lake is way too overcrowded on the weekends." Julia huffed and then took a sip of her tea. When she finished drinking, she added, "The extra boat traffic is polluting our clear lake, too. Many of the boaters don't follow the rules and wash their boats before launching, which is corrupting Pine Lake with algae and zebra mussels. It makes me so mad." She clenched a fist and punched her leg with it. "I wish people wouldn't be so irresponsible."

"A new condo development? You really think the town would go for it?"

"Hey, money talks." Julia rubbed her thumb and index finger together. "And Lofty Pines is no different than any other small town when it comes to filling their pockets."

Rain agreed with a nod. "I suppose."

"And apparently Thornton had money. A lot of it, according to Nick." Julia continued. "At least he flaunted that attitude around town with his swanky apparel and fancy car."

"Well, I guess a condo development won't be happening now . . . will it?" Rain grimaced as an image of Thornton's distorted body re-entered her mind.

Julia shrugged. "Unless there are other bids out there to buy the campground, which we're not yet privy to. Maybe Thornton wasn't the only one interested in this kind of development? I for one, am hoping that's not the case. The lake needs to stay the way it always has . . . zero condos!"

"That could prove to be a motive," Rain said pensively. She took a sip of her coffee and held it in her mouth briefly before slowly swallowing to avoid aggravating the burn on the back of her throat. "Wouldja get a load of us!" Rain's eyebrows danced in amusement, "We both read all those Nancy Drew novels as kids, and now suddenly, we have a real-life puzzle on our hands. Who knew this would be in our future?"

"Yeah, nothing like a good whodunit," Julia said reflectively. "Money is always a strong motive for murder. So are power and prestige. Which do you think is the greater motive? The money? Or the condo development?" Julia shifted on the bench and crossed her legs at the ankle before taking another sip of her tea and letting out a sigh.

"Both," Rain said.

A middle-aged woman holding a leash attached to a small white husky approached and the excited puppy rushed toward them, bringing their conversation to a sudden halt. The woman jerked the dog back at the last second. "Toby, stop!" she said sternly.

"No worries." Rain smiled at the woman and brushed the top of the pup's head before the woman shook her head at her overly friendly dog and redirected the husky to move along.

"I'm sorry!" the woman added over her shoulder as she attempted to direct the puppy to stay on the sidewalk, and not run out into the street. The inexperienced dog owner seemed to have her hands full.

Rain took one last sip of coffee and decided to drop it in the nearby trash can.

"Done already?"

"No, it hurts too much to drink it. I sorta burned the back of my throat this morning. Long story . . ." she added when Julia looked at her questioningly as she rubbed at her throat and grimaced.

"Boy, you're just an injury-a-minute today." Julia playfully jabbed Rain with her elbow. "Do I need to cover you in gauze?"

Rain laughed along. "Probably wouldn't hurt." She looked down at the wound on her arm covered with the Band-Aid.

"Okay, if you're done with your coffee then I'll just bring my tea inside the store. Let's get going in case Jace needs to take off soon. I know my brother, and he won't step foot off your property until he knows you're completely safe. I don't want to hold him up any longer than we need to." Julia rose from the bench and Rain mimicked her action before the two stepped through the entrance of the hardware store.

"I figured I'd check to see if they have bags of dirt in here first. Hank might have topsoil, and then I won't have to make the extra stop at the greenhouse," Julia said over her shoulder as her eyes darted through the aisles. "I'll go sneak a peek and check, but Hank should be at the back of the store. If you want, I'll meet you back there." Julia shook her finger toward the back of the store before heading in the opposite direction.

"Sounds good," Rain said and continued down the center aisle. She walked until she came upon a long counter that extended almost the entire length of the store.

An older man with salt and pepper hair and a thick beard to match was bent over the counter looking down at a notepad in front of him. He reached for a carpenter's pencil tucked behind his ear and began to write something down.

Rain unintentionally cleared her throat to ease the burn and the man looked up.

"Can I help you?" His eyes narrowed as if he was trying to place her.

"Are you Hank?" Rain asked.

"Yep," he looked down at his navy shirt where his name was embroidered into the fabric in bright yellow and pointed. He then looked up and shared a friendly smile.

Rain returned the smile. "I was wondering if you had time today to change the locks at my cabin. I seem to be missing a key, and I'd feel much better if the locks were changed before nightfall." She wondered if Hank had heard the news about the murder, or if the chatter hadn't reached his ears yet. She hoped for her sake it hadn't.

Hank looked over his shoulder as if to look for something he'd misplaced. He then stroked his beard as if petting a stray kitten. "Let me see if Ted's here the rest of the day to cover for me. If that's the case, then it should be no problem." He looked around, but still couldn't seem to focus on the elusive Ted, so he turned back to her. "Where do you live? Are you here in town?" He pointed a finger down and pressed it to the countertop.

"I'm close . . . over on Pine Lake? The Russo family cabin. Maybe you know it?"

His eyes suddenly popped with recognition, and Rain instantly wondered if Hank *had* heard the horrible news.

"Oh! Are you Willow's kid?"

"Yep, that's me." Rain placed her hands on the counter and leaned into it, rebalancing her weight.

"Great to meet you. Your family's been coming in here for years." Hank nodded. "I took over the hardware store when my granddaddy passed away a few years ago. Yes, I'm very familiar with the Russo cabin, isn't everyone?" he chuckled. "It's one of the most beautiful properties on Pine Lake. A real standout."

"Oh, I'm so sorry to hear that." Rain said.

When Hank seem confused, she added, "About your grandfather."

"Ahh, don't be." Hank waved her off with a casual hand. "Granddaddy had a great life. He sure did." The hardware store owner tapped the counter twice as if to seal the comment. His lips came together in a fine line at the remembrance.

"Well, I'm sure he's really proud you took over. It's the only hardware store around for miles, this community certainly needs you." Rain shifted the weight on her feet and then rested her elbows casually atop the counter and laced her fingers.

"I appreciate that. I really do." He nodded. "Your folks sure talk fondly of you, too. It's really uncanny, you could be your mother's twin. Now I *really* see it. I was wondering why you looked so familiar to me." Hank's smile grew, showing aged teeth, which she hadn't noticed due to the fullness of his beard. His one front tooth was completely gone, and Rain secretly wondered if it hurt when he had a cold drink or if he needed to use a straw.

Hank's animated welcome made Rain think he hadn't heard the news of Thornton's murder. It wasn't possible.

He would've said something by now, wouldn't he?

"Well, I'm surprised your father sent you in here instead of stopping in himself to hire me for the job." Hank scratched the side of his head with the end of the carpenter's pencil before setting it to land back behind his ear.

"My dad's not in town this summer, so here I am." Rain leaned away from the counter and displayed jazz hands.

"Whad'ya mean? Of course he is!" Hank leaned in closer, folded his hands together, and waited with a friendly smile.

"I'm sorry? Did I miss something?" Rain chuckled. "I think one of us is a little confused?" Rain wasn't sure where Hank was going with this.

"I just seen your father in town this mornin' . . . comin' out of the coffee shop next door." He flung a sausage-sized finger toward the front of the store, where she and Julia had recently bought their hot drinks.

Rain slowly shook her head and smiled. "Nah, you must be mistaken."

"Am I? No ma'am I'm pretty sure it was him." Hank nodded his head vigorously as if he was thoroughly convinced and then began stroking his beard again.

Rain was growing slightly irritated. "That's impossible. My father is away on business in Japan, far, far from Lofty Pines." Trying to be amiable, she patted his laced hands as if to soothe a child. As if she was saying, there, there little one.

"I think you're the one mistaken. He's the only guy in town that would dare wear that old Cubbies jacket. Especially given the heat!" Hank grinned. "Besides, no one could ever mistake that limp. I bet he's on his way over to the cabin to see you right now, this mornin'. Geez, I hope I didn't crush the surprise." He lay a weathered hand aside his cheek. "I sure would feel like a heel if I did. In any event, I'll be over just as soon as I can get outta here. You're on your way home after this, yes?"

Rain nodded as a trickle of sweat ran down her spine. Hank was right. Her father was the only Wisconsinite brave enough to proudly don Chicago Cubs apparel. And he most definitely walked with a limp, due to a long-ago water-skiing injury, when he'd hurt his back.

What on earth was her father doing in Lofty Pines and why hadn't he stopped at the cabin first thing?

Chapter Nine

The ride back to the cabin was unusually quiet. Rain's mind bounced back and forth as if she was watching a professional tennis match in her head. Views volleyed, making her afraid to voice aloud some of the dark questions bobbing around her mind.

Was her father in Lofty Pines? If so, why hadn't he come to the family cabin? Why would he lie about a business trip? She needed to call him, just as soon as she had a moment alone.

Was Hank just imagining things?

"Hey, it's great Hank has time to change the locks for you today, right? He's a great guy, he really is. Always willing to help wherever he can." Julia looked in the rearview mirror and then over her shoulder out the driver's side window, before safely taking the final turn onto Birch Lane.

"Huh? I'm sorry, I missed that. What did you say?" Rain spun toward Julia after readjusting her seatbelt and shifting to face her squarely in the driver's seat. She brushed her dark hair away from her eyes that had fallen from her long ponytail, and then smoothed it with her hands.

"What happened back there? You've barely said two words all the way home? Something wrong?" Julia reached over as if she wanted to check her temperature. "You feeling all right?"

Rain debated whether she should tell Julia what she'd heard in town, and then the words finally spilled from her lips. "Hank said he saw my father this morning coming out of The Brewin' Time."

Rain cleared her throat and then swallowed. She wondered how long the back of her throat would burn as she touched her hand to her neck and swallowed again with a frown.

"That's impossible." Julia held back a sneeze by cuffing a hand over her mouth and holding her breath. "Didn't you mention that Stuart was away on business? Surely, Hank must be mistaken."

"Bless you," Rain said before continuing. "The man is awfully convinced he saw my father in that old tattered Cubbies jacket. You know, the old nylon one that he wore when we were kids? Honestly, I didn't even know he still had it. I'd hoped he threw that old thing away years ago." Rain rolled her eyes and then turned her focus on the police personnel that were littered across both ditches, on either side of the road. She counted three of them. Apparently, they were still hard at work and she secretly wondered if they'd found anything that would help move the investigation along. She really hoped they'd wrap this up soon, as having a murderer on the loose in Lofty Pines was very unsettling. Then Rain's eyes darted in search of her father's car, which as she'd thought, proved to be noticeably absent.

Julia's body shook as she fought back another sneeze. "Didn't you say Stuart was in Japan?"

"Yep."

"Hank probably saw someone with a similar jacket and misjudged. If your dad was in town, certainly he'd have stopped over at the cabin by now. I'm sure it's just an honest mistake."

After another sneeze, Rain looked at her friend and was about to ask when Julia said, "Allergies. I forgot to take my medicine last night before bed. After the pollen settles later in the summer, I'll be totally fine. I've got a few more weeks of this unfortunately." She moped.

Rain felt bad for Julia as she noticed her friend's labored breathing and saw her red nose was running like a stream. "You better take one of those allergy pills as soon as you get home."

"Trust me, I'm all over it." Julia said then redirected by saying, "I don't see your dad's car in the driveway. See, he's not here. I wouldn't worry about Hank, clearly he misunderstood what he saw."

The two were silent for a few moments and Rain wondered if Julia was thinking the same awful thing and just not voicing it. What if there really was a relationship between her mother and Thornton. And if her father had found out about it—and come to investigate for himself? She'd often heard it said that anyone was capable of murder. Not someone from her family, though. It just *wasn't* possible. She couldn't believe she let the thought even cross her mind. Rain could feel her palms growing moist. No. Clearly, she was letting her mind spin out of control yet again. The thought that she could even consider her father could hurt another person sent a wave of nausea to her stomach. How could she even think such a thing? How disloyal! Her father was in Japan. He'd so much as told her so. She felt awful for mistrusting his word. And to even have let the thought cross her mind made her feel so ashamed. With all the lies from her past not yet fully confronted, Rain found it difficult to trust anyone—even those closest to her. And she hated that.

Julia blew her nose with an old balled up tissue she'd resurrected from inside the truck's door. "I know one way you can find out," she said, as if reading Rain's mind.

Rain looked at Julia and mirrored the puzzled look that had washed across her friend's face. "How?"

"Look in the closet. If your dad's jacket is in there, then maybe you'll know." Julia lifted her shoulders in a slight shrug, as she gripped the steering wheel. She then eased the truck slowly onto Rain's driveway, as if not to kick up dirt or stones on the nearby police car.

Rain slapped a hand to her leg. "You're brilliant! Why didn't I think of that? Instead, I've been stewing all the way home, defending my father's trip to Japan in my head. Besides, I know it's only a light nylon jacket, but why would he have been wearing a jacket this morning, when it's so humid outside? Why would anybody? It's not supposed to cool down until later this afternoon." Rain felt instant relief. She was wasting her time worrying over something she knew was impossible anyway. If she found the Cubbies jacket, it could certainly answer the disturbing questions that were bothering her.

"I'm gonna go help Nick unload the topsoil so he can continue his landscaping project, but then do you want me to come over? Maybe we should take a boat ride this afternoon?" Julia wagged a finger between them. "The stress has been overwhelming for all of us, and I think we both could use a diversion. Besides, I wanted to see if Portside Bar and Grill is open for the season yet. I've been craving their food all winter long. How about we do lunch? Hopefully Hank will be finished with your locks by then. What'ya say?"

"You know, I say that sounds amazing. I'd love that. And the weather is perfect, you're right, we shouldn't miss it." Rain said as she hopped from the pickup truck and added, "Just as long as you get that allergy pill in you . . . stat!" She lifted her hand in a friendly wave and Julia slowly maneuvered out of the driveway in an attempt not to hit any police cars or personnel that might cross her path.

Instead of heading into the cabin right away, Rain walked out into the street until she locked onto a visual of Jace. She thought she might ask if he'd seen her father's car this morning, since he and his coworkers had been out there since dawn. She found him hunched over the tall grass along the tree-lined shaded road and she walked over to meet him. Had her father been the one who had taken the key? She didn't think so, because the rule always was, if anyone took the key out of the outhouse, it was to be immediately returned after opening up the cabin—no exceptions.

Jace abandoned his position and turned to face Rain when she arrived at his side. "Everything go okay? Hank coming over?"

"Yep, he's not long behind; he asked if I was heading home right away." Rain nodded. "I appreciate the suggestion; I think I'll sleep better tonight knowing the locks are changed. My luck, I'll find the lost key just as soon as they're replaced." She smiled and held her hands up in defense even though she knew without a shadow of doubt that'd be impossible.

"Isn't that always the way?" Jace grinned.

Instead of asking specifically about her father, something held her back. Alternatively, Rain asked, "Anyone pull into my driveway while I was gone?"

"Nope," Jace confirmed. "I told you I would make sure your locks were changed before I let anyone near your property, and I'm a man of my word." He said with an official air to his tone. "To be honest, it's been eerily quiet out here this morning. I thought we'd have some rubbernecking—but that's not been the case, thank goodness." He added, his tone lightening.

Rain breathed in and let the air out slowly. She didn't want Jace to sense what was churning in her head.

Hank must've been mistaken. He had to be.

Rain redirected her own mind by returning to the present and what was right in front of her. "How about you? Find anything interesting out here?"

Jace leaned in closer and lowered his voice and said, "I probably shouldn't share this," his eyes traveled over both shoulders to confirm no one was within earshot before continuing, "Wyatt bagged a small piece of fabric that we found over there." Jace flung a hand in the opposite direction, across the street from the outhouse.

"Really? What would you conclude from that?"

"The grass was flattened in that area, too. It could've been where a scuffle took place. We can't be sure yet if the swatch of fabric has anything to do with our case though. For all I know, it could just be a random thing." He raised his hands to the air and shrugged. "Who knows."

"What do you think the fabric is from?" Rain shifted on her feet and slipped her hands onto her narrow hips causing her fingertips to almost touch.

"Hard to tell. It could've been a kid running through the woods back there and getting hung up on some thorns. Or a dog playing around with its owner a little too rough." Jace bobbed his head in the direction of the thick pines and brush. "We've bagged it, but honestly, it's a long shot whether or not it has anything to do with the investigation. So far, that's about all we've found." Jace rubbed the back of his neck as if to soothe the growing tension.

Rain absently reached for the Band-Aid Julia had applied to her arm after they'd finished their hearty breakfast. "I could definitely see how that could happen. Getting tied up on the brush, I mean."

Jace shifted and his eyes darted to the ground after the two heard a ruffling in the grass and movement caught Rain's peripheral attention. A chipmunk scattered close to their feet, causing her to jump back and fling a hand to her heart. Jace reached out to comfort her, before resting his hands comfortably at his sides.

"Still a little jumpy there. You okay?" Jace's eyes softened, and Rain smiled to let him know she was fine. She was going to have to get over being so jumpy. She secretly wondered how long that would take. "I'm sure the last twenty-four hours are beginning to take their toll. I can put you in touch with someone to talk to—if you need it."

Rain diffused with a casual wave of her hand. "I appreciate your concern but no, really, I'm fine." She shifted on her feet and clasped her hands in front of her. "Do you have any thoughts as to when I'll be able to open the library, though? Julia and I were getting things ready before all this happened. You think I should wait another week or so to open? Or what are your thoughts on that? I don't want to bring added traffic here to mess with your work." Rain's eyes traveled up and down the road covered in spent brown pine needles that had fallen from the soaring pines. Since Birch Lane wasn't technically a through road, traffic wasn't all that common.

"That would probably be best. We should be wrapped up by then, and you can go ahead and reopen the library. I know many townsfolk are probably looking forward to the reopening," he added with a smile.

Rain then leaned toward Jace and whispered, "By the way, who are the rest of these people out here today? Besides you and Wyatt?" She turned her head to see one of them walking straight spined in rapid speed, headed in their direction.

"State crime lab, CSU team. We haven't had a murder in Lofty Pines in over twenty years. This crime is big for up here." After noticing the seriousness of the person walking in their direction, Jace added, "I don't want to be rude, Rain, but you probably should go."

"I understand." Rain took the cue to step aside before CSU made it to their side. After turning to walk away, she turned back and said. "Five or five thirty works for all of us. We'll wait for you to start the grill," she said and then quickly moved in the direction of the log cabin, eager to dig through the closets and clear her father's name.

Chapter Ten

After unlocking the cabin and stepping inside, Rain had only one thing on her mind. She took a direct route to the closet located by the back door. She needed to confront the uneasy thoughts once and for all that had flooded her mind. Desperate to confirm that her father was indeed far away in Japan, her legs couldn't seem to get her to the closet fast enough. She flung open the heavy wooden door and began sliding hangers wildly, sifting through multiple winter coats, sweatshirts, and rain slickers.

Rain didn't initially find what she was looking for. She did, however, resurrect the waterski jacket from her youth, adorned with an emblem of the ski team's logo on the back. When she removed the hanger and held it up, the small size reminded her of so long ago and how much had changed for her family up north. Her fingers grazed across the emblem affectionately. So many hours spent gliding across Pine Lake. Instead of returning the memory back to the closet, she tucked the waterski jacket under her arm to show it to

Julia. She wondered if she, too, still had her matching one hanging inside of her closet.

Despite a very thorough search, the hunt came up empty. The infamous Cubbies jacket was glaringly missing from the closet.

After the frustratingly thorough sift through the closet, and not finding what she'd been hoping to find, Rain was left with a feeling of dread. She really wanted to erase Hank's impression that he'd seen her father, completely from her mind. She snapped her fingers and decided that, knowing her father, he probably kept his prized Cubbies possession hanging safely in the closet inside the master suite. Her mother had attempted on several occasions to sway Stuart from his favorite team and have him donate the jacket to Goodwill. But Willow had failed, because as a diehard Chicago fan, the well-worn walking billboard was a relic her father refused to part with. Willow was never able to sway him to the side of the Milwaukee Brewers, either, despite her best efforts.

En route to verify her latest notion, Rain slung her old waterski jacket on the back of a chair, plucked her cell phone from the kitchen counter where she'd left it to charge, and hit the speed dial number for her father. Ready to squelch the idea of him in Lofty Pines once and for all, she could end this nonsense with one quick call. She blew a breath of frustration when she heard her father's voice:

"You have reached Stuart. I'm sorry I missed your call. I'm either away from my desk, in a meeting, or traveling without reception . . ."

Rain irritably clicked off rather than listen to the rest of her father's long-winded voicemail message. She could almost rattle off his message verbatim, she'd heard it so many times before. She thought about reaching out and attempting to phone her mother, too, but Willow had promised that she would call and leave a message about the best ways to get hold of her while she was away digging water sources. Her mother had insisted not to rely on her cell phone either, as she was doubtful it would work. Rain would just have to be patient and wait. Although, a quick email alert that something was desperately wrong certainly wouldn't hurt and might catch her mother's attention. Rain kept it vague. This was something her mother shouldn't learn via email and besides, she wanted to hear the tone of her mother's voice when she shared the details of the horrible tragedy. In Rain's opinion, her mother had a lot of explaining to do regarding her relationship with the victim. And she wanted to hear it firsthand.

So much had happened within the last twenty-four hours, Rain hadn't even considered entering the master suite since arriving to the Northwoods. She'd had no reason to step inside—until now.

To free her hands, Rain tossed her cell phone atop the queen-sized bed in the master bedroom upon entering. A crisp blue and white quilt with matching pillows in geometrical shapes, which almost had a nautical feel to it, covered the bed. This replaced the handmade multicolored afghan that her grandmother had crocheted, and what she'd remembered as a child had always covered her parents' bed.

She rubbed her hand along the fabric to feel the new crisp change. Rain wasn't sure if she was psychologically trying to distract herself from looking inside the closet or not. She wasn't exactly sure she was ready for the answer to the missing jacket, and this was the only other room in which she imagined her father might keep it. Finding the jacket didn't exactly prove a thing. Although it would provide a bit of verification to settle her own mind once and for all.

It felt foreign to enter the privacy of her parents' bedroom and sift among their things after so many years, and without them present. It felt as if she was intruding on their private space. When Rain was a child, the master suite was considered sacred. A place where she knocked before entering, and here she was standing inside the room without them. The whole thing felt off somehow.

The interior wall was the only drywalled area in the oversized bedroom, and it had been repainted a pale blueish white. The rest of the walls were similar to the newer part of the cabin. Thick stacked logs shone like burnt butter from the light that streamed through the two oversized windows facing the lake, adorned with white muslin curtains.

Rain stepped in front of the walk-in closet and took in a much-needed deep breath before opening the door. The shock of what she discovered made her gasp aloud. Her father's jacket wasn't the only thing missing. ALL her dad's clothes were missing.

Rain desperately pushed hangers aside, one by one, revealing rack after rack of only her mother's clothing and a shelf of women's shoes. Even though they didn't live at the cabin year round, the closets were normally well stocked for any season they decided to take a trip. They called it their Northwoods attire, and had the luxury of leaving clothing behind, so they'd never have to pack a suitcase. Especially in the last few years when Lofty Pines was becoming a year-round tourist destination with snowmobile trails popping up and talk of a new snow ski hill in the works. Where were all her father's things? Normally a full wardrobe for both of them would be hanging in the closet. Where did it all go? After shoving her mother's slew of sundresses aside, she came upon an expensive-looking men's suit jacket, hidden deep within the closet. The smoky tweed blazer wasn't something she'd ever remembered her father wearing. A luxurious silk tie wound casually around the top of the hanger and draped in front of the suit, as if it'd been worn. Rain quickly pushed the maroon tie aside to view the size of the blazer and was inwardly embarrassed to not be sure if this would be something that would fit her father.

Frantically, she dug her hands deep inside the suit pockets and found an obituary program from a funeral her mother mentioned that she and her father had attended several years ago. She sighed, feeling relieved, but only for a brief moment, as it was the only thing of her dad's she had found. Her heart thumped loudly in her chest as she stumbled backward out of the closet.

Rain spun around and took in the master bedroom again with fresh eyes.

Everything in the master suite had been remodeled, and the room held a more feminine flair. A tiffany lamp sat atop one of the two matching whitewashed bedside tables that flanked the queen-size bed. Something she knew her dad must've scoffed at. He always wanted to keep the cabin in more of a rustic motif, and this was anything but "cabin-ish." The look was far more feminine. Her parents had argued about this on more than one occasion. Rain recalled a time when her mother had put her foot down, refusing to let her father hoist an oversized taxidermic animal to the living room wall. Willow couldn't stand having a large deer head with fake glass eyes hanging in her home because of her love of animals. She had only compromised on the lighting in the library as she said the antler sheds didn't hurt the deer, they were naturally shed in the woods, so that was okay in her opinion.

Sadly, Rain realized she only saw her parents' relationship in the way she wanted to see it, even throughout her adulthood, not in the way it really was. But now seeing the truth firsthand, it hit hard. This room was no longer a room shared by husband and wife; it was a single master suite designed only for her mother. It had to be. Rain stumbled backward and sat on the edge of the bed and held her head in her hands, taking in this new revelation. She knew her parents were having marital issues, but were they no longer sharing a bedroom? Had it really come to that? She was stunned.

"Knock, knock!" Rain heard the distant holler of a familiar voice.

"I'm back here!" Rain said and quickly shoved the suit back on the rack. She abandoned the master suite before Julia had a chance to enter the bedroom. Rain wasn't at all ready to disclose what she'd just unearthed.

Julia was placing the box of brownies from The Brewin' Time on top of the countertop and spoke over her shoulder. "You forgot these in the truck. If I leave them at my house, *trust me*, they won't make it to dinner, especially if Nick sniffs them out. The man's like a hound dog when it comes to food! As it was, I didn't even take them out of the truck, but I feared if I left them in there any longer, they might melt." Julia laughed to herself, caught in her own world, before turning to Rain who was moving quickly in her direction.

"Hey? You okay? You look a little flushed?"

Rain self-consciously waved air at her face as an attempt to fan herself and cool down, and then said, "I think I'm just accustomed to air-conditioning back in Milwaukee." She chuckled. "Max used to keep our place like a meat locker. I'm hopefully a little young for hot flashes, wouldn't you say?" she added, attempting to keep things light.

Julia turned to pluck a tissue from a nearby Kleenex box by the sink. With her back facing her, Rain conspicuously stuffed the water ski jacket deeper into the chair so Julia wouldn't see it yet. She didn't want to share that she'd already been vigorously digging into the closets. The last thing she wanted to discuss with Julia was her parents' marital woes. Or the missing jacket. She needed time to process all of this before voicing it all aloud. Voicing it would make it real—too real. Right now, she wanted to live in fiction. Maybe she should head over to the library, pluck a book off the shelf, and immerse herself in it.

"I hear you; it can get pretty humid. Even though we're in the Northwoods, we're not immune to the sticky heat." Julia waved the Kleenex in the air before blowing her nose. "Although, maybe you want to open up the windows. The dry air is approaching and it's actually cooling off a bit out there," Julia said. "You'll either get used to the sticky or bump up the air in here." She added, lifting a thumb to the ceiling fan and then tossing the crumpled tissue in a nearby trash can. Julia then turned on her heel toward the back door.

"Yeah, good idea." Rain said.

"Hey, off topic, but Hank's already here. Jace was talking with him in the driveway, and it looks like the big elephant's outta the room. From what I saw, I think he noticed the crime scene tape—I mean, how could you not? Sorry." Julia frowned. "I'm sure by now Hank has heard the official reason of why you're really wanting to get the locks changed."

"I'm not sure we can hold back a murder investigation from the Lakers, no matter how hard we try. News, I'm sure, is going to travel like fan-to-flame real soon. I guess that's something I'm going to have to prepare for."

"Yeah, I suppose you're right." Julia said.

"Hey, just so you know, I talked to your brother about opening the library and he said we'll have to wait until next week. We can still work on some administration stuff, though, if you're interested. It might be good to take some time and organize this week. We have a lot to do, no?"

Rain could tell by the look of surprise on Julia's face, that the reopening of the library wasn't what her friend had expected to come out of her mouth. It was a great diversion away from her parents though and would give her some time to internally process. Organization and order always had a way of making Rain feel in control. Especially now, when everything was the complete opposite. She was desperate to get off this tilt-a-whirl.

"I have a few things to help Nick with, but how about we turn our lunch meeting into a library meeting? Shall we?" A new spark of light danced in Julia's eyes. "I'll meet you on your pier at say twelve thirty-ish. Sounds good? Hank should have your locks changed by then."

Rain's change of topic worked, as Julia didn't even ask about the Cubbies jacket before retreating out the back door. She exhaled a sigh of relief.

Rain followed Julia out onto the deck, closing the screen door behind them. A large shadow had fallen upon the wooden boards, causing the two to tent their eyes and look to the sky.

"Look! An eagle!" Julia pointed to the top of a nearby white pine tree where a large Bald Eagle had landed and perched. His pure white head and yellow beak stood out proudly, not at all camouflaged by the branches.

Rain looked up at the majestic bird, awestruck, and whispered so as not to spook him. "Wow, he's beautiful, isn't he?"

"Sure is," Julia said. "Did you know that the nest on the south side of the lake where we used to waterski is still there? I think there are eaglets in it, too. I see both mama and papa in it from time to time." Julia smiled. "So cute, I can't wait to see the babies grow."

"It's still there? After all these years? Aww, that's sweet."

"Yep, the nest is awe inspiring. You should see the size of it now! It's so incredibly huge. Nick and I call it the eagle condo complex." Julia chuckled. "I've been trying to get a good photo of one, but they keep flying away every time I attempt it. We'll have to boat over there one of these days so you can see the nest. It's very impressive."

"I'd like that," Rain said as the two watched the bird's giant wings extend as it soared from the tree and grazed across the water, picking up a bellied-up fish in his talons, before rising again and gliding away.

"You know they mate for life?" Julia asked.

"I do. I think I remember my grandfather, Luis, telling me that." Rain said. And she couldn't help but think of her parents and wonder if they were no longer sharing the same nest.

Chapter Eleven

Rain stood patiently waiting as the hardware store owner checked his work, one last time, by slipping the key into the new lock, before turning the set of keys over to Rain.

"That should do it," Hank said confidently. He then placed his tool bag by his feet when Rain handed him a bottle of water.

"Sorry I don't have any lemonade or anything, I still need to head to the market."

"This is perfect." Hank nodded as he rose the water bottle up in a "cheers" motion as if she'd given him a large mug of beer. "Thank you," he added as he uncapped the bottle and took a welcome sip.

"How much do I owe you?"

"If you don't mind, I'll have Vivian send you a bill. My wife handles all that, and your folks usually have an ongoing tab back at the shop. I hope it's okay to handle it that way?" His peppered eyebrows came together in a frown.

"Sounds perfect," Rain said as she watched Hank pick up his tool bag and toss the capped water bottle into the bag. She then followed him outside. Life was so different up north. Back in Milwaukee, she'd have to pay a bill in advance to even get a handyman to show up at her house. It was one of the things she could grow to like about life back in Lofty Pines.

"Make sure and tell your father hello for me, I was expecting to see him pop in or out while I was working," he said over his shoulder as he ambled along. "But don't tell him I ruined the surprise."

Rain took in a slow breath and smiled. She didn't know how to respond. Clearly, the hardware store owner was adamant about who he'd witnessed walking out of The Brewin' Time. But she couldn't help but think maybe Hank had been right, maybe her dad had the jacket *and* the missing key in his possession. She just wasn't sure of it yet.

Hank halted his stride and nodded in the direction of the police tape still glaringly draped in front of the outhouse and flapping from an upswing of breeze off the water. "Man, what a darn shame, eh? Nothing like that ever happens in these parts." He hung his head and shook it sullenly.

Rain sighed and held a hand to her heart. "I know. It's a horrible tragedy." After a slight hesitation Rain asked, "Had you met Thornton? He wasn't considered a Laker, right?"

Hank chuckled. "No, he wasn't at all a Laker." He scratched the side of his head and smoothed his beard with one hand. "Although I think he wanted to be . . ."

"What do you mean by that?" Rain was relieved his answer didn't seem to cast any reference in her mother or father's direction.

"Thornton was renting a place across Pine Lake." Hank turned and flung his hand in the direction of the rolling water, but Rain couldn't gauge which direction he was pointing. "I think he was trying to get the owners to sell it to him."

"An Airbnb? Or what?"

"Nah, he was in a longer-term rental, over at the Browns' estate. You know it?"

Rain had been familiar with the Brown family growing up but wasn't exactly sure which house they owned across the lake. She remembered one of the older Brown boys had been on the waterski team a year or so before she'd joined. "Oh? How long had he been renting there? Do you know?"

Hank squinted his eyes and looked to the sky as if to recall a memory from the Rolodex of his mind. "I wanna say a little less than a year? He's been around for quite a few months now. I'd seen him in town on more than one occasion," Hank said as he turned away from the lake and resumed the walk toward his car.

Rain began calculating the timing in her head. *How long have my mother and Thornton . . .? Was it going on all while I was mourning Max?* Rain shuddered at the thought. As the horrible image crossed her mind yet again.

Was that the real reason we avoided each other while I've been in mourning? Rain had always through it was because of the rift between them, but this new revelation made her think otherwise.

"Still hard to believe," Hank said, interrupting her thoughts.

"I heard he had some interest in the campground," Rain suggested. "You know anything about that?"

Hank didn't answer and shut down the conversation by opening the rear car door and shoving his tools inside. "Well, I best be getting back to the store. Ted will be wanting to take a lunch break, I'm sure." He opened the driver's side and slid into the seat.

Rain wasn't sure if Hank hadn't heard her or he just wanted to end the conversation.

"Wow, is it lunchtime already?" Rain said, leaning into the car.

"Sure is." Hank eyed the clock on his dashboard. "Looks to be twelve fifteen. If you need anything else, just holler." He tipped his head before Rain took the cue and closed the driver's side door for him. She then held up a hand in a friendly wave.

Rain gazed out beyond the driveway and noted the police cars were now gone. She wished Jace would return before supper, as the crime scene tape was still flapping and making noise in the breeze which didn't allow a vacation from the thoughts that had completely barraged her mind in the last twenty-four hours. She turned away from the tape and instead turned her attention to the sound of lapping waves rolling subtly along the shore. It was a welcome sound that replaced the feeling of dread with a little peace. She watched as the water curled onto the shoreline.

Since they'd had such a hearty breakfast, Rain decided to phone Julia and ask if they could meet later for lunch than they'd originally planned. She wanted to head to the grocery store before the barbeque, so she could marinate the meat with pesto, and have something besides water and crackers to serve her guests. She retreated inside the cabin and began the hunt for her cell phone. After a few minutes of panic, she remembered leaving it on the bed in the master bedroom. She sighed heavily as she entered the room again, the truth now settling in her bones, that her parent's relationship was in deeper trouble than she'd initially thought. She'd believed that the summer with some time apart might do them both some good. But seeing all the changes first-hand was all too real. She plucked her phone from the bed and noticed a missed call from her dad. Immediately she hit the voicemail:

"Hey, Rain, sorry I missed ya. I'm not really in a good area to talk. I've got a meeting coming up, but I noticed you called. Hope everything is okay. Talk to you soon, love."

Rain decided to believe her father was indeed heading into a meeting, despite the missing jacket. She had to. For her own sanity, she had no other choice than to believe it.

After phoning Julia, Rain walked over to her SUV to do one final sweep before going to the market. She'd emptied the remaining remnants of her life in Milwaukee into the cabin while Hank had changed the locks. It hadn't taken very much time at all, and her life's worth basically filled only one corner of the living room. She was still unsure if she'd unpack anything or leave it all in boxes and store it away in the shed until making more lasting decisions. Currently, life decisions evaded her. Rain had also scanned every closet inside the cabin in search of the illusive jacket. If the Cubs jacket was somewhere in the cabin, it was definitely well hidden. She thought about this as she drove to the Lofty Pines Market, the one and only grocery store for many miles.

The parking lot was bustling with pedestrians and carts wheeling in and out of the grocery store. Rain found a spot far from the entrance but didn't mind the extra walk as she felt she needed the exercise. Her muscles had tensed from the recent stress, and her limbs were stiff and awkward as she stepped from the vehicle.

An outdoor garden center was attached to the market, and colorful hanging baskets of every color of the rainbow seemed to scream "pick me!" and Rain decided she'd bring one back to spruce up the deck. She immediately spotted Marge attempting to place an oversized garden pot into her own cart and rushed over to greet her.

"Hey, do you need some help with that?" Rain asked, stretching out a hand.

"Well, fancy meeting you here." Marge looked up at her and smiled. "Good to see you again."

At closer look, the flowerpot spilled hues of oranges and purples and cascaded over a plastic terracotta pot. "Looks like you picked a beauty," Rain said as she helped place it into the cart.

"I sure did. It's my favorite time of year, finally seeing some life come out of this frozen tundra," Marge said proudly and then leaned in closer and touched a hand to her arm. Her hand was ice, despite the warm weather. "Speaking of life . . . how you doing? You okay, dear?" she whispered.

"Never mind me, I'm actually more concerned about you?" Rain said as she gripped the woman's colder hands and attempted to warm them in her own.

"Oh, I'm fine. I know it was a shock, it's true. But life has a way of taking us all when we least expect it. None of us know the time nor day," Marge said, wagging a finger after she let go of Rain's hands and then gripped the cart tight. "It's a horrible way to go, though. Indeed, Thornton didn't get the best exit from this life."

Rain agreed with a sad shake of her head, her eyes downcast. She noticed Marge's feet shuffle a few steps ahead, and she asked, "Can I help you to your car and load this inside?" Just as the words fell from her lips, a grocery store clerk was at Marge's side.

"Oh, thank you, dear, but I've got it covered." Marge said with a smile. "Although, my trunk is still full of books. I'll just set this in the back seat on a blanket."

"Julia and I will be working at the library this week. If you're up for it, we'd love to have you join us."

"Today?"

"More like tomorrow?"

"I'll be there." Marge nodded firmly. "You take care, Rain, you hear?" Marge patted her arm before setting her attention back to the grocery store clerk.

"Sorry to interrupt, one more thing before I let you go." Rain's eyes journeyed from the clerk back to Marge. "Join us tonight for dinner? I'm hosting a barbeque, and I'd love for you to join us at say five thirty?"

Marge's eyes brightened. "Why, I'd love to come! Rex, too?"

"Rex, too," Rain smiled.

"I'll see you tonight then." Marge turned back to the clerk, and Rain watched as the two chatted amiably and moved away from her, out into the parking lot.

Rain made a mental note to add dog treats to her grocery list. She turned and walked into the store, grabbing a small cart along the way. While in the produce section, deciding whether she wanted a red onion or white, she overheard two women talking in low voices about the murder. It was not hard to hear Thornton's name being uttered. She swallowed hard, hoping neither of them knew that the incident had taken place on her property. Rain moved in closer and examined the fruit section, hoping to overhear a hint of their chatter.

"I know! He didn't have the right to accuse Frankie. He's not even a Laker! Who does he think he is anyway?"

"He certainly won't be a Laker now, will he? And Frankie can finally move on with his life," one of the women said as she tossed an orange into her hand and caught it expertly.

126

The other looked up and curiously studied Rain.

It was then Rain understood the women knew something about Frankie.

Move on with his life? From what?

What had Thornton accused Frankie of? Whatever it was, was it a motive for murder?

Chapter Twelve

The warm breeze brushed her skin as Rain stepped out onto the pier. She readjusted the beach bag on her shoulder, filled with suntan lotion, a towel, and a pair of bejeweled slides to wear inside Portside Bar and Grill. She was wearing a lime green casual sundress that she'd stolen from her mother's closet, atop her black bikini, just in case Julia wanted to sunbathe on the boat after their lunch meeting. The ankle length skirt fluttered in the breeze and tickled her ankles as she walked. The pier felt hot on her bare feet, and she danced her way closer to the pontoon boat, relieved to feel the carpet beneath her upon boarding.

"Hey, thanks for lowering the boatlift," Rain said.

Julia had her nose in a book, and her eyes lifted from the page. "No problem, I figured you'd want to pull the pontoon out as soon as you got down here." She lowered the book, closed it, and rested the novel on the seat beside her. "Isn't it absolutely gorgeous out here? I love when the humidity lifts." Julia removed her large-brimmed hat and tucked it alongside her canvas bag so it wouldn't blow away when Rain pulled away from the pier.

"It really is," Rain agreed. "How are your allergies?"

"Better. The pill kicked in, thank God." Julia smiled. "I couldn't stay inside and miss this, now could I?" She said, rising from the seat. "I did pack a box of Kleenex, just in case." Julia pointed to her bag before leaning in for a quick hug to greet her. "You look terrific."

"Thanks, I stole it from Mom's closet," Rain let the words fall out of her mouth before she had a chance to rethink the consequences of her remark.

"Oh! Did you find your dad's jacket?"

Instead of answering right away, Rain stepped in front of the controls, put the key in the ignition, and started the motor before taking a seat in the captain's chair. "Still workin' on it." She lowered the motor into the water, revved the engine, and backed the pontoon off the lift, before turning the boat in the direction of the restaurant.

The wind whipped at her long dark hair as the boat cut through each wave and splashed along the tubular sides. Rain had the engine going full throttle. She had waited so long for the feeling of freedom when the boat danced across the lake. This is what she loved the most about coming up north—being out on the water. The sun beat down, but the breeze cooled her skin as they traveled toward the center of the lake. She turned against the wind, her hair now flying freely behind her. As they passed an oncoming speedboat,

Rain slowed the throttle to accommodate the looming larger waves that the oncoming vessel had created. The pontoon rocked back and forth with each onrushing wave.

Rain turned the boat away from the center of the lake to direct them closer to the shore. They then traveled slowly, hugging the shoreline, admiring each of the various additions or home improvements to the many cottages that dotted the lake as they passed. Rain cut the engine when the restaurant's dock finally came into view.

A young dockhand was navigating boats as they approached the pier, and Rain tossed him a rope. She watched as he expertly tied them on, and then quickly moved along to help the next approaching boat.

"Thank you!" Rain hollered then turned to Julia and suggested with a pointed finger she tuck her bag beneath the pontoon seat for safe keeping, while they were inside the restaurant.

"Nice service, huh?"

"It's perfect!" Rain agreed before slipping her feet into her slides. She fished for a clutch purse inside her tote bag, then tucked her beach bag beside Julia's beneath the seat. "I think we're all set."

"I can't believe that after the big breakfast we had I'm actually admitting this, but I'm starving," Julia said with a grin.

"Maybe it's the fresh air making you hungry, although it must be close to two thirty by now." Rain frowned. "Sorry to keep you waiting. I really needed to get to the market."

"No worries, it's all fine," Julia looped her arm through Rain's and the two walked from the wide extended pier toward the restaurant.

Rain noted a newer outdoor tiki bar where a bartender was wiping glasses with a towel and stacking them on a shelf behind him. "Is that new? I don't remember it?"

"Yeah, they just added the outdoor bar last year," Julia answered as they passed. "Sometimes they have live music, too, out on the lawn at night. It's really a fun hangout!"

The air-conditioning hit them like a tidal wave as they opened the door. A large sign welcomed them to Portside Bar and Grill, and they ducked beneath it before Rain gazed toward the long wooden bar that overlooked Pine Lake. Sets of multicolored tables littered the center of the room, packed with patrons despite the late lunch hour.

"Maybe we should eat outside," Rain said as she noticed her arms now rippled with goosebumps. "It's freezing in here." Her eyes rose to the back wall that was covered in fish. Various sizes of bass, perch, and walleye, transformed into stuffed taxidermy, watched diners with beady eyes.

"There're tables outside, too, why don't you go and check and see if one's available, I'll flag the waitress to let her know and meet you out there."

"Sounds good," Rain said and retreated out of the restaurant, relieved to be back in the warm sunshine. She immediately found a table for two on the outer deck next to one of the round orange-and-white ring buoys attached to the thick nautical roped railing. The life preservers were wound on with white rope, more for decoration then lifesaving, but could probably be used in a pinch. The wind had calmed, and Rain was thankful for the thatch umbrella overhead that shaded her from the direct sunlight.

"Oh, this is absolutely perfect!" Julia said as she took a seat across from her.

The two picked up the menus located beside the napkin rack to quietly review their selections. "Don't order anything too big, I have chicken marinating in pesto to throw on the grill for supper," Rain said setting down her menu. "I think I'll just get a salad."

"Okay, I'll order some fried shrimp on the side because I've been craving them *all* winter long," Julia laughed and then put her hand beside her mouth, "Don't tell Nick, but his shrimp recipe doesn't hold a candle to theirs. I'm not sure what spices they use, but it's impossible to replicate it, despite my husband's best efforts."

The waitress came to take their orders and after her departure Rain said, "I saw Marge at the market today and invited her to the barbeque. I also suggested she come by tomorrow to work in the library. If you're not around or have other plans, it's no worry." Rain waved a hand airily. "I wanted to invite her, so she can have her trunk back. I felt bad we hadn't unloaded those books for her yet. Today, the poor woman had to put a flowerpot into her backseat because she had no room."

"I can come and help, too. That should be no problem at all. I'll have to double check with Nick first, but I'm sure I can make it work."

"Listen, I'm sorry I was hesitant at first to reopen the library. I hope you know, it's nothing personal. It's just that I've been going through some stuff—"

Julia interrupted her by tapping her gently on the hand. "I know, sweetie. I can't even imagine what you've been going through . . . how hard it's been for you to lose Max. He was so young . . . such a shock." She slowly shook her head.

Rain wasn't sure if she was ready to unload all the hefty feelings she'd been carrying regarding her deceased husband. She'd lugged the weight around so long now that she'd grown somewhat accustomed to it. The blame she felt toward Max gave her an excuse not to move forward. And if she moved forward, he would be gone for good. She was happy for the interruption when the waitress delivered their iced teas and then quickly retreated. It gave her the opportunity to change the subject.

"So . . . you want to fill me in on the workings of the library? Do you know what system my mother has in place thus far? I feel like you're far more well-equipped than I am to open it up to the public as you've seen the drill, I'm sure, countless times. Please tell me she's not still using that ole' log book that I found on the shelf?"

Julia laughed, "Did you really find that ole' relic? No, Willow upgraded from the log book, but still kept it pretty simple. She just used an Excel spreadsheet to keep track of who borrowed books. She'd look over the spreadsheet from time to time to see if anyone hadn't returned materials after around a four-week period and send them a letter in the mail as a nice warning instead of issuing citations. Keep in mind that most that frequent the library are locals, Lakers mostly, so it's a pretty simple system. Unless the list of library patrons grows by leaps and bounds, we could probably just keep the same system in place. Although an upgrade in internet would be nice as sometimes people like to use a public Wi-Fi, especially while out on the deck. And besides, I think an email for a warning would be much more efficient than snail mail, don't you?"

"Yeah, my parents weren't big on Wi-Fi back in the day, but times are definitely changing. I agree, a stronger signal may be in order." Rain nodded as she toyed with her straw in the iced tea.

"I'm pretty sure Willow left a laptop with the Excel spreadsheet on the desktop back at the library. Have you found the computer yet?"

"Yeah, I've seen one on the side table by the door, but I didn't give it much thought. To be honest, I didn't even power it up. I'm sure it'll be fine, though."

"I think Willow bought a new one last summer. I agree, it should power up, no problem."

A lull fell between them and Rain began to fidget in her seat.

"What's wrong? It seems your mind has already left our library meeting. Is there something else you want to talk about? You're obviously restless."

Rain leaned in toward the table, resting her weight on her elbow and then looked over both shoulders to see if anyone was within hearing distance before asking, "Do you happen to know where the Browns live on the lake?"

"Yeah, why?" Julia leaned in closer and mirrored her stance.

"Apparently Thornton had been renting their place before he passed, and I was just wondering if you wouldn't mind pointing out the house to me before we head back home?"

"Sure, I'd be happy to show you. We can boat over there after lunch." Julia sipped through her straw and then turned pensive. "May I ask why, though?"

"I have something bothering me, that I can't seem to let go of." Rain admitted after she took a sip of her tea.

The two leaned back when the waitress came with a tray and set the salads in front of them. "Shrimp will be out in just a sec," she said and turned quickly on her heel, causing her long red ponytail to bob up and down.

"Thanks," they said in unison, and then chuckled, as if they hadn't been apart for years. Any awkwardness Rain initially felt reconnecting with Julia had melted away.

After the waitress was out of earshot they continued with their conversation.

"What is it, Rain? You look distraught." Julia smoothed the paper napkin on her lap and waited.

"It's nothing, I'm sorry. We're here to discuss library business and instead my brain keeps getting sidetracked. Let me refocus here . . ."

"Don't worry about the library right now. We'll have plenty of time to catch up about that. Spill it. I can see you're upset."

A long pause ensued between them and Julia patiently waited for Rain to continue.

"Have you ever felt so disillusioned by life, that everything you'd had lined up, and everything you counted on your entire life, just burst like a bubble? And you're left wondering how you missed the clues? How you missed the truth of everything, right before your very eyes? But you're too damn afraid to take off the rose-colored glasses for fear your life would shatter into a million pieces? That's how I feel." Rain said with conviction.

Julia nodded sympathetically and held her gaze but allowed Rain to steer the conversation.

Rain shrugged her shoulders. "I'm beginning to think it's possible my mother might have been tangled up with Thornton in some sordid affair, and it's really not sitting right with me. I want to *know*. I need to know. It's eating me alive." Rain balled her fists and clenched them atop the table.

Julia didn't speak, it was as if she didn't want to break the spell, and merely waited for Rain to continue.

"I wanna share something with you, that I probably shouldn't but . . ."

Julia leaned closer and reached for her hand and gave it a quick squeeze of encouragement before letting go. "Tell me. I know it's been a long time since we've confided in each other, but I'm your friend, Rain, and I'm here for you. What's going on?"

Rain saw the sincerity in her friend's eyes and felt safe to share. "Max had an affair before he died. Before the motor-cycle accident."

There, she'd said it.

"Oh." Julia sank back in her seat. "I had no idea. Your mother never mentioned anything to me. That's why this is doubly hard for you, isn't it? The possibility of your mother . . . with another man . . ." Julia bit at her straw nervously. "You don't have room in your heart for that kind of behavior. You're wounded."

Rain's eyes filled and she nodded.

"Oh, my dear friend, I can imagine how you must feel. I'm so sorry," Julia said with a tone of deep sympathy. She reached out and rubbed Rain gently on the arm. "Honestly, I don't know what to say . . . I wish I had the right words."

"You don't have to say anything. Thank you for letting me unload. I'm carrying all this around and it's driving me nuts. My mother doesn't understand how I can be grieving Max and angry at him at the same time. How could he do that to me? While we were trying to have a baby together! My emotions are all over the place. Sometimes I feel like I'm on the tilt-a-whirl desperate to get off."

Julia nodded slowly. "I see."

"But knowing that my *own* mother could be capable of doing the same thing to my dad? I mean, it's just too much." Rain blew a breath out slowly like a blowfish. "I'm sorry, I shouldn't have dumped this on you over lunch. This is a terrible lunch conversation." Rain waved a hand toward her salad. "Please go ahead and eat."

Julia lifted her fork and said, "So, because Willow knew what you were going through, you don't understand how she could make the same mistake as Max. Is that right?" Julia took a bite of her salad and slowly chewed. "Am I fully understanding what's bothering you?"

"Exactly." Rain pushed the salad away, suddenly not very hungry.

"Have you asked your mother? Maybe we're creating things that flat out just aren't true. You can't let town gossip be your guide." Julia said with a dismissive wave of her hand.

"It's not just gossip . . . I don't think. I mean, even *you* noticed them together." Rain held her breath and reached for her necklace and toyed with it. "It seems my mother has taken over the master suite at the cabin."

Julia sat straighter at this news. "What do you mean?"

"I didn't find my father's jacket. And the rest of his clothing I found hanging in the spare room closet. It's as if he's taken up his own room which is strange because all my life my parents have shared one. It's just weird, that's all. To me it seems their relationship is in deeper water than I thought." Rain sulked.

The waitress arrived to place the shrimp between them on the table. "Something wrong with your salad?" she asked, pointing to the plate.

"No, it's perfect. It's just that, suddenly, I'm not very hungry," Rain admitted. "Would you mind boxing it for me?"

"Sure," the waitress said. "I'll bring you a box with the check."

"That would be great, thanks."

This seemed to prompt Julia to hurry and finish her lunch, knowing she was now eating alone. They sat in companionable silence as Rain watched the boats and wave runners skate across the lake. She noticed the deckhand and the waitress talking several times and wondered if they were in a relationship. After a sip of iced tea, she turned back to face the dock. Something she overheard caught her attention.

"Hey Frankie! Wait up! You forgot to shut the tackle box and my prize lure is in there!"

A flicker of adrenaline surged through her. "It's him!"

"Him? Him who?"

Rain turned to Julia. "Do you know that man?" She inconspicuously pointed out the older gentleman approaching the restaurant, with another man lagging a few feet behind. Frankie's wide shoulders almost took up the entire width of the dock. His bulging arms and solid build looked as if he could've been quite an athlete back in his day.

A look of confusion washed across Julia's face and she set down her fork. "No, why? Should I?"

"I overheard someone at the market say that Thornton was accusing Frankie of something."

The question that burned through Rain's mind:
What exactly was Thornton accusing him of?

Chapter Thirteen

Rain studied the man called Frankie and his cohort who leaned a casual elbow against the outside tiki bar. They were each nursing a beer and throwing their heads back in collective laughter.

"Maybe we should go and get a drink? You think?" Julia suggested. "See what they're laughing about."

"Should we?" Rain chewed on the inside of her cheek while not taking her eyes off the two men. "They're probably just talking nonsense, but after what I overheard at the local market, I'd be curious to see if one of them brought up the recently deceased. Wouldn't you? I mean, how many Frankies can there be around this lake? He seems older to me than I'd expected." Rain squinted her eyes to see if she could get a better determination of the man's age.

Before Rain and Julia had a chance to make their move over to the outdoor tiki bar, the waitress arrived at the men's side with what looked like a takeout bag and handed it to one of them. Rain watched as the two men then slammed the remainder of their beers in one fluid motion, abandoned the empties upon the bar, and ambled back down the pier toward their fishing boat.

"Crud, so much for that plan." Rain turned to Julia and threw up her hands. "Looks like they're leaving. Not much we can do now."

"Bag up your stuff, let's follow them." Julia said, taking one last bite of her salad before ditching her fork and tossing her napkin on top of what little remained of her lunch.

Rain liked her friend's idea and was totally on board. "Here, let me buy." She reached into her clutch and plucked out more than enough money to pay for lunch and a generous tip. She slid the money beneath the iced tea glass, so it wouldn't blow away.

"Nonsense. Let me at least pay for mine," Julia attempted to hand Rain a twenty-dollar bill, but Rain held a firm stance by holding up her palm in defense. "Next time, you can buy. Quick, let's just get a move on."

Rain abandoned her uneaten salad, not waiting for a takeout box, and the two hurried from their table. They quickly navigated their way back down to the dock and reboarded the pontoon. Rain wanted to be sure her boat was out on the open water and not hung up on someone trying to navigate their way in. The last thing she wanted was to lose a visual of Frankie and his friend.

While waiting for their turn to depart the dock, Rain followed the two men with her eyes and observed them boarding a fishing boat with a flashy red Lund decal reflecting on the side. Frankie and his friend were bustling around the boat, moving fishing poles and adjusting their gear in order to get situated before their departure. To Rain, they seemed completely oblivious to the fact that were under surveillance by a couple of thirtysomething women. The two men finally settled in and shared a bag of French fries, while they, too, seemingly waited their turn to pull away from the restaurant's dock.

Rain unmoored the pontoon to a spot where they could inconspicuously float. She cut the engine, and then lifted the sundress off her head to expose her bikini in order to make it look as if they'd stopped merely to sunbathe. Julia noted and followed suit. This gave them a perfectly good reason for the pontoon to bob idly in the water. As soon as she noticed the Lund pulling away from the dock and planing out atop the water, she flicked the ignition on and hit the throttle in full pursuit.

The Lund fishing boat was clipping along at a decent speed, creating a large wake behind them. A wave runner, outside the appropriate lake rules, attempted to squeeze between the Lund's wake and the front of the pontoon, giving Rain no other choice than to back off the throttle. Then a sailboat came between them, causing her to cut the engine completely. She threw up her hands in frustration and shook her head in disgust as the pontoon bobbed along idly, being pushed back by each oncoming wave.

"See what I mean about the lake traffic getting to be a little too much?" Julia asked. "This is borderline ridiculous! It was never like this when we were kids. We practically had this lake to ourselves! Remember? Not anymore. Pine Lake has officially become a hotspot. And I for one am not exactly happy about that," she added, adamantly tapping a finger to her chest.

"I can't *be-lie-ve* we lost them! Ugh!" Rain slapped her palm to her forehead. She then reached under the seat, plucked a beach towel from her bag, and wrapped the towel around her middle before slumping down in the captain's chair.

"Oh well, at least we know Frankie owns a fishing boat, right?" Julia asked defeatedly. "At least it's something to go on."

"Yeah, and it's a Lund. Maybe we'll be lucky and there won't be fifty more of them today on the lake just like it." Rain rolled her eyes.

"Actually, the red decal on the side is 'extra,'" Julia said throwing her fingers up in air quotes. "My dad had an estimate once to put on that added bling when he bought his new boat and declined because of the cost of it. That's an expensive boat." Julia wrapped the beach towel tighter to her midriff to cover her one-piece swimsuit. "Besides, what are the chances we'd hear them talking about Thornton anyway? Pretty slim, to be honest. I doubt they were throwing back beers talking about the guy's murder in public. Especially, if there was any hint of guilt on their part. Do you?"

Rain's shoulders fell. "Yeah, I suppose. So far, it's the only lead I have; I was hoping to poke the dragon for more." She didn't add that it was the *only* lead away from her own parents' potential involvement. She kept silent on that little tidbit.

"Hey, at least we're getting some sun." Julia smiled and then reached for her suntan lotion and began to apply it to her legs and the tops of her feet. "Want some?"

"Nah, I usually only burn once, then tan the rest of the summer. I'll take my chances," Rain said, turning her face toward the sun and closing her eyes to block it.

"Suit yourself," Julia said.

The breeze off the water felt refreshing and Rain breathed it in. "Wow, I forgot how much I love being out here. It's gorgeous on the lake today."

"Me too, friend. Me too. No place I'd rather be than out here on this lake with you!" Julia's tone carried a smile. "I've missed you, Rain, seems like forever since we've done this."

"Julia?"

"Yeah?" Julia was covering the bench seat with her towel and then rested on top of it. She turned then, shielding her eyes from the sun, in order to face Rain.

"I'm sorry."

Julia sat up and leaned on one elbow, "For what?"

"For letting our friendship slide. For not coming up here as much. For letting my life with Max get in the way." Rain sighed. "I never should've done that. It wasn't right."

"Nonsense! Don't worry your pretty little head about it, we're here now, aren't we?" Her friend grinned. "I can imagine how you'd miss this, though; we grew up here." Julia shaded her eyes with her hand and then dug around until she reached her hat and placed it firmly on her head. "I get the feeling Max didn't like coming up north, did he? Not a fan of the Northwoods in general? Or just here on Pine Lake?"

"Not really. He was born on the west coast, and he never really got the salty sea out of his veins," Rain admitted. "To him, this lake wasn't the same . . . Anyhow, I just want you to know that I'm sorry. I feel like we missed so much."

"No need to apologize. Life does that to the best of us, I was busy with Nick, too. It seems like we kept missing each other. Every time I was up here, you guys weren't and vice versa. Besides, I could've tried and visited you down in Milwaukee, and I didn't. Let's just agree, we're both happy to be spending time together again, and we'll make a stronger effort not to let life get in the way again. Deal?"

"Deal." Rain reached out and they fist-bumped, extended their hands like an explosion and then laughed aloud like two of Julia's teenage students.

The boat drifted slowly across the water, led by the slow current, as the two sunbathed. After a while, Rain noticed that they'd drifted clear into one of the many hidden coves, and soon she'd have to either anchor the pontoon, or navigate their way out before they hit shore.

"How about pointing me in the direction of the Browns' cottage? I'd like to see where Thornton's been living the last few months. Wouldn't you?"

Julia reached for the suntan lotion on the floor and tucked it back into her bag. "Umm," Julia stood up, steadied her stance, and then looked both east and west before pointing right. "Hug the shoreline and head that way." She sat down on the bench seat before Rain stepped in front of the controls and hit the throttle.

The two traveled along the edge of Pine Lake, admiring each residence as they toured. They watched as folks gathered lakeside, drinks in hand, throwing a frisbee, or sunbathing upon their docks. Every now and then they'd see a few kids with fishing poles in hand.

"I love that house," Julia said, pointing out a weathered gray McMansion set back a few hundred feet from shore. "Look how much frontage they have," she added in a dreamy tone. "They keep the landscaping so nice, don't they?"

Rain noticed a woman in a large straw hat tending a nearby flower garden along the side of the house. "Yeah, that sure is a beautiful property." She also noted the flowering baskets that hung from the porch were similar to the ones Marge had purchased earlier in the day at the market. The lawn leading to shore looked as green and plush as emerald Ireland.

"Oh, wait. Here's the one you were looking for." Julia pointed three estates down from the McMansion to a large, but modest in comparison, two-story home that sat back from the shore about seventy-five feet. "That's the Browns' house. I remember it well, we used to have waterski club meetings there. Remember?"

"I don't remember that?"

"Oh, it must've been before you joined the club then," Julia squinted her eyes for confirmation. "Yeah, that's definitely the one. I remember the tree swing that hangs out over the water, see it?" She pointed to a tire swing that did just that and sat idly waiting for its next guest.

Rain backed off the throttle to the slowest trolling speed to take it all in. "What road is the house on, do you know?" It was hard to catch her bearings, to define land and subdivision from the water side.

Julia pointed to the small peninsula that jutted out to the next house. "I know that's Bark Lane that comes right here to the point, so it must be the road parallel to it. I'm not sure what the name of that street is, though."

"Oh, okay. No worries, I think I know where that is."

"Rain, look!"

Rain turned her attention to where Julia was now pointing. The fishing boat with the bright red Lund decal bobbed idly, attached to the dock adjacent to the Browns' property.

"Looks like your friend Frankie and Thornton were neighbors before he died."

Chapter Fourteen

The smell of chicken searing on the grill wafted in the air and, for the first time in a long time, Rain was hungry. Even with the chaos of the last few days, things seemed to be finally settling and as she gazed out across her deck at Julia, Nick, Jace, Marge, and even her new furry friend, Rex—she felt blessed. Rain couldn't believe how completely familiar this group of people already felt to her. It was as if time had slipped backward, and she and Julia had picked up where they had left off during their teenage years. In a mere few hours together, the two were connecting again like long-lost family members.

Before the arrival of her dinner guests, Nick had assisted Rain in resurrecting an old patio table out of storage, to place upon the deck for the summer. She knew the moment she'd seen him put the table in place, she could foresee many meals would happen beneath that umbrella. After a thorough wipe down, the table was brought back to its original glory.

"Do we have enough room?" Rain asked as she handed Julia a stack of napkins.

Julia ducked her head from beneath the umbrella, her pink hair now gleaming in the sunlight. "Plenty of room," she said. "And if we don't, we'll squeeze in tighter," she winked and smiled before returning to the table to arrange the plates and cutlery.

Rain looked toward the grill and noticed Jace was standing in front of it and was flipping the chicken, while Nick chatted with him and uncorked a bottle of wine. It was as if each of them had stepped into roles in a production; each already knowing his or her own part. If it hadn't been for the murder of Thornton Hughes, Rain would've thought them all the perfect dining companions for a normal dinner party. She leaned over the deck railing to find Marge taking Rex out to do his business beside a tree and noticed the grass had been cut. Why hadn't she taken note of that earlier? Had her parents hired a landscaper for the summer? Who had cut it while she and Julia had been out on the pontoon?

Since everyone seemed to have a job to do, Rain suddenly felt out of sorts, despite the dinner taking place at her own home. She shoved her hands deep into her denim shorts pockets and looked out onto the lake. She watched as a flock of gulls squeaked over an abandoned bellied up fish atop the water. They each fought for it, until one gull won and flew off protectively with its dinner.

Nick seemed to catch on to her awkwardness, walked over, and handed her a glass of white wine. "Looks like you could use this," he said before nudging her playfully.

Rain willingly accepted the glass and took a sip, "Thank you, Nick."

"How you holdin' up? You all right? It's only day two for you in the Northwoods, and so much has happened."

Rain turned to him. "Despite everything, I'm more than all right. I didn't realize how I'd been socially isolating myself since Max's death. This feels surprisingly normal, and to be honest, I haven't felt that in a long while, so thank you for coming over to barbeque with me." She lifted the glass in cheers before taking a sip.

"That's good to hear, Rain. We sure are happy that you've decided to come up for the summer. I know, for one, Julia really missed you." The two turned their focus on his wife who was bustling about. Julia was uncovering a large cobb salad that she'd brought from home. They watched as she added a vinaigrette, tossed it with tongs and placed the salad in the center of the table.

"Yeah. I've missed her, too."

"You're welcome, by the way." Nick's attention left his wife and he turned, bobbing his head and pointing a finger past the deck railing.

"I'm sorry?"

"I really thought you would've noticed when we were bringing the table up. But in all fairness, I guess you've had a lot to contend with since you arrived. I'm sure you're a bit overwhelmed." Nick rubbed at his arm absently before readjusting the ballcap on his head.

Rain had absolutely no idea what Nick was talking about. She wondered if her forehead mirrored his and was wrinkled in concentration. She noticed lately in the mirror how her thirties seemed to be taking its toll on her usual flawless face, and stress was now showing itself in deep waves.

"The grass?" Nick questioned with raised eyebrows.

"You?" Rain pointed in his direction and then touched her fingers to her lips.

"Yeah, while you and Julia were out to lunch, I took care of it. It was getting long; I hope you don't mind. Landscaping is a bit of my thing, it sort of relaxes me."

"Oh, my goodness, can I repay you somehow?"

Nick chuckled. "That's what neighbors do. They help each other!" He playfully jabbed her with an elbow. "Plus, Julia said you bought her lunch. Really, it's the least I could do to help you."

Rain was not accustomed to this. Back in the city, of course people were friendly, but cutting an acreage for their neighbor would be unheard of. Neighbors would be too busy for that sort of thing. Or find something better to do.

"How can I thank you?"

"You just did." Nick grinned and then tapped his wife playfully on the backside as she rushed past them.

"Well, I might just have to hire you for the entire summer. If you're up for it." Rain smiled and then a surge of smoke caught her attention. "Can you excuse me for just one second," she held a finger in the air. "It looks like Jace might need a plate for the chicken pretty soon." Rain turned from Nick and headed over to Jace who was waving a plume of smoke away from the grill with one hand.

"I better not burn supper; I'll never hear the end of it from my sister. Nor will I be invited back. I guess, I shouldn't've taken over from you. You were doing quite fine on your own before I got involved." Jace grinned wider when Rain reached closer to his side. The hint of his cologne was quickly replaced by the smell of smoke.

Rain pinched the bridge of her nose and smirked. "I may have overdone it with the olive oil, you think? Too much in the marinade causes the chicken to burn?"

"I don't know *what* you bathed this chicken in, but I near ate it raw. It smells amazing! What is it? No one warned me you were a trained chef?" Jace's light eyebrows danced jokingly, and Rain was happy to see the officer letting his official guard down and enjoying the makeshift gathering.

"Just homemade pesto I threw together."

Jace's eyes narrowed.

"You don't know what's in pesto?"

"Uh uh"

"Basil, olive oil, parmesan cheese . . ." Rain was ticking each item off on her fingers when she noticed Jace smiling down at her.

His grin widened.

"Oh." Rain elbowed him jokingly, "You do know what's in pesto! You stinker!" She then remembered back to her youth how Jace had always had a bit of a teasing side. She'd long since forgotten, as she hadn't spent as much time with him when they were kids. He was a few years older than Julia and was far more interested in "older girls" at the time, to give either one of them the time of day.

"Uh, yeah. We do eat stuff other than crawfish and walleye around here. I for one have a very mature palate." Jace plucked at his faded Abercrombie T-shirt and gave it a shake as if he needed to cool down from the hot grill. He then shifted his weight and his smile faded. "Just to let you know, I left your grandfather's book inside the house on the kitchen island." His head nodded in the direction of the cabin.

The conversation was thrust so quickly back to the murder that Rain had to steady herself by resting a hand beside the side burner on the grill.

Was he uncomfortable with the teasing? Or was he flirting and stopped? The ease and banter between them had felt so natural, Rain almost didn't want it to end. She hadn't had fun like that since Max . . .

"I thought you wanted it back, so . . . I put a rush on it," he said, interrupting her thoughts.

"Thank you, I appreciate that very much. My grandfather Luis's work is very important to our family. His book is irreplaceable, because it's long out of print." Rain took a sip of wine and held the fruity liquid in her mouth for a moment before swallowing. "The publisher went out of business years ago," She added, fluttering her hand in order to wave off a new plume of smoke that floated in front of her.

"I could understand that, which is why I took it from evidence. They're finished with it anyway." Jace picked up a beer from the nearby cooler, popped the top, and took a sip.

"Did they find anything of value? Fingerprints? Anything helpful?"

"A partial to Thornton was all we could lift. Unfortunately, the pollen from the air dusted the book— therefore prints proved inconclusive." He said as he began to peel away the label on the beer.

"Oh."

"In your case though, it's good news, right? It allowed me to return your book. Otherwise, your grandfather's novel would've sat in evidence for who knows how long." Jace took another sip of his beer and then set it down beside the side burner on the grill and flipped the chicken. "You ever read it?"

"No, I haven't yet. I wasn't interested in his writing when I was younger. I only liked to trade Nancy Drew books with Julia back then." Rain chuckled, gesturing a hand toward his sister. "And because my grandfather's books were always kept up here, and didn't leave the safety of the library, I never had a chance. But now that you've returned it, I'm pretty sure I'll be digging into it real soon. Do you like to read?"

"Nah, not much time for that. I work out in the morning before work," Jace lifted his bicep and hardened his muscle and then dropped his arm as if embarrassed he'd shown off too much. "After work, I'm too tired. I'd rather watch something mindless on TV, catch up on sports, or go fishing." He shrugged before lifting the beer to his lips. He then set it back down and wiped the condensation from the beer off his hands onto his shorts.

"I can understand that." Rain ran her finger along the top of the wineglass, making an ethereal sound. She then took another sip.

"By the way, the chicken is done," Jace said, centering them both back in the present as he turned the knob and shut the grill top to keep it warm.

"I'll go grab a plate," Rain said. Grateful for the diversion, she rushed into the house in search of a platter.

* * *

The group gathered around the table, shared a delicious home-cooked meal, and talked casually about nothing of importance until Julia turned to Jace. "Anything new on the investigation front? I speak for all of us when I say, I think we'd all like an update. Yes?" Julia's eyes bounced around those at the table, looking for an agreeable nod. "Care to share?"

Jace took a bite of his chicken and slowly chewed, taking his time, before dodging his sister and turning his attention instead to Rain. "This is delicious. Best pesto chicken I've ever had." He lifted his palm in the air as if he was taking an oath. "Hands down, I swear. Thanks for the invite." He smiled, causing deep dimples to form on either side of his face.

Rain smiled in response but felt an uncomfortable stillness hovering around the table. Everyone gathered could tell that Jace was avoiding his sister's line of questioning, but Julia persisted.

"I think you owe us something, Jace. Cheese Whiz, it happened only a few hundred yards from here." Julia flung a hand in the direction of the outhouse. They collectively lifted their eyes in the direction of the yellow tape that still flapped in the breeze.

Jace raised an eyebrow but didn't comment.

"Come on," Julia pushed. "Don't you think we have the right to know why the guy was bludgeoned to death over there? Do you have any leads or what?" She placed her hands firmly on the table and leaned toward her brother expectantly.

Jace cleared his throat. "It's not really something I'm supposed to be talking about. You know better than that, Julia." His eyes warned as he lasered in on his sister. The whole table felt the vibration of the table from his leg shaking in agitation beneath it, and he caused a slight tremor to the deck floor next to Rain.

Julia didn't heed the warning. "We heard that Thornton was planning on tearing down the campground and putting up a condo complex, and that had a lot of people upset. Myself included." Julia set her fork down and turned a thumb to her chest. "I guess that makes me a suspect." She swirled the wine in her glass and then lifted it to her lips. Her eyes danced toward Rain, and her smile widened.

Marge nodded her head in agreement. "I'm sure Jace and the entire police department have their hands full with this investigation. I imagine the suspect list is long—real long. You may as well just get in line," she said before leaning down to pat Rex on the head. Rain plucked a dog treat from the Tupperware on the table, and then discreetly handed one to Marge in case the owner wanted to share with her dog.

All eyes turned toward Marge when Jace asked, "What do you mean, get in line?" Jace wiped his mouth with a napkin and then took a sip of beer before leaning his elbows on the table and tenting his fingers and waiting for the older woman to explain further.

Marge finger tapped the tabletop. "He thought he would just move to Pine Lake and become a *Laker*? It doesn't work that way. You don't just rent a house on the lake and think you're part of us." She lifted her chin with indignation. "There are generations here. History! That shouldn't just get wiped away!"

Rain was surprised by the older woman's response and pressed, "Because he rented a house you mean? And didn't own?"

Marge's expression pinched. "It was wrong of Thornton to think he could come up here and try and buy up all the property around the lake." She lassoed a finger in the air. "The campground and these homes have been here for generations!" She pounded a fist on the table, shocking them all. "That man was trying to buy up half the lake! And he probably wouldn't have stopped until he succeeded." Rex barked at his owner's elevated voice, and she looked at the dog and uttered, "Tsk Rexy!"

"Well, if anyone looks like a suspect, I guess add me to the list, too," Rain said. "A dead man is found on my property, I'm sure that makes me trump you two as a suspect."

Julia held up a hand to interrupt her. "In your defense, Rain, I saw your car pull into the driveway and you walked immediately to the pier, where I talked to you for the first time. There was no blood on your shirt. The only stain I noticed on your T-shirt was coffee from your drive up to the Northwoods. I wouldn't worry about it, I'm your alibi . . . and it's tight." She winked. "Besides, I saw your face when you saw Thornton for the first time, and it was obvious to me you didn't know the guy! And lastly, you barely had enough time to shower and change. Certainly not enough time to commit a *murder*," she drawled dramatically.

So, the coffee stain that had embarrassed her had also quite potentially saved her from a life behind prison bars, Rain thought inwardly. How's that for irony?

Nick turned to Jace, "In any event, bro, it looks like you're going to have a long list of suspects, there buddy." He said out of the side of his mouth as he teasingly pounded the officer's shoulder. "Two sitting right here at this very table," he added with a laugh, wagging his finger between his wife and Marge. "How about you cuff 'em right now? Boy wouldn't that be fun." He slapped his knee and threw his head back in laughter. Julia's response was to swat her husband with the back of her hand, but she barely attempted to hide her smile.

Jace instead cornered the women by pointing each one of them out and saying, "In all seriousness, all three of you were on the property and found the deceased. "Who do *you* think killed Thornton Hughes?"

Rain didn't want to utter a word regarding the horror that had been going on in her head. Thinking either one of her parents, and their mess, could provide potential motive was bad enough. Saying it aloud to an officer of the law was another thing.

"Now isn't that the million-dollar question?" Julia asked, puckering her lips and setting her empty wine glass back on the table. She looked into the empty glass longingly as if already ready for a refill.

Marge straightened in her chair, turned to Jace, and said, "I certainly hope I'm not on your suspect list. It's a known fact that the person who discovered the body is usually considered a suspect, no?"

"You mean Rex?" Jace cracked a smile. "Didn't your dog find our victim? You don't have anything to worry about Marge. You have two women sitting at this table who I'm sure would provide a tight alibi, right ladies?" He grinned as his eyes traveled between Rain and Julia who nodded in agreement.

"Officer Lowe, if you share the evidence with us, maybe we can help you solve this crime. We're all readers here. All three of us love a good mystery novel." Marge pointed to herself and added, "I for one can usually figure out who the guilty party is despite any red herrings the author tries to mystify me with. Share with us what you have so far for evidence, and we'll assist you." The older woman leaned in eagerly and expectantly.

Jace pushed his plate aside and lifted from his chair and then turned to Nick. "I think we can still get a few hours of fishing in before dusk. Yeah? Whaddaya say partner?"

Rain piped up, "Wait, you're ignoring her? Marge has a good idea here." She flung a hand in the direction of the older woman. "Us girls, if we put our heads together, could probably provide valuable insight to your case."

Jace turned to Nick and held out his hands in defense, seemingly looking for a way out.

Nick caught on, mirrored Jace, and leapt from the chair with newfound enthusiasm. "Fishing? Now, your speaking my language!" He turned to his wife for permission with puppy dog eyes and his hands out like drooping paws. "Pleeease, honey?"

"Get outta here, boys." Julia whisked the men away with her hands before gathering the littered plates around the table and stacking them.

Jace and Nick shared a happy exchange when Rain added, "Go fellas, we got this. We'll clean up."

The two men exited faster than Road Runner before anyone could change their minds. Their behavior morphed from adults to childlike excitement before their very eyes. Like two underage boys heading for their first drink, they rushed down the stairs. "Thanks again for supper!" Trailed after them in unison.

"Men!" Julia huffed as she gathered the plates, Rain collected the glasses, and Marge opened the sliding glass door, leading back into the cabin with Rex at their heels.

"Just throw it all in the sink," Rain directed when they reached the kitchen. "I'll clean it up later. While we have a few minutes let's unload Marge's trunk and start planning the reopening of the library."

"If you gals unload my trunk of books, I'll load the dishwasher. How about that?" Marge was already handing Julia the car keys before Rain could argue with the plan. Marge shooed Julia away with her hands. "Go on now. And don't you listen to what those boys had to say." Marge shook her finger in annoyance. "We're gonna solve this crime." She added with determination. "Those boys know nothing when it comes to women and a good mystery." She uttered under her breath. "Nope, they have no idea what they're in for."

And they didn't either.

Chapter Fifteen

R ain's mind was churning like butter. While she and
Julia unloaded the trunk of books, she couldn't help
but reflect on what Marge had mentioned around the dinner table about everyone in Lofty Pines having a beef with
Thornton. She, too, loved a good mystery novel. Maybe it
was up to the three of them to solve the murder of Thornton
Hughes.

"What? I can tell something is going on in that noggin
of yours." Julia followed Rain in the direction of the library
with her arms stacked with so many books it looked as if she
might topple over with a strong wind.

Rain was piloting her own large stack, being careful
not to drop any books herself. She didn't want one precious
novel to fall in the dirt and get soiled, nor did she wanted to
damage a brand new cover. Getting new release books for
the library felt like a Christmas morning of her childhood.
She couldn't wait to escape in one of them, with multitudes
to choose from.

"Come on, tell me. Gosh, you remind me of my brother. You get all up in your head sometimes!" Julia teased. "Spill it or I'll nag you until you do. Don't worry, I'll wear you down, I'll wear Jace down, too." She grinned. "Don't you worry your pretty little head about it."

Rain remained silent, deep in her own thoughts.

When they arrived at the entrance to the library, Rain set the stack of books carefully by the door before returning to the cabin for the key. "Hang on a sec," she said as she doubled back after retrieving it and slipped the key into the lock. She held the door for Julia to enter. The smell of aged books—a faint mix of grass and vanilla, was a welcome scent. She really needed to spend more time in here.

Julia set the stack of books on a side table directly inside the library door and waited for Rain to fully enter with hers. "Come on . . . I can tell, you have a lot on your mind. Will you please just spill it?" she ordered. "You're driving me crazy."

Rain retrieved the books, two by two, and stacked them neatly atop Julia's pile. Then she turned to her friend and whispered. "I can't get this potential affair between the victim and my mother out of my head. Is that really what you want to hear?"

Julia sat down in the nearby loveseat adjacent to the bookshelf and tapped the seat beside her. "Drop the books and come over here for a second, will you please?"

Rain placed a book atop the stack and then acquiesced to her friend's bidding. After taking a seat, her shoulders drooped and she leaned forward, putting her head in her hands.

"I hesitate to even talk to you about this. I should've mentioned it when you first brought it up over lunch, but I couldn't. I needed to ask Nick's permission before we came over for the barbeque, if it was okay to share this with you. It's private between us, not another soul knows."

Ran sat upright and turned to face Julia. She tucked one leg beneath her and picked up one of the throw pillows and held it on her lap.

"I feel like if I share this with you, maybe it'll help somehow." Julia picked on the thread of her shirt and then her gaze fell to the floor. "Here goes, I'm just gonna say it." She took a breath. "I almost cheated on Nick once," she said quietly. So quietly, Rain wasn't sure if she'd heard her friend correctly.

Rain didn't know what to say, but the words she thought Julia had uttered made her grip the throw pillow tighter, causing the anchor pictured on it to skew.

"It was before we were married, but Nick and I were engaged. That still doesn't make it right but . . ."

"With who?" Rain asked.

Julia rolled her eyes and chuckled. "Actually, it was the father of one of my students. He was much older than me, but we had this weird connection, I can't explain it . . ." Her voice trailed off.

"And he almost cheated on his wife with you?" Rain could feel herself twisting harder at the pillow. She'd never heard firsthand this side of an account. She hoped she was ready for it.

"No . . . he wasn't married. At least that's what he'd told me." Julia waved a hand airily. "He'd recently divorced. Honestly, I felt bad for the guy, which was probably part of the draw at the time." She threw her hands up in frustration. "Honestly, I don't know. There was just something about him . . ."

"And you wanted to sleep with him? Because you felt *bad* for the guy?" Rain was incredulous. "Why are you telling me this, Julia?"

Julia reached out a hand to touch her leg. "Because I want you to understand the other side of it. I want you to understand that despite me being sooo in love with Nick, this almost still happened. Sometimes these weird universal connections happen. But that doesn't negate the fact that you still love your spouse or fiancé as was my case."

Rain didn't know what to say.

"And I know you don't think there's room for forgiveness, but Nick has forgiven me, and it's actually made our relationship stronger. We talk about things we often avoided in the past. Instead, we're head on in our conversations . . . we're candid . . . I love him, Rain, and I'd never intentionally hurt him that way again."

Rain buried her head in her hands.

"I know Max hurt you deeply, Rain. I can see it on your face when you talk about what may or may not be going on with your parents. But you're gonna have to try to keep those things separate, or you'll drive yourself nuts. You're gonna have to find a way to forgive Max, even though he's no longer here. Forgiveness is for you," Julia added gently. "It's not for the person who wronged you."

"How do you expect me to do that? Huh?" Rain squeezed the pillow tighter. "I loved him, and he cheated on me. Me. He did it to me. All while I was trying to get pregnant with *his* child." Her voice began to quake. "I was going through infertility treatments for him! He wanted a baby even more than I did!"

"I hear you. I do. And in no way am I negating your feelings or saying that you can't feel them. No way." She flung out her hands like an umpire calling safe. "I guess what I'm trying to say, after being on the other side of this, and Nick and I having worked it out . . . I learned you can still love someone deeply and do something incredibly selfish and wrong. But it doesn't change the fact that I love Nick and I always have, and I know Max loved you. He just made a very bad judgment. He fragdaggle'd up."

"Fragdaggle'd?" Rain felt a chuckle bubble to the surface unbidden.

"You know the word. I still can't swear because of my students, otherwise I'll go back to work in the fall like a drunken sailor and nobody wants that." Julia grinned.

"What ever happened to him."

"To who?"

"The guy, the student." Rain rolled her hand in the air looking for more information.

"They moved. He took a new job, so the student was transferred out of my classroom. I was very happy about that actually. I didn't know how I would face my kids every day otherwise. It was a painful time. Do you think differently about me, after sharing this with you?"

"Not at all. I love that you're so transparent. It's another thing I've missed about you and I appreciate it. I do." Rain reached out and squeezed Julia's hand.

"Do you think differently about you?" Julia asked.

"How so?"

"Can you see how Max still loved you. Or how Willow may still love Stuart very much?"

"Yeah, but what if my mother *was* having an affair. And what if it made my dad crazy? What if all of this got taken a little too far?"

"I don't think so—"

"What do you mean, you don't think so? What about the owner of the hardware store adding to this mess, saying that he saw my father?" Rain threw up her hands, tossing the throw pillow to hit the floor. "I can't even believe I'm saying this out loud, but what if my father isn't in Japan? What if he's *here* in Lofty Pines? And what if he had something to do with this?" She covered her mouth with her hand as if she'd made a mistake by sharing the deepest chasm of what had been plaguing her head. Somehow Julia's confession made it easier. Julia had a way of making her unload all the dirty truth from her own skull. It was an unusual gift.

"You really believe that?" Julia rose from the seat and placed her hands firmly on her hips and leaned away from her.

"No!" Rain rose to her feet, mimicking her. "But I need to prove otherwise, because I can't help but think ONE of my parents could be the prime suspect!" Rain hissed in a whisper.

"Well, what about the Chicago Cubs jacket? Surely, finding that would ease your mind. I told you—"

"I never found it." Rain's shoulders slumped and she sighed deeply. "I never found any of my fathers' clothes. Remember I told you? The master bedroom closet is void of anything belonging to him."

"It has to be in the cabin somewhere else, besides the master closet. It didn't just disappear! Maybe your dad has it packed away somewhere. Or maybe all his clothes are in a spare room closet somewhere."

"It's not. *Trust me.* I've looked everywhere. Yes, as I mentioned to you on the boat, I found some clothes in the spare room closet, but no Cubs jacket." Rain shook her head.

"Well . . ." Julia blew out a frustrated breath. "What now?"

Rain looked to the ceiling and then faced her friend squarely. "I need to go over to Thornton's place. The one he was renting—the Browns' place. Maybe I'll find something belonging to my mother that can help explain things. She tapped a finger to her lips. ". . . I *need* to find something. Or find nothing. Either way, I need to either confirm or deny my suspicions. I need to prove to myself that this town is just full of gossips."

"I'm sure the police have already gone through everything over there," Julia said flatly. "Don't you think? They've probably gone through it with a fine-toothed comb."

"Yeah, but they're not looking for something belonging to my mother. I *am*," Rain said, jutting a firm thumb to her chest.

"And that will help how exactly?" Julia shifted on her feet and then leaned her shoulder against the bookcase, careful not to shift any books by doing so.

"I don't know," Rain admitted. "Do you have any other suggestions? I need to do something. I can't just sit around here and wait for a confession from someone. Besides, one way or another, I have to figure out what my mother's connection was with the victim."

Julia turned away from her and ran her hand against the spines of the books on the shelf contemplatively. She readjusted the books neatly on the shelf as she spoke. "I noticed that Jace brought back your grandfather Luis's book. You guys didn't tell me it was found out under the bush not far from Thornton. I knew Jace found a book, but not one written by your own grandfather. Do you think that has anything to do with all of this? Could it provide some sort of clue perhaps?"

"Like what?" Rain asked, smoothing her hair away from her eyes. "To me, it only proves that Thornton was deeply connected to my mother somehow. You know my mother wouldn't let that book leave this room." Rain gazed around the shelves of novels that surrounded them. "Unless a lot has changed since my childhood, she didn't let anyone remove my grandfather's work from this room. Ever. Am I right? Please correct me if I'm wrong."

Julia confirmed with a nod of her head. "That's right. Your grandfather's books were under strict instruction not to leave the property. Maybe Willow would allow them to read one of them out on the deck, but honestly, I'm not even sure she allowed that. I know for sure she wouldn't let anyone take one to the outhouse!" She giggled at an attempt to ease the tension.

Rain smiled at the outhouse comment. "So, what does that tell us? To me, it tells me there was something in that written work that was important. Something in my grandfather Luis's book . . ."

"Like what?"

"I don't know." Rain sighed and then bit at her lip.

Julia moved over to the shelf where Rain's grandfather's books were stored. "Why that particular book? And not one of the others?" She began to sift through the small pile to view the titles.

"I left the one that was found by Thornton in the kitchen. The one Jace brought back from the police station. Should I go and grab it? So we can have a look?"

"Yeah. Let's take a closer look. Maybe it'll tell us something?" Julia suggested.

"Okay, wait here."

Julia stepped away from the shelf, held a book to her heart, and spun around like Julie Andrews in the entrance song from the Sound of Music. "What? And leave me here among all this?"

Rain rolled her eyes and laughed as she turned out the library door.

Marge was wiping the last of the dishes with a towel and setting them alongside the sink but turned to greet Rain when she arrived.

"Dear, can you reach the glasses up there to put away? You have a few inches on me that would help, otherwise I'm going to need to find a stepstool." Marge's eyes darted around the floor seemingly looking for one.

"Don't worry about this mess, I've got it!" Rain rushed to take over. "You're doing too much. I thought you were going to just load them in the dishwasher?"

"Old habits die hard dear. I wasn't raised on machinery; I was raised on these two hands doing the job." Marge shook her head and smiled. "Boy, sometimes when I watch you it's like you're the spitting image of your mother." She squinted. "Sometimes I can see the same mannerisms of your grandfather, Luis, too . . . it's uncanny." She smiled affectionately and watched as Rain loaded the glasses into the cabinet.

Rain turned to her and leaned her weight against the counter. "I miss my grandfather," she said wistfully. "I'm starting to lose things he used to say to me. You know how one day that suddenly happens? After you lose someone you love?"

Marge nodded knowingly. "Yes. Yes, I do." She reached out and tapped Rain affectionately on the arm. "I can still hear your grandfather's voice sometimes . . . He was a character that fella." She looked off to a faraway place that Rain would never be able to join.

Rain nodded in the direction of her grandfather's book lying atop the counter. "I'm looking forward to reading his novels and getting to know him on a deeper level this summer. I've heard the old saying that writers "write what they know." She threw her fingers up in air quotes. "Maybe I'll learn to know him as an adult, something different from my childhood memories."

Rain couldn't discern the peculiar look that washed over Marge's face and the sudden stiffness in her spine. It seemed the older woman was suddenly holding back or something she'd said had upset her, and she couldn't understand why or what.

Marge confirmed it when she said, "I probably should be getting home. I don't particularly like driving after dark, and it looks as if dusk is upon us." She pointed to the window. The orange sun was slipping quickly out of sight as if the water was soon going to swallow it. In the same way, Rain felt totally in the dark of generational family secrets that even Marge seemed privy to. And she was desperate to shine a light on them.

Chapter Sixteen

Rain jammed the SUV into park and then reached into the backseat for the bucket filled with cleaning supplies and two sets of rubber gloves. "Thanks for reaching out to the Browns. I mean, it's a bit of a stretch, telling them you were starting a cleaning business, but it worked. I guess we'd better do a bang-up job to convince them they hired the right pair, huh." She feigned a laugh.

"Are you sure you want to do this?" Julia squished her face as if she'd just smelt something putrid, like rotten garbage. "Maybe we should've just asked Jace to bring us over here to check things out." Julia stopped brushing the emery board across her fingernails, and then tossed the nail file on the dashboard after blowing the dust from her fingers. "I guess I could use the extra money, but cleaning wasn't exactly what I had in mind for a side job this summer, thank you very much." Julia bounced her eyebrows and then grinned. "The lengths I go to for my friends." She rolled her eyes dramatically. "Don't say I never did anything for you."

"Hopefully, this will be our one and only hired cleaning job. Besides, after the way your brother was acting at dinner last night, I highly doubt he'd just let us snoop in Thornton's rental to our hearts content. Do you? What are the chances? Like less than zero?"

"I know. I know. Highly unlikely," Julia said blowing out a deflated tone as she shut the door of the SUV and walked to the front of the Browns' estate carrying a bottle of window cleaner in one hand and a full roll of paper towel in the other.

"Actually, I'm surprised the police cleared the house as of part of the crime scene already. Aren't you? They must've taken all the evidence they needed from here, you think?" Rain looked up to take in the large two-story colonial. The black shutters looked as if they'd been recently been replaced, flanking numerous windows that filled the front façade. She lost count and gave up after counting ten windows. She inwardly hoped they wouldn't all need to be washed. Julia would be so upset with her if that were the case.

Julia readjusted the roll of paper towel in her hand as it looked as if she was soon to drop it. "The owner of the rental, Jeremy Brown, is friends with the chief of police. Jeremy insisted he needed to put the house back up for rent for the summer. This is prime-o season, you know. I guess when you have friends in high places, you can pull all kinds of strings."

"I wish your brother would let us pull his strings. Then we wouldn't have to be hired cleaning help to get inside here," Rain said teasingly.

"Right? So much for that!"

Rain waited and watched while Julia set her supplies down on the stoop and unlocked the front door. She took the extra time while Julia fiddled with the lock to crane her neck toward the neighbor's house but didn't catch a visual of Frankie.

Julia's head turned over her shoulder and did a double take as she caught Rain looking toward the neighbor's house and said, "Don't even think about it. Don't tell me, you want to offer to clean Frankie's house, too, in order to get in there." She huffed. "It's NOT happening." Julia gathered the window cleaner and tucked the paper towel under her arm while she held the door wide for Rain to step inside ahead of her.

"Hey . . . now, that's not a bad idea!" Rain grinned and elbowed her friend.

"The things you get me into, lady." Julia shook her head dismissively.

"Me? I seem to remember it was *you* that got us into trouble as kids." Rain shot a finger in Julia's direction. "Remember the time we went out in the kayak after dark? After your father gave us strict orders not to. Man was he ticked at us. I don't think he warmed up to me for like a week after that incident!" Rains eyes grew wide. "I didn't think he'd ever talk to me again!"

Julia laughed, slapping her knee with the roll of paper towel. "I forgot all about that! Too funny."

"Oh, not me. It's seared in my memory!" Rain laughed as she pointed to her forehead.

Their collective focus shifted when the two turned and took in the space they had just stepped into.

"Wow, I wasn't expecting this," Julia said, moving deeper into the house. "It's different than viewing the house lakeside, that's for sure."

"This is beautiful," Rain agreed.

The oversized living room was decorated in monochromatic hues in varying shades of white and off-white furniture and walls. The muted color scheme allowed the panoramic view of the outdoors to catch immediate attention. The large window bathed the room in sunlight.

Rain instantly noticed the striking blue-green color of Pine Lake out of the floor-to-ceiling windows leading to the rear yard. "What a view!" she said, as a magnetic pull caused her no other choice than to walk over to the window to take a closer look. Sparkles danced atop the water and shimmered in the light like dancing jewels.

Julia whistled simultaneously. "It's gorgeous," she sighed. "Breathtakingly beautiful, what a view." She let out a sigh. "Man, I'd kill for it."

Rain snapped her head toward Julia. "Bad timing on that comment there, friend." She teased.

Julia covered her mouth as if she could take the comment back, but it was too late.

Rain pulled back the gauzy looking floor-to-ceiling curtain further and noticed Frankie out tinkering by his boat. The man was turned away from the house, bent over the back of his motor. "Hey, I found him," she whispered even though the two friends were indoors alone. "He's out on the Lund."

Julia must've known exactly who the "he" was that she was referring to, because she plucked the back of Rain's shirt to back them away from the window after joining her there. "We'd better back off before he catches us watching him."

"Are you kidding me? I'm gonna go talk to him." Rain walked over to the screen door leading to the lake and was halfway out of it when she heard Julia's squeal behind her. "Wait! Now? We have a huge house to clean! Don't offer any more services, you hear me! This is the last house I'll clean for you! I'll stay back in case I need to dial 911!"

Rain walked with purpose to the neighboring property and Frankie was so preoccupied with his engine work on the Lund that he didn't even regard her until she stood a foot away from him, standing on his dock.

"Hello, excuse me," Rain cleared her throat.

Frankie rose to his full height to greet her. The man was taller than Rain remembered, and when standing within arm's distance, he trumped her in height. His arms bulged from his T-shirt, filled with a lengthy tattoo that she couldn't place. And the weathering of his face made his true age show. "Something I can help you with?" He wiped greasy hands on an aged hand towel as he waited.

Rain swallowed. She suddenly wondered if she should've made Julia join her for back up as she struggled for the right words. "I just wanted to offer my condolences . . ." she stuttered ". . . for your neighbor . . . Thornton."

His eyes narrowed. "And you are?"

"Oh." Rain wiped sweaty hands on her legs to dry them before offering a hand to shake. "I'm Rain."

"*Rain*?"

"Yeah, like the storm," she looked to the sky and then back again, as she held her hand out waiting for him to take it.

Instead, Frankie continued to wipe his hands with the towel. "I don't think you want to do that. I'm a bit of a mess. The name's Frank but Lakers call me Frankie," he said, looking at his grease-covered hands, and Rain quickly dropped hers to her side.

Rain waved a hand toward the house and noticed Julia standing at the screen door summoning her with her own hand for Rain to return. "That's Julia," she said when she noticed Frankie's eyes follow to the back side of Thornton's rental. "We're just here to clean, so Jeremy can get the house back on the market to rent, and I didn't want you to be concerned that someone was in your neighbor's house, unannounced." She cleared her throat again. This time, she noticed the burn in the back of her throat seemed to be healing.

A look of understanding swept across Frankie's face. "Ahh, I see, you're here to clean."

Rain nodded.

"Any suggestions of how to get blood out of carpet?"

"Excuse me?" Rain could hardly believe what she'd just heard. Frankie must've seen her shock and continued.

"My buddy bludgeoned a few carp and made a bloody mess." He pointed to a dark stain on the floor of the boat next to what looked like a stained wooden club inside a bucket of rags.

"Oh? Carp are starting to invade the lake again? I do remember that was a problem back when I was a kid. Ah, no. I've heard maybe club soda helps with wine stains but I'm sorry. I . . ." Rain gulped and took a step backward.

"People don't know when to quit or how to clean up their own messes, you know what I mean? That's what I get for allowing that guy on my boat."

"Yeah, I hear ya, and speaking of that, my friend won't want me down here gibber-gabbing. We have a large estate to tidy." Rain rolled her eyes. "Well, again, I'm sorry for your loss."

Rain turned on her heel and was about to walk away when she heard Frankie utter under his breath, "not really . . ."

Rain turned back to face him. "Did you say something?"

"Hey, I'm sorry, that was wrong of me." He tossed the soiled towel that he'd used to wipe his hands into the nearby bucket covering the blunt object. "He was a bit of a snob. A bit standoffish is all. I tried to be friendly with the guy, but I guess he just wasn't having it. Ah well, not my place to talk ill of the dead. That's not right of me."

"No, it's okay, I've heard Thornton wasn't too popular with the Lakers." Rains eyes darted across the dock as she searched for the right words, then she went for it. "Didn't like the guy, huh? Any reason why?"

"I wouldn't take it that far, it's not that I didn't like the guy. He was private is all. Hard to really get to know him, even after I'd offered him a few beers on several occasions. He did have one friend, though, that he seemed to get along with. I didn't recognize his friend as one of the Lakers, though. Some German guy. I can't remember his name; I only remember his family came over on the boat. I only talked to him once."

"Oh."

He smiled sheepishly. "Anyway, I appreciate your condolences, but really, it's not warranted."

"No, I get it." Rain rushed, hoping she could get him to open up more. "I didn't actually know Thornton either, but I heard he was frustrating a lot of Lakers. I guess I thought he got to you, too?"

"Nah, the guy was harmless, just standoffish in my opinion is all." Frankie waved a hand of dismissal. "The only time the guy rubbed me wrong when he got a little up in my business. Thought he could tell me and everyone else around here what was acceptable on their property. Hey, it's my property. I can do whatever I please with it." He flung his hand in the direction of his yard toward the thick pine trees.

Rain nodded vigorously and then rolled her eyes, "Yeah, you're not the only one," she scoffed. "I hear he was after the campground, too. Wanted to tear it down and build a condo? The nerve of the guy!" She hoped by taking his side, she could get him to unload more.

Frankie frowned. "Yeah, that would've never worked, Lakers wouldn't have let that pass. Ahh," He waved a hand of disgust. "Don't even get me started."

"His friend? Who is he again?"

"Some guy who speaks multiple languages, as if that was supposed to impress me. All hoity toity and dressed to the nines all the time like he was ready to attend a wedding or something. And he'd said these foreign words and I had no clue what he was saying or if he was talking about me. Give me a break. If you're gonna live up here in the Northwoods, you gotta dress casual like the rest of us, and speak our language. This is our vacation spot, not a competition. Those types just get under my skin is all. Think they're better than everyone else, well I tell you, they're not. I work hard for what I've got!"

A wave runner pulled up to the dock and a guy summoned with a whistle, "Hey Frankie! Tie me on!"

"Hey, look, I gotta go, my mechanic is here to take a look at my engine. Nice meeting you, Storm." Frankie said as he rushed over to dock the wave runner.

"It's Rain!" she uttered after him, but gave up, as he'd already turned away from her.

Rain quickly took the cue for an exit and jogged up the backyard and then re-entered the house.

"Well?" Julia said, with her hands on her hips. "What did you dig up on our guy Thornton? Please tell me you didn't offer cleaning services to the entire neighborhood!"

Rain grinned. "No worries there, I assure you, I didn't offer to clean. Although he asked how to remove blood from his carpet," she added with a smirk.

"Come again?" Julia cuffed a hand by her ear and waited with eager expectation.

"You heard correctly. He says the blood was from carp, but the other thing that kinda bothers me is what was sticking out of a nearby bucket. A mini baseball bat looking thingy. You don't think . . ." Rain slowly rocked her head from side to side and chewed her cheek.

"That it's the murder weapon!" Julia gasped and then covered her mouth with her hands.

"Could it be?" Rain grimaced.

"Come on, let's be honest here, no one would be stupid enough to leave a murder weapon out in the open for anyone to see." Julia waved her hands dramatically in the air.

"Yeah, of course not. We should take Frankie at his word. Right?"

"Right," Julia said, although not convincingly. "Innocent until proven guilty, and all that . . ." she added with a tad more conviction.

Rain wasn't sure she agreed with that last comment. Instead more thoughts tumbled from her mouth. "No doubt Frankie has the physical build to pull off a murder. The dude's built like a brick house." Rain said and then bit her lip to stop herself yet again. "And what if he's so narcissistic he thinks he can easily pass off the murder weapon as a carp tool?" She was letting her imagination run away with her and thinking the worst of everyone around her. It was as if everyone she encountered was guilty, guilty, GUILTY. And this train of thought had to stop at the station. She breathed in deeply and said, "You know what, let's just get on with what we came here for."

"Alrighty then. We'll just have to keep diggin' and see what Thornton's beef was with the guy. If we find enough motive for Frankie maybe then we'll be on to something. Until then, you have no other choice than to take him at his word. Julia spun on her heel and then huffed. "Jumping Jehoshaphat this house is huge. We have a lot of cleaning to do." Julia squished her face after her eyes rose to the elaborately high ceilings and then cornered Rain with a scowl.

Rain blew a breath from the side of her mouth. "Yikes. We may have bitten off a little more than we could chew, huh?" she agreed with a nod and sheepish grimace.

"Yep. I can't believe you talked me into this," Julia said placing her hands on her hips and surveying the space.

"Sorry but not sorry about that," Rain said with a wink. "You wanted to read a new mystery novel? Well, it seems to me, we've stepped right into one." Rain mirrored her friend by slipping her hands on her own hips. "We're bound to discover something in here. Where do you want to start?"

"Jeremy said he wanted me to empty the refrigerator. One of his main concerns was that the leftover food would spoil. I can't half blame him there."

"Oh." Rain deflated and her hands fell to her sides. "That job alone could take all day." She then surveyed the living room with fresh eyes. "To be honest, it's not too bad. It's actually quite tidy in here; I'm thankful at least Thornton was a neat freak."

Julia scanned the room and walked over to the side table next to the white couch where a golf magazine lay open. "Yeah, almost too neat? You know what's missing here?"

"What?" Rain moved over to join her.

"I don't see any personal photos. I mean, I understand this is a rental." Julia threw her hand on a hip and leaned in. "But don't you think it's a little strange there are no personal snapshots? Of anyone? No one he loves. Who is this guy?" She spun around the room for another look. "It's not like he was here for a long weekend. He lived here for months!" Her eyes traveled the walls seemingly looking for photos there, too, and she flicked a finger in the direction of a large sailboat painting. "Wouldn't he display something personal?"

The comment from Julia made Rain wince. The *last* thing she wanted to find was a photo of her mother with that man. That would be just plain awful. "Maybe Jace took them?" she suggested, but Rain really hoped not. She wasn't sure she was ready to explain her theory to the police either.

"Let's take a quick tour of the house to get our bearings. Whatddaya say?" Julia asked as her eyes darted around the space.

"Sounds like a good place to start," Rain answered, taking the lead. She traveled up the open loft stairs and down a long carpeted hallway, where bedrooms flanked both sides.

As she opened each door to peek inside, she noticed the beds were perfectly made, as if they'd never been slept in. She then shared her musings with her friend over her shoulder. "I don't think these rooms were even used. Maybe Thornton wasn't too keen on company?"

"Who knows. Doesn't seem like he was making a lot of friends here in Lofty Pines except for . . ." Julia stopped short and cuffed her hand over her mouth.

Rain heard her friend stop short and knew exactly what she was implying—her mother. She shook her head when Julia replied with a sheepish look.

When they finally arrived at the end of the hall, they both took a collective breath before stepping inside the master bedroom. The room was bright white, just like the others, and Rain wondered how anyone could get any sleep, as she almost had to shield her eyes from the starkness of it all.

Julia walked around the queen-sized bed and stood by the bedside table. "Seriously, who lives like this? There're no personal items? No photos? It's weird, isn't it? It's like walking into a freaking hotel room." She picked up a small blank notepad and flapped it in the air. "Nothing."

"Let me see that." Rain reached for the notepad and squinted. "If you look closely, the top sheet has indents. I'm going to take this home and shade it with a pencil. Maybe I can lift a phone number or something."

"You do that, Nancy Drew," Julia teased, brushing her pink hair off her forehead and then tucking it neatly behind her ears.

Rain ripped the top sheet of paper and slipped it inside her back pocket before laying the notepad back on the bedside table. "Hey, you never know. Right?"

"Do you think the police took everything? This is crazy? I wonder if the Browns came over and took stuff out to donate after the police were done? It really doesn't even look like anyone was living here." Julia's eyes tracked floor to ceiling before walking over to the closet.

Julia opened the closet door, flicked the light, and ducked her head inside. "There are clothes still in here. So, I'm guessing *someone* has been living here." Julia's words started to muffle as she walked deeper inside. Rain followed to see for herself. She was thrilled upon quick inspection not to see any women's clothing hanging there, including anything belonging to her mother. She just wasn't ready for that kind of heartbreak.

"Lots of suits for living in the Northwoods. He never would have made it as a Laker. Check this out," Julia said, pulling out a suit jacket for a closer view. "This looks like it could be Armani."

"You sound like Frankie. Clearly, Thornton didn't understand the casual attire people wear up north," Rain said as she fingered a silk tie hanging on a tie rack. "He had great taste, though, if not better for city living. Or living on either coast."

"Yeah, these clothes must've cost a fortune. Maybe money is the motive? You think?"

"That's what we're here to find out, *Nancy Drew*," Rain said, returning her friend's earlier jibe.

Julia rehung the suit jacket and then retreated out of the closet. "All right, let's go clean that refrigerator or we're going to be here all day." Julia waited for Rain to step outside before flicking off the light and closing the closet door.

Rain followed Julia into the kitchen where her friend continued to search for snapshots along their path. "No photos? I just think it's weird, that's all," she said. "That in itself is a clue. The lack of something can be just as telling as pure evidence. I can't remember where I heard that, or read it, but it stuck with me."

"Makes sense to me. So, what is it telling us?"

"Maybe it's telling us he doesn't want anyone to know anything about his past. Maybe it's seedy and dark!" Julia rolled her hands together and made a spooky face.

"You're a goof." Rain laughed. "And I love you for it."

Rain opened the oversized stainless-steel refrigerator and was relieved to find it wasn't chock full of food. "Looks like our victim preferred take-out," she said after eyeing a Chinese takeout box.

"Thank God. Otherwise we'd be here all day!" Julia huffed.

"What do you want to do with all of this? Take it home with you?"

"Yep, that's what I was told to do. If there's anything worth saving." Julia hung on the door of the refrigerator, waiting. As if she didn't even want to begin the task at hand.

Rain opened a lower cabinet door beneath the sink and found a box of trash bags. "Wanna use these?" she waved the box in the air and Julia gave a thumbs up.

"Sure. I'll hold the bag open." Julia took a bag and shook it open and held it with two hands waiting.

"This is weird, right? Emptying the contents of a dead man's fridge? Like he's never coming back? Poor guy," Rain said reaching for the carton of milk. When she did so, Julia bumped her arm accidentally, and the carton flew out of her hands and crashed to the floor.

"Oh no! What happened? Did I do that? I'm so sorry!" Julia jumped backwards dropping the trash bag to the floor and reaching for a nearby towel that hung neatly on the stove.

"Not your fault, it was as light as a kite for some reason. It literally flew outta my hands." Rain went to grab the carton off the floor, and something made her stop short. "Wait. Didn't you just mention that the absence of something means *something*?"

Julia stared at her with incomprehension before coming to an understanding. "Oh, I get it. Why isn't the carton leaking milk all over the floor?" she asked as she handed over the towel.

"Exactly my dear Watson. You're reading my mind" Rain said as she plucked the carton from the ground and felt its lightness again. After shaking it she said, "It's empty?"

"Why would someone put an empty carton of milk back into the refrigerator? That's ridiculous!"

"You're asking me to climb into the mind of a dead man? And figure out Thornton's lazy cleaning habits? Seriously?" Rain huffed before attempting to toss it into the trash bag.

"Hang on, listen to what you just said. That's just the thing. Look around this place, it's neat. It doesn't fit his profile to put back an empty carton. Do you see any garbage laying around here? Hold on a second." Julia reached for the carton and dropped the empty trash bag to the floor. "Give it here."

Rain folded her arms across her chest while she watched Julia open the milk carton and give it a sniff. She then investigated the carton closer by eyeing the inside. "This doesn't smell like milk; it smells like *cash*."

"Cash?" Rain took a step backward.

Julia gasped.

"What?" Rain threw up her hands, but a chill ran down her spine when Julia began to empty the contents upon the kitchen counter.

A slew of five-hundred-dollar bills fell from the carton onto the counter. There had to be hundreds of them.

"Are these real?" Rain stuttered. "I've never seen a five-hundred-dollar bill in my life!"

"Sure, looks like they're the real deal." Julia frowned. "I hate to say this, but I think we may have just found our motive. I bet these are worth a whole lot more than what's printed on them. I bet they're rare. I think we better call Jace. We are so busted. He's never gonna believe that we were here to clean. Mom couldn't even get me to clean my room when I was a kid."

"Yeah, and while he's here I'll alert him to the neighbor's boat. Maybe then he can find out if Frankie has more than carp blood on his hands.

Chapter Seventeen

After a long day of cleaning, and then a tongue lashing from Jace about why they never should've entered Thornton's rental and used a cleaning business as a ruse, Rain was ready for an escape from reality. Jace had mentioned that the discovery of so many large bills was a significant clue in the case but had refused to elaborate. She and Julia would have to dig deeper into it to find out, but for now, her mind was numb.

Earlier, she had blasted the air conditioner in the library to seventy degrees, with the future promise that she'd be able to snuggle deep within her nylon sleeping bag long into the night. How she longed for Max's solid arms, that formerly wrapped her tight. Tonight, the sleeping bag would have to suffice. The nights were the toughest for Rain. Too much time for her to be alone, to feel the starkness of an empty bedside. And too much time in her head, to think, to feel, and to grieve.

Instead, Rain made a conscious decision to revert to memories from her childhood and allow the comfort of the library and escape of books to encircle her as it once had. She didn't feel so isolated when encouraged by the words that had been put to page, as the result of an author's dream. And she was aware she was never alone in her pain. She knew if she searched for printed validation, she could find pain similar to hers, shelved among one of the many books that surrounded her. Pain that could only transfer from the page to the reader, because a pain like it had certainly, at one time, been felt by the author.

Rain wriggled her toes and nestled deeper into the soft polycotton fabric, wrapping her icy feet in, and feeling nice and toasty. She held her grandfather's book, *Always You*, in one hand, and sipped a mug of tepid herbal tea in the other. The comfort of the hand-hewn logs of the library walls engulfed and protected her, as if her great-grandfather, Lorenzo, stood watching over her. Instead of using the overhead deer antler chandelier, that often cast a shadow when lit at night, Rain resurrected a dim reading lamp from the storage boxes that had traveled with her from Milwaukee. The beam of light kept the room bright enough to read but still provided a comfortable muted glow and shadowed the rest of the space.

Rain flipped to the next chapter, surprised at how much she could relate to Grandfather Luis's words. So stunned was she that her eyes lifted from the page to the tongue and groove pine ceiling in order to reflect on the sentences she had just read:

"I long for you, my love. An ache so deep, I can barely breathe. I'm suffocating, and I don't know how much more my heart can take. Missing you doesn't provide ample words to express . . ."

What was her grandfather talking about? As she read deeper into the novel, Rain discovered that the book that had been found near the body of Thornton Hughes was that of a tragic love story. A story of death and sadness. A love story so wrought with emotion, Rain hardly believed a man had written it, never mind her own grandfather. She knew the book was a work of fiction—but still. The feelings hit too close to reality, to not hide some sort of hidden buried truth.

Rain remembered her grandfather, Luis, as a kind man, a man whose bulbous nose had twitched, whose hazel eyes had always danced and crinkled in laughter as he'd chased her playfully around the yard. A man who liked to tinker with old things and build bird houses for her to paint to then dangle in the trees. A man who had crafted a wooden swing to hang from a mighty oak for Rain to spend hours pumping her legs, until her leg muscles would burn, and she could no longer take it. A man whose stark white hair had often been disturbingly askew and flapped haphazardly in the breeze. That was the man she remembered. And she missed him.

Rain hadn't experienced a man who could write with such sadness and desperate longing for another. So much melancholy was infused in the written words, that the book surprised her. She flipped the cover to see the date of publication, remembering back to the year when her grandfather Luis was born. After doing the math in her head, she realized he had published *Always You,* long into his forties. But he couldn't have been talking about her grandmother that he'd been aching for? She'd outlived him by eighteen months. So, how did grandfather get the emotions of anguish so vividly right? Had Luis known such pain? He must've experienced something similar, as the words were so raw and relatable. She couldn't fathom how a "little research" could transfer so knowingly, so vividly and honestly, to the page. She'd known her grandfather only as a jolly figure and couldn't recall ever having a deep conversation with him. It was as if she was getting a peek behind the curtain, to understand him on a more intimate level. One that she'd never had the chance to experience growing up.

After some thought, she realized she could ask Marge about all these musings in the morning, when the older woman was due to arrive for her shift at the library. After all, Marge had grown up with Luis, and probably discussed at length with her grandfather how he'd come to write this book. Maybe Marge would be able to provide a backstory.

With new resolve, Rain bookmarked the page and closed the novel. She drained the remainder of her tepid tea and then set the mug aside. Her eyes were growing heavy despite her mind still needing to ponder. She inched deeper into the sleeping bag and reached to turn off the light. Even in the darkened room, she felt safe, as the scent of long-ago written novels and rugged pine boards, lulled her to sleep.

*   *   *

A knock at the library door sent Rain to shift inside the sleeping bag. The knock grew louder and more insistent, and then Rain blinked her eyes when she heard, "Rain? Hellooo? Are you in there?"

Rain unzipped the sleeping bag and crawled out from it. She then stumbled toward the door, "I'm coming!"

Rain heard a muffled, "Oh, thank God!" before opening the door to Julia who stood juggling a reusable shopping bag which dangled from one arm, and a tray holding two disposable cups in the other hand. "I ran into town for doughnuts at The Brewin' Time and when I knocked on the cabin door over an hour ago and you didn't answer, it sent my mind in a tailspin. Especially with your car in the driveway, I figured you went for a walk or something, so I came back, and you still weren't answering the door. Are you all right? You scared the crap outta me! What are you doing in the library before breakfast? Didn't I mention last night that I'd bring breakfast over?"

Rain smoothed her tongue over her teeth and then blew into her hand to check to see if she had morning breath before opening the door wider for Julia and her twenty questions to enter.

"Wait," Julia said as she stepped deeper into the room. "Did you sleep in here last night?" Rain watched Julia's eyes move over to the rumpled sleeping bag in the corner and then back to her.

Rain shrugged sheepishly.

"You did, didn't you?" Julia looked at her as if she'd fallen off the deep end.

Rain nodded. "I did." She brushed the hair out of her eyes and smoothed the static to lay down by licking her fingers to tame the few flyaway strands. She then rubbed at her eyes to remove the sleepy crusts to awaken fully.

"How late were you up? If you wanted to work at the library last night you could've called. I would've come over in a heartbeat and helped, you know?" Julia set the tray down on a nearby table and pointed. "I brought you coffee. Looks like you could use some," she chuckled. "Although, it might be cold by now . . ."

"Thanks, I'll take it!" Rain said reaching for the cup with coffee scribbled in loose handwriting on the side. "No, it's not that; I wasn't working," Rain said accepting the doughnut hole that Julia was now handing her to go with the beverage. "I wanted to hang out in here alone and do some reading. Although I normally shy away from romance, I started reading my grandfather's novel. It's a rather interesting read. Have you read it?"

Julia nodded and took a bite of a chocolate-covered doughnut hole, covering her lips in dark smears, and then licking it off. "Man, I love these." She said as she looked at the pastry longingly. "Try it," she encouraged, lifting her doughnut so close to Rain's face, the pastry almost hit her on the nose.

Rain stepped back and then took a bite of her own. "Wow, I can see why they do quite a business. This is delicious, thank you. It's every bit as good as their brownies, eh?" She licked her finger where the chocolate had dripped. "So, have you ever read Grandfather Luis's books? Or specifically, have you read *Always You*?"

Julia polished off her doughnut and with a mouthful mumbled, "Yeah, but it was a long time ago. You know I read so many books a year . . . You'll have to refresh my memory. What's it about again?"

"It's a love story about a man who loses his first love because their families didn't approve of their relationship. It's so wrought with emotion, it's almost hard to believe a man wrote it. Never mind my own grandfather. It's a bit telling. To be honest, I didn't expect it. Totally different from the man I remember, I can't imagine the man I knew from my youth even writing it."

"Well, it's fiction, right? Oh yeah! Now I remember . . ." Julia snapped her fingers. Her eyes moved to the ceiling as if to recall more. "Is that the one where the girl finds out she's pregnant and his parents want her to get rid of the baby? Right?"

"I didn't get that far, I'm only on chapter ten, so . . . maybe?"

"Oh shoot, I'm sorry. I hope I didn't ruin the plot for you?" Julia grimaced and then wiped her hands on a napkin that she'd found after digging inside the bag. "Let me see it. May I?"

"Sure," Rain finished her doughnut, licked her fingers, and then reached for the novel beside the sleeping bag and handed it to Julia.

Julia wiped again with the napkin before accepting the book. She flipped through the pages. "Yesss, of everything your grandfather wrote, this was my favorite. The characters just leapt from the page! Your grandfather had a way of sucking you right into this book. If I remember correctly, this one was incredibly giving, and realistic. This one made me cry at the end!" Julia said, holding it to her heart and then handing back the book. "I hope you enjoy it; I'm not gonna give away more, you'll have to see for yourself." She smiled. "I think you should read in its entirety—even if I did spoil it a bit. It's so cool that you have an author in your family, I can't help but say I'm a bit jealous." She grinned.

Rain looked down at her rumpled attire and then back to Julia. "Are you here to work already? Or just to drop off a delicacy from town?" Rain asked when she noticed Julia rolling up the sleeves of her denim shirt and reaching for one of the new books they had dropped off the previous night.

Julia's eyes darted to the large clock on the wall, "Didn't you notice? It's nine o'clock already. Marge called me and said she'll be here in about an hour. By the way, it's freezing in here. I know you mentioned turning on the AC, but it's like an icebox." Julia said, unrolling her sleeves and buttoning them taut to her wrists. "I'm glad I dressed for it. And here I had planned on wearing a light blouse," she chuckled.

Rain's jaw dropped. She hadn't slept that long in ages. "Is it really nine o'clock already? You must be kidding me?"

"Yep, sure is," Julia smiled. "Sounds like you needed a through night of shut eye. Good for you."

Rain tucked the sleeping bag under her arm. "I'm gonna run back to the cabin and quickly change clothes, okay? I'll turn off the AC and you can leave the door open if you want to warm it up in here before Marge arrives. Otherwise you're right, it'll be too cool for her, I think."

"Good idea. I'll start cataloging the new books while you're gone, if you're okay with that." Julia stood waiting for approval before touching any other books on the stack.

"Perfect, sure. Whatever you need to do, and thanks," Rain said over her shoulder as she headed out the door and into a rush of warmer air. After a quick change of clothes, a comb through knotted hair, and brushing her teeth, Rain hurried back to the library to help Julia catalog the new books before Marge's arrival. She hoped the three of them would have a chance to talk hours of operation and work out some minor details of when and who would staff the library when she was unable. As she stepped through the door, she heard grunting noises and noticed Julia looking flushed and flustered, standing beside the bookshelf.

"Something wrong?" Rain asked, rushing to Julia's side. "Do you need a hand?"

Julia pointed to the log wall located behind the bookshelf that had been exposed when her friend had removed a book from the shelf. Rain noticed that it looked as if a few flies had traveled inside and had a funeral as they lay limp behind the books in a pile.

"Oh, gross!" Rain said. "I wonder how they got in here. Maybe the chinking is loose outside, and the flies burrowed in. I'll have to go and check that out." Rain was about to turn toward the door, to go outside and verify, when Julia grabbed her firmly by the arm.

"That's not the issue."

Rain shook her head in misunderstanding.

"Come closer." Julia summoned her with her hand. "Look at this." Julia pulled at a chunk of the log that had come loose and wasn't fully sealed within the chinking. "When I started picking at the fly that was stuck in that white caulking stuff, I noticed the log shift, as if it was loose. I found something hidden in the wall behind the bookshelf."

"*Huh*? You did? What is it?"

"I don't know, but it looks like I might've just uncovered a family time capsule hidden within the wall of the library."

Chapter Eighteen

R ain couldn't believe her eyes. She had to blink several times before fully accepting reality. A rectangular shaped item wrapped in brown paper was tucked into the cutaway log that Julia had dislodged behind the shelf of books. She reached for the object and held the wrinkled brown paper between shaky hands.

"A time capsule?" Rain shook her head in disillusion-ment. "My parents never mentioned anything hidden inside any of the logs. This is nuts! If my family had partaken in this kind of family tradition, surely I would've heard about it by now! Wouldn't I?"

"If it wasn't for the bug funeral, I would've never found it!" Julia exclaimed. "It'd still be hidden I think."

"Yeah, crazy, eh? Dead bugs lead to a family treasure? That's the last thing I would've expected." Rain chuckled. "Maybe it's gobs of money! Wouldn't that be fun!" she said in a teasing tone.

"Open it! Open it!" Julia could barely contain her excitement as her friend began to lift in rapid movement up and down on her toes and clap her hands as if she was awaiting a rock band to begin their worldwide concert on opening night. Julia's eyes were growing as big as sunflowers by the second.

Rain removed the aged, yellowing string, and the dry paper crinkled at her touch. She gently tore away the paper and revealed a fresh copy of *Always You* by Luis Russo. The hardcover had preserved well over the years, and Rain ran her fingers lovingly across the gilded words.

"It looks brand new, doesn't it?" she said, her eyes filling. "I guess my grandfather just wanted to be sure he always had a pristine copy on hand," Rain suggested. "Evidently, this book meant the world to him, more than the others, because it's the only one here. Unless he has other books buried within multiple logs in this room." She shook her head in dismay and then her eyes traveled across the room to the shelf that held the rest of his written work. "I wonder why he kept this one. It's so weird."

"Was it his first novel? Maybe that's why?"

"No, it's not. I only began reading this one first because it was the one found near Thornton. Like you suggested, I wanted to see if there was any connection, you know? I guess I was looking for a reason why my mother would've lent that particular book to our murder victim." Rain's face burned. She didn't want to tell Julia that the thought had crossed her mind that Willow and Thornton might have been working through their own unrequited love, similar to the story. She swallowed back a gag.

"Wow. That's gorgeous, look at the workmanship." Julia said tapping a finger to the book in Rain's hand. "If I were you, I'd have to sniff it too." She laughed. "Nothing like sniffing an old book. Don't tell my husband, but it's better than his cologne." She batted her eyelashes and tilted her head back . . . ooh la la . . ." she teased as she clasped her hands to her heart.

Rain joined her friend in laughter. "Boy, we really are book nerds, aren't we? I was thinking the exact same thing," she said as she opened the book to take a whiff and an aged envelope fluttered to the ground from its pages.

"Son of a monkey! Look at the inside of that book!" Julia clapped her hands over her mouth.

"*Son of a monkey*? Seriously? Who says that?" Rain teased.

"Hey, trust me. As I said before, when you're a teacher, you quickly learn to improvise your swear words in front of your students." Julia grinned and then pointed. "Look!"

Rain opened the book wider and held it in both hands as if she were a priest holding the Holy Bible and noticed the inside of the book had been completely gutted. It wasn't a book; the novel was just a ruse. The book had merely been a place to hide something of importance; the hardcover just held an empty shell of cut out pages. An inch of text was all that remained around the cut-out edge—that was it. Her eyes darted to the floor where the yellowed envelope had fallen. She reached for it, her heart thumping erratically in her ears.

"What do you think it is?" Julia asked.

"A million-dollar check? A lifetime of free McDonalds?" Rain said finally, with nervous laughter. "I don't have the slightest idea. I'm not sure it's something I should open. Should I leave it for my mother? Obviously, her father put this here for a reason. Maybe I'm not the person that should be opening this." She frowned.

"Are you crazy? You have to open it! Talk about a mystery, this is getting better by the minute." Julia rubbed her hands together in anticipation. "We're going to have to co-write our own novel! No one would ever believe this!" She grinned, looking over Rain's shoulder, waiting. "A treasure inside the log! Shut the front door!"

"Oh, all right. What harm could it do? Right?" Rain said as she carefully peeled open the unsealed envelope. She unfolded the sheet of paper, and a gasp flew from her mouth.

The first printed word Rain's eyes caught was that of Thornton Russo and she sucked a breath. Instantly her eyes began to blur from tears. "Wait. What is this?"

"Shiitake mushrooms!" Julia said, her eyes widening. "It's a birth certificate! Thornton wasn't a *Hughes*! He was a Russo!"

Rain's eyes flew to Julia and then back to the formal sheet of paper for confirmation.

"Thornton wasn't my mother's lover." Rain held her hand to her heart. "Thornton was my uncle." She whispered as she leaned against the bookshelf and slowly slumped to the floor.

"Wait. Who's listed as the mother?" Julia asked, reaching for the birth certificate.

The two were interrupted by a knock on the open door, "Hellooo! Ladies, are you in here? Good morning!"

Rain's eyes flew to Julia. "Quick! Hide this stuff!" Rain scrambled to her feet and dusted the dead flies from the shelf to land upon the wooden floorboards. She snatched the birth certificate from Julia's hand, tucked it safely back inside the envelope, and shoved the book back inside the wall. She then rushed to hide any evidence of the open wall behind the bookshelf by shelving random books to haphazardly block it. "The piece of log! Hide it!"

Julia reached for the missing piece of log that had held the secret book hidden inside the wall. She held it in her hands like a quarterback not seeing the wide receiver. "Where do you want me to go with this?"

Rain pointed to the corner of the bookshelf along the floor. "Just stick it here for now. We'll hide it with a pile of books. Hurry!" she added under her breath.

"Wait. Why are you dead set on hiding this from Marge?" Julia whispered, setting down the log and then removing books off the nearby shelf to hide it. Rain handed her another book to use to complete the cover job.

"I'm not ready!" Rain whispered. "I need time . . . I need to process all of this!" she waved her hands nervously. "It's my family . . ."

"Okay, I respect that." Julia held up a hand in defense. "Don't worry, I won't say a word." Julia zipped her mouth

Holly Danvers

with her fingers and then held two fingers crossed in the air. "Scouts honor, we'll keep this between you and me." Julia then turned away from her, blocking Marge from view. She rushed toward the older woman and directed Marge back toward the pile of new books still waiting by the door.

Rain heard Julia say, "Marge, this looks like such a great collection for the library. I absolutely love what you chose! Show me which one of these novels is your favorite? Have you had a chance to read any of these yet? Or were you saving them all for the grand reopening?" Julia's eyed darted over her shoulder to check with Rain before continuing to hold Marge's attention.

Rain held her beating chest and willed her heart to stop hammering. The room began to sway, and Rain grasped the bookshelf to steady herself. She'd jumped back to her feet too quickly, after slumping to the floor, for the blood to rise to her head where it belonged. She took a few slow breaths and pasted a smile on her face before joining the others.

"Good morning, Marjorie!" Rain said in an elevated tone. Even to her own ears, the words came out croaked, like she was attempting to hide something. She shared a knowing look with Julia before reaching to clasp the older woman's hands. "Oh, your hands are freezing. I just turned off the AC, and we're keeping the door open for the time being. It should warm up here soon, I hope. Sorry about that." She grimaced.

Marge smiled and squeezed Rain's hands tighter before fully releasing. "I don't care how cold it is in here. I can't

206

tell you how excited I was to wake up this morning knowing we were coming back to the library. I'm so happy you're opening it up again to the public this year. It's such a special place." Her eyes twinkled like stars in the night as she gazed lovingly around the room.

"That it is!" Julia agreed and then shared another knowing glance with Rain. "Special indeed!"

"Julia has been working on cataloging the new books you brought over, and I was hoping to discuss coverage, library hours, and that sort of thing, before we reopen next week. I want each of us to still enjoy the summer up here, without being so tied down that we don't get a chance to enjoy the sunshine," Rain said.

Marge tapped each of them on the arm. "Anytime you gals want to whoop it up on the lake, you just call me. I can be here faster than flies on roadkill if need be." She nodded firmly.

Marg's comparison to flies made Rain and Julia share a puzzled glance.

"What's up with you two? I feel like I'm missing something." Marge squinted and eyed Rain and Julia intently. "Did you hear more on the investigation that you're not sharing?" She slipped her hands to her hips and leaned toward them. "Listen, ladies. I'm part of this investigative team. Just because I'm older than you by a few decades doesn't mean I don't have my wits about me!" she waved her finger between them.

"Well . . . we went over to clean . . ." Julia said, before Rain interrupted holding up a hand to stop her.

"What can you tell me about *Always You* by Luis Russo? I started reading my grandfather's book last night, and it's just so incredibly different than the man I knew. Do you think maybe you could share some of the backstory with me?" Rain asked.

Marge's eyes journeyed intently from Julia to Rain before she blew out a breath and said, "Rain, sweetheart. I have something to tell you."

Chapter Nineteen

R ain and Marge decided to talk lakeside, out on the wraparound deck, leaving Julia to continue working on cataloging books inside the library. As the heat rose, a stickiness hung in the air. Rain knew from previous visits to the Northwoods, it meant something could be brewing. Like the air could grow so heavy, it would have no other choice than to weep and dump a storm.

Marge had expressed to Rain, when they spoke in the library, that she wished to speak with her privately, and that whatever the two discussed, would be up to Rain's discretion to share with her immediate family only. Marge had explained that she'd kept a long-hidden secret that she'd promised to herself she'd spill to Willow and Stuart before summer's end. But with both of them far from Lofty Pines, she voiced, it was best if she spilled the beans to Rain.

Rain encouraged Marge to take a seat beneath the umbrella-covered table, but due to the sun moving across the eastern sky, the canopy did little to cover them. She

209

adjusted the umbrella so that the sun was no longer smack dab in Marge's eyes, causing her to squint. "Is that better?"

Marge nodded solemnly. "It's fine, dear, thank you." she spoke so quietly, that Rain barely heard the words uttered from the older woman's mouth. She hadn't known Marge long, but this somber demeanor was something she'd yet to observe.

Rain hadn't witnessed the woman being anything but animated, so the new subdued Marge gave her concerned pause. "Would you like something to drink? I have lemon-ade—" Rain pointed toward the cabin and licked her lips at the thought. With the rising heat, a tall glass sounded very refreshing.

"No, thank you. Not just yet." Marge patted her hand on the chair beside her. "Sit, dear, please have a seat, will you? We can share a drink and snack afterward, if that's okay with you?"

Rain took the seat, noting Marge's sense of urgency, as if the older woman couldn't hold in what she needed to share for another millisecond.

Marge nodded in approval and smiled when Rain had finally succumbed to her bidding.

Rain folded her hands upon the table. "Okay, talk to me. I feel like whatever this is, it's weighing heavy on your heart right now. I get the sneaky suspicion that this might have something to do with my grandfather's book. I saw it in your face back there in the library when I asked about *Always You*." Rain watched the older woman intently to see if she was right. "Is that it? Do you have something to tell me about my grandfather, Luis? You mentioned growing up with him, is there something I need to know? Something I missed from my childhood?"

Marge's spine stiffened at the sound of Rain's grandfather's name, and she shifted in the patio chair. "I've carried this secret so long now, sometimes I don't even think it's real anymore. It seems as if it happened during another lifetime . . . another chapter in another book, other than my own." Marge gazed wistfully toward the lake, and Rain's eyes followed, taking in the soft lapping of the water against the shore, and the green-blue hue that mimicked the older woman's watery eyes.

"My grandfather's book isn't fiction, is it? I suspect it's more of an autobiography. No?" Rain asked, redirecting her.

Marge's gaze abandoned the lake and her eyes then dropped to the table.

"It was *you* he was writing about, wasn't it? The girl that he once loved. I know it wasn't my grandmother. And I can tell it isn't fully a work of fiction." Rain clasped her hands to her heart. "It's too good—the pain is too real. So wretchedly real." Rain's voice softened. "I feel it within my own heart."

Marge's eyes rose to meet Rain's and filled, until a tear drop spilled between them on the table. "No, dear, it wasn't me that he loved." She paused for a moment, wiping her tear. "But close." She hung her head again, and her breath began to labor, and her shoulders trembled as if resigned.

Rain was confused by the answer and reached her hand to touch the older woman's arm. "What do you mean, *close*?"

"Luis loved my sister once." Her lower lip trembled as the confession fell from her mouth.

"Your sister?"

"Yes." Marge wiped the tear from her eye with the back of her hand. She then leaned back in the chair and resurrected a rumpled tissue from her pocket, blew her nose, and clasped it so tightly that her hand turned almost translucent.

"I didn't know you had a sister. Where is she? I'd love to meet her. To talk with her, and get to know my grandfather's lost love —"

Marge interrupted with one swift comment, "Dear, Maggie's dead. She's been gone a long, long time now." The older woman dropped the tissue into her lap, and then tapped Rain's hand gently.

"Oh," Rain said, slumping in the chair. "I'm so sorry. I didn't know." But the words seemed hollow somehow. She knew the feeling of loss, and sorry just didn't cut it. Not when she witnessed and felt the enormous sadness sitting next to her.

"My sister has been gone so long; I've begun to lose the sound of her voice. You know how that happens? Remember how you told me you've forgotten, too? The sound of your grandfather's voice? Or words the deceased once spoke. I can't even hear the tone of her voice anymore. Maggie used to be such a great singer . . ." A smile began to form on her lips. "Sweet, sweet Maggie-pie." Marge sniffed. "That's what Luis used to call her; you know . . . Maggie-pie." She brushed her hand across the edge of the table and then folded her hands in her lap, balling the tissue between them.

"What happened?"

Marge continued. "The novel your grandfather Luis wrote, *Always You,* was a love story about his relationship with my sister Maggie."

"Wow." Rain leaned forward and rested her elbows on the table and then tented her hands, resting them to cover her mouth.

"Yes. Even your grandmother didn't know that the book wasn't a work of fiction. She believed Luis just had a gift of the written word. And, surely, he did. I'm not at all discounting his accomplishments." Marge smiled and then her smile faded. "But *Always You* was not a work of fiction, I assure you that," she added firmly.

Rain rested her chin on her closed fist, "So, nobody knew? No one ever put the pieces together. Besides you?"

"No."

"But how then? How do you know for sure it was a love story about my grandfather and your sister? Did Luis affirm that to you before he died? Did he tell you the truth himself?"

"No, dear, he never admitted it to me. But I knew." She raised a pointed finger to the air, and then leaned forward and whispered, "Because in the story, the protagonist's lover, the very love of his life, dies in childbirth, just like my sister Maggie did." Marge's lip quivered. "And I know for a fact, my sister loved Luis and never made love to another man. Luis was her one and only. Maggie confided that to me, in secret." She rose her finger to her lips as if to remain hushed. "But Luis never knew that she'd told me."

Rain's heart thundered in her chest. "I didn't get to that part in the book yet . . . but Julia mentioned something . . . about a baby . . . what happened to the child? After your sister died."

"I was told the baby was stillborn and my sister died not long after giving birth. I think your great-grandfather Lorenzo was relieved to be honest." She scoffed and then lifted her chin in indignation. "Our family wasn't considered good enough by Luis's parents. Your great-grandfather completely disapproved of the relationship. When he knew my Maggie was never coming back, that made Lorenzo happy. Very happy indeed." Her lips turned downcast.

Rain couldn't help but feel the generational shame on behalf of her family. It made her heart hurt. "Was it a boy or a girl?"

Marge's shoulders lifted in a slight shrug. "I never learned the sex of the baby. No one would tell me," she said sadly. "It was as if the baby never existed at all. It was as if Maggie died another way . . ." Her voice trailed off and her eyes moved toward the lake and then back to Rain. "Sometimes, I can still picture her out there on water skis, you know. She was so incredibly talented. I always envied her." She smiled. "She had so much promise. So much life ahead of her."

Rain didn't speak for fear of interrupting the spell.

Marge's smile faded, and a heaviness took over once again. "They sent her away to stay with extended family out east. I almost didn't believe my parents when they told me Maggie had died. I kept waiting for her to come home." Marge waved a hand airily. "I never saw her again."

Rain slumped back in the chair.

"I didn't mean to upset you, Rain. And I'm certainly not trying to talk ill of your great-grandfather Lorenzo, I hope you understand. I just think it's important the secret doesn't die with me. I think it's important for someone to hear Maggie's side of the story. And I always wanted someone else to know, she's alive in that book." Marge tapped a finger to the table.

"No, that's not it."

"What is it dear?" Marge leaned toward Rain, her eyes studying her intently. "The color has drained from your face, child. It looks as if you've just seen a ghost!"

"I think I just did," Rain whispered.

Chapter Twenty

The spell dissipated, and the deep discussion between Rain and Marge ended rather abruptly when the screen door opened. Julia poked her head just outside the door.

"You ladies need a drink? I brought iced tea! I came inside to grab some after leaving the library door open. It's getting awfully stuffy inside there pretty quick. I think it's gonna take a few minutes for the air-conditioning to catch up again, so you might wanna grab a drink before heading back to the library." Julia's eyes toured the sky. "I can't believe how quickly it heated up out here, I guess we're in for another doozy today!"

Marge lifted from her seat to regard Julia. "No, thank you, dear, I think I'll pass." The older woman then turned to Rain. "Do you mind if I come back later to work in the library? I think I might need a rest. Suddenly I'm not feeling the best, to be honest. Maybe the heat is getting to be too much for me."

Rain rose to meet her. "Of course. You take all the time you need. We won't open the library to the public until next week anyhow. And honestly, there isn't much pressing except for discussing the hours of operation and shifts to split between us. Please, go on ahead," she encouraged, before waving Julia back inside who was still waiting by the door for an answer.

"Julia, I'll be in, in just a minute, okay?"

"Sure thing," Julia said before disappearing back inside the cabin.

Marge opened her arms for an embrace and the two grasped each other tight.

"I'm so sorry for the way my great-grandfather behaved. And I'm deeply sorry for the loss of your sister. I wish there was something I could do to make up for my family's poor judgement." Rain held Marge at arm's length. "They had no right to treat Maggie that way." Her gaze dropped to the ground in shame.

"Sweet Rain." Marge patted her lightly on the cheek. "I didn't share all of this to upset you or blame your family for anything. It was a long time ago. I just wanted to be sure that my sister's love story lived on in *Always You*, the book your grandfather wrote, and that the secret didn't end with me because now you know it, too." She smiled. "For that, I'm eternally grateful."

Rain noticed the beads of sweat forming on the older woman's forehead and took her by the arm to lead her away from the deck. "Do you need me to drive you home? You sure you're okay to drive?"

"Yes, I think I'm a little overcome, that's all. It's been a long time since I've talked about Maggie." She smiled weakly. "I'll blast the AC in the car, no worries, dear. I'll be happy to get home to Rex real soon. I didn't want to bring him back over here, instead I left him home to stay inside where it's nice and cool, and I wasn't sure how you felt about me bringing him inside of the library when I work. I tend to baby him, you see. Thank you for your patience and understanding."

"Of course. And Rex is welcome inside the library anytime. I bet the patrons would love to meet him," Rain said as she walked Marge to her car and opened the door for the older woman to slip inside. "You just take care of yourself, and Rex, and call me if you need anything. Promise?"

"Thank you," Marge said as she adjusted herself behind the wheel. She then grasped Rain by the wrist before shutting the car door. "I know I probably don't look like it, but I feel so much better unloading the secret I've carried for so many years. Thank you for letting me tell it. And don't worry, I'll be okay, dear. A little rest, and I'll be good as new."

"I'm glad you felt safe to share the secret with me, and in some ways you and I are even more deeply connected now. We're almost like family," Rain said. "Thank you for opening up to me. I won't tell a soul, I promise." She held a hand to her heart and closed her eyes momentarily taking it in.

"Yes, I appreciate that. I would like to be the one to tell your mother if that's okay. But if something ever happens to me . . . before I get the chance . . ." She let the implication linger.

"No worries. If something happens to you, Marge, I will be sure my mother learns the truth. You have my word." Rain held up her hand as if she was taking a sacred oath.

Marge turned the key in the ignition, signaling it was time for her to go. Rain lifted her palm in a wave. Her mind battled between what she had learned from Marge, and what could potentially blow her life wide open. Pieces of the puzzle were beginning to shift and come together in her mind. She turned and dashed up the deck stairs and hurried into the kitchen through the backdoor. Her entrance was so rapid, Julia stopped mixing the batch of iced tea and looked at her, alarmed.

"Did I offend you by using your kitchen? I'm not trying to overstep, I'm sorry. Willow always lets me bring my tea over here and—"

Rain stopped her with a raised hand. "Are you kidding me?" she laughed. "No worries, you're welcome to use anything here, in the kitchen, or anywhere, you should know that by now." Rain slipped her hands onto her narrow hips. "But I think I just learned something that could change everything." She looked over her shoulder to see if anyone was there, knowing full well, they'd be the only two in the room.

Julia took her cue. "Nick's not here, we're alone." She put down the ladle she was using to mix the tea and set it beside the carafe. Her eyes narrowed, waiting for Rain to unload.

"I'm not sure what's happening right now, my mind is working a mile a minute!" Rain rolled her hands around her head like she was going crazy.

Julia's eyes skirted around the room and then she moved over to the back door, "Wait. Where did Marge go? Is she not right behind you?"

Rain shook her head.

Julia persisted. "Did she quit working at the library or something? What happened between you two? I've never seen the poor woman so upset. What did she need to talk to you about? Is that what this is about?"

"Hang on a sec, you're firing too many questions." Rain chuckled.

"Hey, I'll try and be patient, but if this is just a way to deflect and not tell me what's going on . . . Well . . ." Julia placed her hands firmly on her hips.

"You're not going to let me get out of this one, are you?"

"Nope." Julia smiled with smug satisfaction.

Rain encouraged Julia to take a seat next to the center island. "I'm not supposed to share this . . . but I guess I have to trust you. I have to trust somebody," she uttered beneath her breath. "And I couldn't tell Marge until I know for sure . . . I need your help." She bit at her thumbnail before adding. "I'm almost too afraid to find out. You might have to do it for me."

"Do what? You're not making any sense." Julia pulled out the stool beneath the island and plopped onto it. "Rain, what are you talking about? Did you tell Marge about

Thornton being your uncle? Is that what this is about? I thought you weren't ready to share that with anyone yet." Julies eyebrows narrowed in question.

Rain vigorously shook her head. "No, I didn't. But wait until you hear this one."

Julia folded her arms across her ample chest. "Go on, now you really have me intrigued." Her eyebrows danced in amusement.

Rain reached for two glasses in a nearby cabinet and handed one to Julia. She then brought over the tea and began to pour, her hand trembling. "Maybe we should have something a little stronger for this conversation," she teased. "Too bad this isn't a Long Island Iced Tea." She rolled her eyes. "Not that I've ever had one, but now, if ever, would be the perfect time to give it a go."

"Actually, a Long Island Iced Tea doesn't actually have any tea in it. It's the amber color that gave the alcoholic drink the name. But I bet Nick has some vodka at home if you want a splash of that to settle you down." Julia's eyebrows danced as she pointed to the glass of tea. "Hey, It's five o'clock somewhere. I'd be willing to join in, too . . . if you need a reason." She smiled.

"I was just kidding," Rain waved a hand of dismissal before taking a sip of tea and sliding onto the stool next to her friend. "Thanks for bringing this over by the way."

"No problem."

"I'm just getting a bit stressed, if you couldn't already tell."

"I can totally tell. You're killing me here. What the cotton pickin' candy is going on?" Julia leaned toward her and shook her by both arms, almost spilling Rain's drink. "Tell me! Please!"

"You have to PROMISE you won't share this with anyone. Not Nick, not Jace, especially not Jace yet." Rain held her finger to her lips in a hushed position. "Not anyone, Julia. Can you promise me that?" Rain studied her friend and waited for final confirmation.

"You have my word," Julia said, lifting upright on the stool and zipping her lips with her fingers.

"God forgive me," Rain said, taking a breath and looking to the ceiling. "I literally just promised Marge the same thing; that I wouldn't tell a soul. But you have to help me make sense of all of this," she added, biting her lip as if subconsciously holding herself back.

"It's okay, God will forgive you this once," Julia said with praying hands and then a nudge of her elbow. "Spill."

"*Always You*, my grandfather's novel, wasn't fiction. Marge just confirmed that. It was a story written about my grandfather, Luis, and her sister Maggie! Can you believe it!" Rain slapped her hand to the table. Saying the words aloud made the implication more real than ever.

Rain watched as the gears turned in Julia's mind and a hush fell between them.

"But the girl in the book, she was pregnant, right? And then . . ." Julia rolled her finger in the air. "Then . . . the baby died, and the protagonist had his heart ripped out!

222

That book was so sad." She said sullenly. "I cried for days over that one."

"Uh-huh, that's how the story goes. But here's the thing. I don't think the baby dies like in the book. I think, in real life, the baby lived, and was adopted out." Rain flung her hand behind them. "I think the baby *just* died! Over there . . . by my outhouse!"

Julia cuffed her hand over her mouth and then dropped her hands in her lap. "Son of a mother trucker. Thornton was the baby in your grandfather's book."

Chapter Twenty-One

Rain and Julia sat at the kitchen island in dead silence while they let the implication of an illegitimate baby sink in. If Thornton really was Grandfather Luis's baby, then she'd have to tell Marge the truth. This wouldn't be something she should ever hide from Marge. It wouldn't be fair not to share that her nephew had in fact lived and indeed had lived a somewhat fulfilled life.

"How would I tell Marge?" Rain finally voiced aloud. "That would be devastating, learning that her nephew actually *was born* but now is *gone*?" Rain sipped her iced tea and then wiped the condensation from the bottom before setting the glass down. "It would be like grieving her sister Maggie, and the baby that she never got to meet, all over again."

Julia blew out a breath of disillusionment. "Yeah, that's a tough one. Especially since Marge didn't speak very kindly of him the other night at the dinner table. Remember? I don't think she was a big fan of Thornton Hughes. Uh-uh, not at all."

Rain winced. "Ouch. Yep, nothing like adding salt to the wound. Gee-wiz, how do you wrap your head around that one?" She removed a hairband from her wrist, combed her hair with her fingers and wrapped it in a ponytail. "Maybe Marge would have felt differently if she knew they were blood related." Rain cocked her head to the side and waited.

"I wish I had better advice, but maybe you'd better hold off. It's not like you have any proof. Really, right now, it's just a theory between us." Julia ran her finger along the rim of her glass and then licked it. She then took a sip of her tea and set it aside.

"Is it just a theory though?" Rain tapped a finger to her heart. "Let's go check right now if what I'm thinking is actually true! Maybe you're right. Maybe I'm reaching, and we can put this to bed right now." Rain slipped off the stool and stood. She took one more sip of iced tea before turning on her heel in the direction of the library. "I think it's just a little too coincidental, don't you?" she added over her shoulder as Julia followed out the cabin door closely at her heels.

The closer the two came to the library, the more urgency Rain felt. She stepped up her pace and flung open the library door. And then headed directly to the bookshelf that hid the birth certificate. Books were tossed on the floor in a random pile until she revealed what she'd been looking to rediscover. She plucked her grandfather's book from the hidden compartment inside the log, slipped out the birth certificate, as her fingers worked overtime to reopen it.

Rains eyes darted to the birth mother's signature listed on the legal document. Her shoulders slumped when she read: Birth mother: Margaret Shay.

"Do you know Marge's maiden name?"

"I don't, why?" Julia asked.

"This states Margaret Shay as the birth mother. Marge said her sister's name was Maggie, which is short for Margaret, so that could fit." Rain chewed nervously on the inside of her cheek. "I was hoping for a slam dunk. Not another question."

"Who else could it be? Unless your grandfather Luis was one heck of a lady's man," Julia said sarcastically and then covered her mouth with her hand. "Sorry, I say inappropriate things when I'm nervous." She slapped herself on each cheek as an act of self-punishment. "I didn't mean to be rude. I just meant Margaret must be Maggie. Right?" she added sheepishly. "Who else could it be?"

"If I'm gonna break this kind of news to our coworker and friend, I'm gonna have to be absolutely positive that I'm right. I'll need complete verification first by asking what her maiden name is. I don't want to upset Marge for no good reason, you know." Rain scratched her head and then readjusted her ponytail, squeezing the band tight. "I mean, can you imagine? This will break her heart knowing that her sister's baby did survive. And that he was living right here, in Lofty Pines? A mere few miles away from her?" Rain snapped her fingers. "Maybe Thornton was trying to find his birth mother? Or better yet, maybe he was looking for

Marge! But Marge just returned from Florida, maybe that's why they haven't connected yet."

"Wow. I never thought about that." Julia twirled her hot pink hair between her fingers nervously. "This is getting pretty juicy. But we'll never truly know what Thornton was up to, the poor man's dead! How will we ever find out?"

"Hang on a second." Rain tapped her finger to her lips. "Thornton had a copy of *Always You* near his body."

"Yeah, so?" Julia nodded. "Go on." She rolled her hand in the air for Rain to continue.

"What if my mother already knew the truth. What if my mother lent the book to Thornton so he could learn more about his father and his parents' love story before talking to Marge? It makes sense, no? That could fit." Rain began to pace nervously back and forth across the antient floorboards that held so many secrets.

"Yeah, but wouldn't Willow tell you? I mean something *that* big, I don't think your mother would hide that kind of stuff from you, would she? And why wouldn't she have introduced him to Marge—his own blood relative?"

"Maybe it's a timing issue. My relationship with my mother has been on a bit of shaky ground lately. I don't want to get into it right now, but our communication has been strained to say the least. Maybe she just wanted to tell me face to face. Just like Marge waited to tell me face to face today, to unload her secret. My mother wouldn't dump that kind of thing over the phone, I don't think. And maybe Thornton wasn't ready to meet his aunt. Maybe he told my mother to wait. My mother probably already knows what happened to Maggie. Maybe she was the one to tell Thornton his mother didn't survive his birth."

"True," Julia replied, and she was happy her friend didn't push the issue regarding the rift between her and her mother.

Rain knew when the time was right, she could share, and she loved that about Julia. Her friend knew just how far to push and when to hold back.

"So many details just seem to beg more questions."

"Yeah, I know. This is a lot to take in," Rain said, folding the birth certificate and placing it on the bookshelf for a moment to think.

"I wish you could get in touch with Willow. That would surely connect a lot of dots for us now, wouldn't it?"

"If only." Rain rolled her eyes. "Good luck trying to locate her in that faraway place. It feels like she's on the other end of the planet. I tried to reach her via email, hoping that she'd at least pick up the message on her phone. But I'm guessing there's no internet connection where she's located because if there is, she definitely would've responded by now. Anyhow, with things the way they are with my parents, she might not have shared this information with my dad either."

"What now?"

"Great question. I'm at a loss. What are your thoughts? Where do we go from here?" Rain asked.

"You're not going to like my suggestion, but maybe we should call Jace. I know you don't want to tell him or anyone else. But to be fair, this information might help him with the investigation. Because maybe Thornton's identity will have an impact on this case. We're borderline hampering if we don't tell him. Right?" Julia frowned and slipped a hand on one hip.

Rain blew up her mouth like a blowfish and slowly exhaled.

Julia must've understood where she stood with her hesitation because she added, "Think on it tonight, and we'll talk about it in the morning? Fair?"

"Fair enough." Rain nodded.

"Hey, off topic, but Nick and I were invited to a bonfire by one of the Lakers tonight. Maybe you should do something to take your mind off all this? Come and have a cocktail by the fire? Why don't you join us?"

"Nah," Rain waved a hand of dismissal. "I don't want to crash."

"Are you sure? It's over at Kim's place. Remember Kim from ski club? You wouldn't be crashing, she'd love to have you, I'm sure of it."

"Red hair? Freckles, kinda short?" Rain asked.

"Yeah, but she's grown up, too. A little bit more mature from the Pippi Longstocking look of her youth." Julia chuckled. "Her freckles have faded, and dare I add she's a bit of a stunner like yourself." Julia flicked a finger toward her. "I'd settle a trade for either one of your faces over this one," she added encircling her face with her finger.

The comment made Rain smile. "Next time? I'm kinda tired." She stifled a yawn.

"No kidding, I can see why after sleeping here on the floor instead of on a comfy bed where you belong. No wonder you're tired. You're lucky one of these flies didn't buzz around your head all night," Julia teased. "I hope you're planning to use a real bed tonight."

"Let's just finish up here so you can get going, I don't want you to miss the bonfire."

Julia swept up the dead bugs from the floor into her hand. "This is so gross!" she said as she headed for the door to dump them outside.

"We have a dustpan for that, you know!"

"I've cleaned up worse from my students." Julia threw her head back in laughter and continued out the door. "Believe me!"

The two worked in the library well into the evening in companionable silence, both lost in their own thoughts. Rain's mind kept whirling back to the death of her uncle. Did either of her parents know? Or had the hollowed-out book with hidden family secrets been locked away from all of them? Did Thornton even know? Did he have a copy of the birth certificate, which led him here? Or had the adoption records been sealed? Was he waiting for the right time to reveal his identity?

Rain returned to the open bookshelf and began to re-hide the birth certificate, back inside its envelope. She tucked the envelope safely inside her grandfather's hidden compartment novel, and then returned it back inside the log for safe keeping. She smoothed her hand over the log once set in place, and noticed that only a small part of the chinking was missing—the part where the bugs had come in. She wasn't sure if anyone would've even found the time capsule if not for the bugs burrowing a nest. With the chinking intact, it wouldn't be so obvious that there was something hidden inside that part of the log wall. It looked as if her grandfather had sealed the hollowed book into the wall, and only he would be able to remember its location. She couldn't help but wonder then if her mother really *did* have access to the truth. After kissing her fingers and touching them upon the sealed log, she replaced the books back on the shelf, hiding it completely once again.

Julia tapped Rain on the shoulder, interrupting her reverie and she jumped, throwing her hands to her chest.

"Oh, I'm so sorry! I didn't mean to startle you." Julia put her arm around her shoulder and gave a squeeze before releasing her. "You okay?"

"I'm fine." Rain nodded. "Sorry, Julia, I'm just lost in my own head again."

"Are you sure you don't want to reconsider and come with us? You look like you could use a cocktail. And Kim's family would love to meet you, I'm sure. Did you know she has a set of twins now? They're three already! Cutest little buggers," Julia added in a baby talk voice. "Every time I see them, I just want to pinch their cherub cheeks. I'm not sure if they'll be tucked in for the night, though. Sometimes Kim does that so she can sit by the fire without worry. I can't half blame her."

"Nah, I'll pass for tonight. But thanks for the offer. Tell Kim to stop by the library when we open, I'd love to see her and the kiddos. Don't worry, we have all summer long to get together. Maybe I'll host another barbeque and invite a bunch of Lakers so we can all reconnect. Wouldn't that be nice? What do you think?"

Julia grinned. "I think that's marvelous that you're wanting to come out of your tortoise shell! Absolutely! And I can help you plan. Okay then, if you're sure . . ." she said after her eyes darted to the clock. "I'm off. If you need anything, just text me. I'll have my phone with me if anything should pop up."

"You know what? I take that back. I'm coming with you," Rain said with a new resolve.

Just as Julia was hitting the threshold, she stopped short and turned, "was it something I said?"

"Yeah. You know what? I think you're right. I think it's time I get outta my tortoise shell even further. Give me a few minutes to get ready, I'd love to join you guys."

Chapter
Twenty-Two

Rain, Julia, and Nick followed the smell of smoldering embers like a train of cars to the backside of the property, until the licking flames were visible. A crowd of people already peppered Kim's lakeside property, the bonfire evidently in full swing. Outdoor lights hung from the open pergola, attached to the house, sending a shimmering reflection to the lake. And tiki torches lined the way all the way to the pier. The lights made everything sparkle, resembling the ambiance of a seaside resort.

Rain leaning into Julia and whispered, "it's my fault we're late, sorry it took me so long to get ready." She'd already felt a slight hesitation when the car had pulled up alongside Kim's place. She secretly wondered if she'd made the right choice to join them, suddenly getting cold feet when she heard the buzz of conversations and laughter bubbling up from around the firepit. How she would've preferred to be snuggled deep into her sleeping bag, with eyes deep in a library book right about now. *What am I thinking coming here?*

Julia bushed her off with a wave of her hand. "No worries, we're not late. People come and go at these things. There's no set time," she said as a petite red-haired woman approached them. Pale freckles, covered in makeup, glittered across her lovely face.

"You brought Rainy!"

"Kim?" Rain said, taking an awkward step backward and then reaching in to greet her with a hug and a smile. The woman standing before her looked almost nothing like what she remembered from her youth. The gangly Pippy Longstocking lookalike of their formative years, now long gone.

"Yes, Rainy, it's me." Kim held her at arm's length. "Look at you! Aren't you a sight for sore eyes! It's so good to see you again. Gosh, it's been decades!" she said, the light of the bonfire reflecting in her excited green eyes.

"Likewise," Rain said with a smile. "It's really good to see you, too. You look amazing, Kim," she added and meant it.

"I guess I've found my footing! And it's no longer on the pyramid, I prefer solid ground now." Kim demonstrated with a little dance in front of them, causing collective laughter within the group.

"She's being bashful," Julia said. "Kim can still kill it on skis." Julia's focus turned directly to Kim. "I see you out there behind the boat, first thing in the morning, sometimes."

"Exactly. First thing, while there's not too much boat traffic and the water is still calm. You won't see me dodging waves in the afternoons when all those crazies are out there on the lake. I'm too old for that kinda stuff now," Kim laughed.

Nick interrupted the fun by saying, "You ladies want anything? I'm going for a beer." After he'd waited for an answer, and was greeted with a few head shakes, he strolled away from them toward the drinks.

Kim pointed out a few large coolers by the pergola, in the direction where Nick was heading. "Please, ladies, help yourselves. There are wine coolers, too, if beer's not your thing. Seth has the coolers well stocked." She shifted her weight and turned to wave across the fire at another new-comer. "I think he bought seltzer, too, so if you go thirsty, it's your own fault!"

Julia pipped up, "I knew he'd have them well stocked. Rain, wait until you meet Kim's husband, Seth, he's an absolute doll." She elbowed Rain and smiled.

Kim returned the smile and then summoned her hus-band from across the backyard. Seth in turn held up a hand for her to wait, as he was deep in conversation with another man holding a beer. "I'm sure you'll get a chance to meet him sometime this evening," she said finally.

Rain looked up at the chocolate brown chalet and the twinkling pergola, taking it all in. "Congratulations, it looks like you, too, have inherited your parent's property. It's beautiful out here."

"Once a Laker, always a Laker," Kim laughed. "Yeah, my folks wanted to winter down in Florida, so we bought them out a couple years ago. They bought a small place here in Lofty Pines, but not directly on the lake. They come over here from time to time when they want a boat ride, or just want to sit on the pier and watch the skiers go by. They still have the best of both worlds—minus the maintenance."

"Oh, that's so nice! Good for them," Rain said.

"Yeah, it sure is nice having them close. And besides, this would be too much for them to give up completely," Kim agreed. "A lot of history here."

"Where are the twins? Bed already?" Julia asked.

"Yeah, they about wore me out today." Kim huffed. "Somedays, I just don't know how to settle them down at the end of the day, but finally they went down." She animatedly wiped pretend sweat from her brow and then smiled.

"I'd love to meet them," Rain said. "Maybe come by the library next week and we'll help set them up—find a few campfire stories or bedtime reads."

"I'd like that, I'm sure they would too." Kim's eyes scanned the lapping shore, and then back to the fire. "Oh, shoot! I just remembered! Before you gals arrived, I was heading inside to grab the gear for pudgy pies. Seth is begging for one." Kim then pointed across the fire to a couple seated in lawn chairs rolling marshmallows on large sticks. "We also have smores fixings, out by the fire. Want anything?"

"No thanks, none for me," Rain answered.

"Speak for yourself! I'll have one!" Julia grinned and then poked Rain teasingly with her elbow when Kim walked away from them. "Hey, is this a party or what? Bring on the sugar and drinks!" she added with a chuckle.

Rain looped her arm through Julia's and moved them out of earshot, "I'm so glad Kim didn't mention anything about the murder on my property. I figured it would be the first thing out of her mouth. To be honest, it kinda surprised me that she didn't mention anything."

"I called ahead and asked her not to. I said it might scare you off."

"You did that for me?" Rain held her hand to her heart. "You really are protective of me. Like a sister from another mister." She shoulder-bumped and teased with a wink.

"Of course! I called Kim while you were getting ready. Now go mingle and have some fun. I'm gonna go grab a beer."

After Julia stepped away, Rain shoved her hands deep in her pockets. When she finally plucked up the courage to look over the crowd, it seemed most were "coupled off" which was exactly what she was afraid of. Mingling without Max had become burdensome, especially in groups of mostly married couples. She didn't want to be obnoxious and hang on Julia's shirttails, but the unease was certainly starting to creep in.

Rain felt a tap on her shoulder and spun around. A stocky man holding a beer stood in front of her. Rain noticed the Harley Davidson tattoo instantly.

"You a friend of Kim's? Or Seth's? I haven't seen you at their bonfires before?" He looked at her quizzically and wiped the mop of dark hair out of his eyes.

"Original Laker." Rain rocked back and forth on her heels, keeping her hands in her pockets. "My family owns a cabin further down the lake. The name's Rain." She flung out a hand, he took it in his, and then gave a firm handshake.

"I remember you." He wagged a finger in her direction, his eyes finally placing her. "I'm Brock by the way. We were in ski team together back in the day."

"We were?" Nothing about Brock looked familiar to Rain. She was rolling through ski team members in her mind, one by one, and still couldn't recognize him.

"I held the base position on the pyramid," Brock said, shifting his weight to one hip. "You really don't remember?" He cocked a brow teasingly. "That surprises me."

"Ohh, I remember you now!" Rain smiled. "Aren't you the one who used to drop us from time to time? You almost got kicked off the team, right?" Before she had a chance to hit the rewind button, the words had flown from her mouth. She hoped he couldn't see the sudden rush of blood she felt to her cheeks and hoped he would think it was just brought on from the fire.

Brock smiled sheepishly and held up his beer. "You guessed it. Yours truly!" he said with a grin. "I'm surprised I haven't seen you around the lake in so long. Where've you been? Hiding under a rock?" he asked, taking a sip.

Rain couldn't half blame Brock for adding a teasing dig after how she'd greeted him. "My husband wasn't much of a fan of long drives. We hung close to Milwaukee mostly, so only a weekend to the Northwoods here or there . . ."

Rain wasn't sure how much to share or what to say. Suddenly she felt incredibly awkward. She pointed to his tattoo. "I used to work for Harley. Great company to work for." She beamed.

A new toothy grin crossed Brock's face. "Yeah? No kidding! I wouldn't take you for a biker chick." He nodded approvingly. "Nice. What'dya do for them?"

"Accounting. Not super exciting, but I was still eligible for the bike discount." Rain had no idea why she'd said that. First of all, she didn't own a Harley, and second of all, her husband had died as the result of one. So why was she trying so hard to impress Brock? Was she really that socially awkward? She swallowed and noticed the burn on the back of her throat had indeed healed.

A woman came up behind Brock and looped her hand through his arm protectively. He turned to greet her. "Lyla, look, it's Rainy . . . an old ski friend of mine!"

"Oh, hiiiii!" The woman's attitude instantly changed at the introduction. "I've heard about you! Your family is somewhat of a legend on this lake, right?" Lyla's blond brows danced in amusement. "Wasn't someone in your family like a famous author or something? I'm right . . . right? Am I right?" She ran her hand through her dyed blond hair to primp it. "We met a long time ago, but I doubt you'd even remember it," Lyla added.

Lyla was right, there was nothing about the woman standing in front of her that seemed remotely familiar to

Rain. She even wondered if the woman was lying about the fact that they'd previously met, to impress Brock or something. She wondered this as she took the woman in for a half hug.

"Oooh, didn't the police find that dead guy on your property this week?" Lyla scrunched her nose and held a hand to her mouth as if the deep secret would be kept only between them and not privy to everyone else that surrounded them around the bonfire.

Brock's demeanor instantly changed. His eyes narrowed in on her. "That was your property? Now, that I didn't know." He shifted his weight and stood gripping his beer tighter, waiting for an answer.

Rain's eyes darted the crowd, seeking Julia or Nick. Neither was nearby. She cleared her throat before answering. "Um, unfortunately, yeah." She rubbed up and down her arms, not because of a chill in the air, more out of a need for protection.

"Oooh, it *was* your house!" Lyla whispered as a coconspirator with a slight nod. "That's what I'd heard. The author's house . . ."

"Did you know the guy?" Brock asked.

"No, I didn't." Rain admitted easily. "Did either one of you?"

Both shook their heads and eyed each other in denial.

"Do the police have any leads?" Brock seemed suddenly intense or agitated. Rain couldn't discern which, as the man kept shifting his weight.

"Not to my knowledge." Rain's eyes surveyed the back-yard again, looking for a Hail Mary from her friends but came up empty. "You know, I'm feeling pretty parched. I think I'll go and grab one of those." Rain pointed out Brock's beer, but the truth was, anything that could provide an escape would help at this point.

"No worries allow me. I'll go grab one for ya, I could use another myself." Brock said. "I'll be right back." He turned on his heel away from them, leaving Rain and Lyla in uncomfortable silence.

"Well, that was awkward," Lyla said. "Nothing usually rattles Brock." She took a sip of her wine cooler and pointed out a few lawn chairs closer to the fire. "You want to join me?"

"Actually, I'm feeling pretty warm." Rain admitted, and she wasn't exactly sure if it was from the bonfire. She guessed more from the sudden rapid-fire questions. Questions that she'd naively thought she could avoid in mixed company.

"Suit yourself!" Lyla said and went to take one of the chairs seated around the fire.

Rain wandered closer to the lake and looked out at the darkening sky. A shooting star shot across her path, and before she could make a wish, a male voice interrupted her.

"Beautiful, isn't it?" The man came from behind and moved past her, making his way closer to the lake, almost to the point of the toe of his sneakers touching the water. "Makes you wonder how anything horrible can ever happen around this place. It's so calming." He stood a few feet from the pier and then stepped onto the wooden boards like he owned the place. Something in his familiar voice prompted Rain to follow.

"How so?"

"The murder out here on Pine Lake, for one. I guess you don't remember me."

Rain couldn't gauge in the dark who she was talking to, as when he'd passed by, a shadow from the lighting had hidden half of his face in the dark. "What's your name?" she asked instead.

"Paul," he said before turning toward her. "Don't you remember me stopping by to borrow a book from the library?"

Before she had a chance to answer, she heard a familiar voice behind her.

"I gotta go, nice to meet you, Paul," Rain said jutting a thumb behind her. "That's my friend calling me, have a good night," she added, before turning on her heel and walking over to join Julia.

"Having fun?" Julia asked, finally coming to her aid.

"You want the truth?" Rain asked. "Or should I give you the sugar-coated version?"

"Yeah, I want the truth, give it to me straight." Julia threw her arm around Rain's shoulder, pulling her in, while still holding a wine cooler in one hand.

"I still haven't gotten used to socializing without Max yet. Especially, when everyone seems coupled off." Rain's eyes traveled back to the bonfire where couples were laughing and licking marshmallow off each other's fingers. "Max was so charismatic, you know?" she continued. "I never realized how much of a buffer he provided in social situations . . . until he was gone . . ." her voice trailed off.

Julia must've realized her predicament when she, too, looked back at the bonfire and confirmed what saw. Which was everyone seated around the fire two by two. "Oh Rain, it didn't even cross my mind. I'm sorry for being insensitive. Honestly, I hadn't even thought of that. But if you're uncomfortable, let me take you home, okay? I can come back for Nick."

"Are you sure?" Rain felt terrible, as they'd just arrived. But the larger part of her wanted to curl up with one of those new books Marge had supplied to the library.

"One hundred percent positive. I'm sorry I put you through this too soon. I'm not being a very good friend." Julia's eyes dropped to the ground.

"On the contrary, you've been an amazing friend." Rain shook Julia by the arm. "It's not that. I know socializing alone is something I need to get used to. I guess I didn't even realize how often Max took the lead in these types of things. I just need to get my footing is all. I'll get there," she added with a weak smile to be convincing.

"I know you will." Julia gave a tight squeeze of her shoulder and then released her as if she completely understood.

"I really do appreciate you allowing me to tag along."

Julia wagged a warning finger and then bopped her on the nose. "You're never just a tag along. You're a Laker again. And us Lakers stick together, remember?"

"Yeah, I remember." Rain smiled.

"Now, let's get you home."

Chapter
Twenty-Three

Julia had not only insisted she drive Rain home, but she also took her by the elbow and led her to the door. Rain had already decided a good book to bring along to bed might settle her down, so the two walked into the house to retrieve the key, and then back outside to the catwalk leading to the library.

"Did you have any fun tonight?" Julia asked.

"Yeah, it was a great first step reacquainting with some of the Lakers. And Kim clearly is a wonderful host. I appreciate it."

"Talk to anyone interesting?" Julia pressed.

"I navigated through a few conversations. I'm an idiot though, I think I'm fresh outta practice," Rain admitted and slapped her hand to her forehead.

Julia looked at her amused. "What happened? Tell me."

"I actually said to Brock, 'Aren't you the guy who dropped us from the pyramid?'" Rain said using an exaggerated dunce voice. She shook her head in disgust. "Can you believe I said that? What an entry!"

"Hey, not your fault that's his claim to fame." Julia grinned. "He's the one who dropped the ball." She laughed aloud. "Nothin' Nimble I think we nicknamed him at one point."

"His wife is certainly insecure. Until she knew who I was, she was like a coyote ready to pounce." Rain shook her head and rolled her eyes.

"Oh, that's just Lyla." Julia waved a hand airily. "They're not married . . . Yet . . . Lyla would like to be, but Brock seems to be dragging her along. Now that I think about it, they're probably considered common law married as they've been together way over the seven-year mark. I would've given him the ultimatum long ago." She blew her pink bangs away from her face.

"You're too funny."

"What? I feel like there's more to the story." Julia asked, shaking a finger in front of her eyes.

"Nah," Rain shook her head. "It's nothing. Well . . . maybe it's something?"

"Spill it."

"What else do you know about Brock besides his clumsy drops?" Rain chuckled. "He acted kinda weird when Lyla brought up Thornton's murder. He acted sketchy, I guess would be the word."

"Oh, nooo . . . Lyla didn't! She brought it up. Why would she do that? No wonder you wanted to bail. I'm sorry!" Julia cringed.

Rain shrugged. "Like I said before, keeping this crime under wraps is gonna be somewhat difficult— if not impossible. It won't take long before every citizen around Pine Lake knows about it," she said with conviction.

"Yeah, I suppose you're right."

Julia started doing that twirling thingy she does with her hair that prompted Rain to ask, "What? I can tell something's going on in that pink head. What's up?" Rain eyed her friend inquisitively.

"It's nothing." Julia disregarded with a wave of her hand. "I'm just taking in what you said about Brock. Nick mentioned when we were out by the cooler that he overheard someone say that he's involved in that whole condo complex debacle. Interesting that he was weird with you. He's pretty even keel . . . not a guy that's easily flustered."

"Huh. Something else to ponder, I guess." Rain threw her hands to the sky.

"Yeah," Julia sighed. "I'm bummed you didn't get to meet Seth. Kim's husband is a doll. Oh well, next time."

"Yeah, next time." Rain agreed.

"There's gonna be a next time, right? You're not gonna let this couple thing scare you off?"

"Of course!" Rain nodded. Maybe there was a book in the library that could help her out with this. If nothing else, a book would provide a great escape right now, and she was ready for it. "You need to get back there. Time's a-tickin'!" she flicked a finger to the clock on the wall.

"Okay, okay, I'm outta here." Julia turned and took a step before hesitating and turning back on her heel. "You sure you're gonna be okay?"

"I'll be just fine. But thank you." Rain smiled and followed Julia to the library door. "Again, Julia, thanks for the invite tonight. I appreciate all you're doing to welcome me back to the Laker scene. It's just going to take me some time."

Julia's look of compassion was so tangible, it almost brought Rain to tears. She swallowed the lump that was forming in her throat.

"You have Jace on speed dial, too, if you need, right?" Julia's eyebrows knit together in concern. "Give me your cell phone so I can check, if not, I'll plug the number in."

"Yes, I have it. Now, go!" Rain smiled and gave her friend a light shove out the door. "Get outta here, go back and hang out with your husband, you're wasting precious time! I'll see you tomorrow."

"Love you, Rain. And I'm so happy to have you back up here with us in the Northwoods," Julia said.

"Right back atcha." Rain winked. "I'm happy to be back, too."

Rain rose a hand in farewell before retreating to the safety of the library. After shutting the door, she leaned against it wearily and let out a tired sigh. The smell of bonfire smoke permeated her clothing and filled the space around her. She wondered if she should pump up the AC and go and take a nice hot soak in the clawfoot tub.

Rain's eyes were gritty and fatigued as she surveyed the shelves of novels that filled the library walls. She pushed away from the door and walked deeper, her eyes traveling up and down the stacked walls of books. So many beautiful leather spines begged her to make another choice, outside her grandfather's work. After talking about Thornton all day, she needed a distraction. She plucked a mystery from the nearby shelf, read the blurb, and then set the book back down, unable to make a choice. If only her eyes weren't so weary, she'd tuck in for another long night of reading. She blinked several times and then dug the heels of her palms into her eyeballs. Despite her best attempt to revive them, she didn't think her eyes would cooperate, and she'd have to settle for a night without books. She let out a resigned sigh. Double checking to make sure she locked the door, she flicked off the chandelier and closed the library door before re-entering the cabin.

The living room was dark when Rain entered the room, but instead of turning on the lights, she was prompted by the rising beam of the moon to walk over to the floor-to-ceiling windows overlooking the lake. The colossal orb was full, casting a sparkling reflection to glow like a lighted path upon the water. The scene before her looked almost sur-real—like something she would find on a computer background photo, and she took in the ethereal scene gladly. She closed her eyes momentarily, hoping to commit the picture to memory, and then opened them.

A dark shadow darted across the front lawn. She blinked her gritty eyes to verify that her eyes were not actually playing tricks on her and stumbled backward momentarily. Rain sucked in a breath and flattened her body against the log wall, when she saw the figure reappear. She crouched down beside the window frame and peered out again to see if she could follow the trespasser with her eyes. The shadow darted again, and then ducked behind a tree on the far end of the yard, and she completely lost visual. Her eyes sprinted toward the screen door. Holding her breath, she crept over to it, and slid the door open a hair crack, just enough for her ears to perk at any sound. The sound of a branch snapping in the distance caused the intruder to yelp and then what sounded like *Depp!* in a foreign tone sung out, interrupting the unnerving quiet.

"*Depp?*" Rain shook her head as if to find the word in her own vocabulary but came up empty.

Could it be Julia sounding off one of her many flowery superlatives? Did she forget something, and then run across the lawn? She wouldn't play that kind of a game, even in a drunken state. Not now, not with everything that's happened. Besides, the bonfire was happening on the far side of the lake, nowhere near . . .

No. Rain confirmed in her own mind. It was certainly a man's voice—and the voice sounded foreign to her ears. Even if she'd heard but a mere syllable.

Rain's heart hammered in her chest as she waited what seemed like an eternity. The deafening silence frightened her as her ears were hypersensitive to the next sound. She focused in on the ticking of the clock which mimicked her thundering heartbeat. She desperately tried to slow her breath to the rhythm.

Finally, she heard a rattling noise coming from the cabin's front door, as if someone was jiggling with the doorknob. After slowly easing the back door shut and locking it, she crept into the kitchen. Her eyes darted the room in search of a weapon to defend herself. She reached for a knife from the block atop the kitchen counter, held it to her side, and moved like a sloth from South America toward the front door. When she arrived, she saw the knob abruptly stop moving. She couldn't help but thank her lucky stars that she'd heeded Jace's advice and changed the locks and added the deadbolt.

The sudden lack of sound or movement made Rain uneasy. She wanted to phone Jace, but she feared the intruder would hear, and for the life of her, she didn't know where she'd last left her phone. Rain clenched her teeth. If only she'd listened to Julia and kept the phone handy, she chastised inwardly.

Rain crawled back to the front window, careful not to slice her hand with the knife, peeked outside, and waited.

It seemed like forever before the dark figure passed the light of the moon that had cast a radiance upon the front lawn. She noticed the figure was wearing a dark hoodie and was now moving away from the cabin at a rapid pace which gave her a slight sense of relief. The figure quickly darted toward the pier. Rain wondered then if she'd hastily left the keys to the boat inside the pontoon. Before she had a chance to consider, she heard the distinct throaty engine of a wave runner come to life and scoot off into the dark night.

Chapter
Twenty-Four

After much searching around the cabin, Rain finally found her phone back inside the library, tucked under one of the nautical cushions in the reading nook. For the life of her, she couldn't remember how her cell phone had landed there. Her fingers couldn't work fast enough across the keypad to send Jace a text. A night alone in the cabin, without an officer of the law coming by for an official statement, wasn't sitting well with her, and was no longer an option in her mind. She told Jace to meet her at the back door, in hope there might be a chance he could lift a fingerprint off the front doorknob. She needed to know who the heck had been jimmying with the knob. And soon.

Every light, in every room of the cabin, was now fully lit, and Rain paced back and forth, wearing a path in the floorboards, until she heard a knock on the hard glass. Her eyes rose to the door where Jace stood with his hands on his hips and a grim look upon his face.

"Hey, You okay?" Jace asked when Rain went to greet him. She opened the door wider to let him cross the threshold. He grabbed hold of her arms, gave them a light shake, and looked intently into her eyes until he felt he had the answer he was looking for, and then slipped his hands back upon his hips. "Fill me in, what happened?"

"I'm still a little rattled, to be honest." Rain wrung her hands, blew into them, and then dropped them to her sides. "I think whoever it was that came here tonight wouldn't have taken a chance if my lights or the neighbors' lights were on. He wasn't that brazen because he was dressed in a hoodie and dark clothing . . . like he didn't want to chance getting caught. And your sister is at a bonfire tonight, so it looked like no one was home at either house. I'm not sure if Julia is back yet, I didn't want to call her and ruin the rest of her evening. I already did that once tonight." Rain ducked her head out the door to see if she could see any lights on next door, and then retreated when she noticed it was still dark.

"And Julia's spotlight didn't go off?"

"No. I didn't know she had one. Does she?"

"Yeah, Nick put one out by the pier last summer." Jace rubbed the side of his jaw hard. "So, we know for sure then that the intruder was on a mission to come only here," Jace pointed a directed finger to the floor. "To your cabin. Otherwise, I'm sure you would've noticed the lights go on over there. It would've lit up like an amusement park." After bobbing his head in the direction of her neighbors' house,

Jace tucked his thumbs into his thick police belt and held a military stance.

"Yeah, no lights came on over there, from what I could see," Rain confirmed.

Jace's face remained serious, and Rain noticed by closer inspection that he had a scar on his chin. She was almost inclined to reach out and touch it, to find out where the scar had come from. Instead, she stepped back and deeper into the room, and then turned back to face him after he'd followed to join her.

"Tell me exactly the timeline and try not to miss any details." The vein by Jace's temple pulsated and she could easily tell he was concerned for her safety.

Rain shared her version of events and then Jace returned to the back door. "The perpetrator went that way. To the far side of the property?" He pointed to the side yard. "You mind stepping outside on the deck and showing me?"

"Sure." Rain followed him out onto the deck. The air was heavy and damp, and she rubbed her hands up and down her bare arms. After her eyes adjusted, Rain noticed how bright the landscape seemed beneath the full moon. It was as if only the shadows from the trees remained murky, leaving the backyard mysterious and dark in places.

"Can you point me in the right direction?"

Rain pointed to the rear yard where she'd lost a visual of the intruder before he'd retreated to the dock and left via the wave runner. She wished she could remember a color of the vessel, but it had been too dark on the far side of the pier to be certain. Besides, the pontoon had blocked her vision of it.

"And he was out by the rear yard then? By the outhouse? By the way, you keep referring to the intruder as a male. How do you know for sure?" Jace turned to face her.

"I had the backdoor open a crack to see if I could hear anything, and I heard what sounded like . . . *Depp*?"

Jace cleared his voice. "Excuse me? You *opened* the back door? Do you have any idea what kind of a chance you took by making that kind of decision, young lady?" His eyes grew even more concerned. "What were you thinking?"

Rain's shoulders lifted in slight defense and she held out her hands. "In the heat of the moment, I guess I wasn't really thinking. Except to find out who was lurking around on my property."

"You're lucky the perp didn't see you. You need to be a little more careful in these types of situations. You have no idea what the intruder's intentions were."

"I know, I know, it was a bad move, I hear you," Rain said. "Look, I know it was a guy, based on his build beneath the dark clothing. And when he shouted out loud . . . the word *depp* . . . it sounded foreign. Also, I know for sure he was alone. I didn't see anyone else with him. Does any of that help?"

Jace plucked a cell phone from his back pocket, hit a button, and talked into the phone, uttering the word "depp." He then turned the phone to show Rain what he'd uncovered.

She read the Google text aloud. "Depp means idiot in German?"

Jace frowned and then tucked his phone back in his pocket. "I know it was quick, but by any chance did the man sound like he could be of German descent?"

Rain nodded slowly. "Could've been. I'm not one hundred percent sure to be honest. It was just the one syllable!"

Jace summoned her with one hand. "Walk with me."

He straightened, throwing his shoulders back, and walked with purpose down the deck stairs out onto the lawn, and Rain followed. He removed a flashlight from his police belt and cast a narrow light to shine her way and then moved the beam across the grass. "Stay close and let me know if you see anything out of place. Even a bent piece of grass, nothing is irrelevant. You hear?"

"Yeah, sure."

The dew on the lawn soaked her flip-flop-covered feet, and Rain tried her best to keep up with Jace's stride. Suddenly, Rain stopped short and gasped aloud, clutching her heart.

Jace turned abruptly and grabbed hold of Rain, tucking her closer to his side in an act of protection. "What is it?" he whispered. The way that he'd attempted to safeguard her caused a giggle to rise from her throat.

Jace turned to face her. "What's so funny?"

"I'm sorry." Rain covered her mouth with her hand. "I didn't *see* something. I *thought* something."

Jace smirked and then his lips curled into a genuine smile. "Care to share instead of sounding off all my alarm bells? You startled me. I thought we weren't alone out here."

"I'm sorry, I didn't mean to. May I?" Rain reached for the flashlight in his hand and took it in her own. "I have a hunch." She quickened her pace and moved without hesitation in the direction of the outhouse all while trying not to blow a flip-flop.

"Where are you going? Back to the crime scene?" Jace jogged alongside Rain to keep up with her directed stride. "We've been through all that. Unless you think the perp was returning to the scene of the crime for some reason."

"Yeah, you might say that."

When Rain reached the outhouse, she turned to the him. Can you lift fingerprints off wood? I don't want to contaminate anything."

"Yes, you can." Jace said. "Thank you for waiting, and not touching anything."

"Would you mind opening the door for me then?"

Jace slipped a rubber glove from his police belt and adjusted it on his hand before turning the wooden latch to open the door leading inside the outhouse.

"Do you have an extra glove I could use?"

Jace retrieved another glove from his police belt and tossed it to Rain, which she immediately stretched onto her hand.

Rain ducked her head inside the outhouse door, removed the roll of toilet paper that hung from the nail and grabbed the key that was now hanging beneath it. "Someone returned the original cabin key tonight," she smirked, dangling the key like a pendulum with her gloved hand for Jace to view. "Whoever came here tonight had a mission to get inside the cabin and then return the key. Because the same person attempted to use this key on the cabin front door, but thankfully you suggested Hank change the locks. You find out who that was, and you might just find out who killed Thornton Hughes," Rain said resolutely.

Jace laced his arms around his broad chest and nodded his head. "Okay, I think you officially have my attention."

"I think this is the same person who's attempting to frame my father." Rain said under her breath with new conviction. "This explains the missing coat." Rain chewed her lip nervously.

"Missing coat? Would it happen to be made of nylon material?"

"Jace, how much time do you have? Do you have time for a beer? I think it's time I share a few things that I've recently uncovered that might be relevant to your case."

Chapter
Twenty-Five

Rain watched as Jace lifted the long neck bottle to his lips and then set the beer down in his lap. He picked at the label aimlessly and then his eyes fixed out onto the lapping shore.

"Beautiful night," he said as his gaze left the lake and instead toured the night sky. The sound of his voice became more prominent than the cicadas buzzing loudly in the distance. The bugs created a rhythmic sound that was almost holy to Rain's ears.

"Do you need anything else from inside?" Rain asked as she momentarily stepped away from the threshold leading to the cabin. Before fully joining Jace out on the deck, Rain decided she'd retreat inside the house and grab a sweatshirt and a light throw blanket. She liked his idea of chatting outdoors, so the two could regroup beneath the light of the moon. And Jace was right, the weather was perfect for it. Maybe he was hoping the intruder would return so he could catch him in the act, but she doubted it. Or maybe he was just uncomfortable with the idea of being alone with her inside the cabin and tossing back a few beers.

"Nope, all good," Jace said with a smile and a hand tap to the cooler of beer beside him. "I have enough here that I'll definitely be crashing on Julia's couch. She won't mind, she'll be glad I didn't attempt the drive home." Her question had interrupted his reverie of the night sky. His eyes returned to it before she walked away.

Rain hustled to gather her things and then stepped back out onto the deck and closed the screen behind her to prevent any bugs from entering the cabin. She took a seat next to Jace on one of the Adirondacks facing Pine lake. It didn't take long for her eyes to readjust to the darkness, as the moon overhead lit the surface almost as if the wraparound deck was under a Hollywood spotlight.

The stars were just starting to pop and sparkle in the night sky. The pollution back in Milwaukee never allowed the stars to shine with the same brilliance despite the fullness of the moon. It seemed to Rain as if they filled the sky in multitudes.

"If it weren't for the circumstances, this would be the perfect night," Rain said as a light breeze came off the water, tickling her legs. She covered her bare skin with the throw blanket, and then tucked it in tight, allowing no wind to penetrate. "I was just thinking how different the night sky is from the city. I've missed this."

"Yeah, I love sitting by Pine Lake on summer nights. Luckily, Julia lets me crash whenever I want."

"You don't own property on the lake? That surprises me, I guess, I assumed you did."

"Not yet, but I want to. Julia bought our childhood home, and at the time, I thought I'd be traveling the world, far from Lofty Pines . . . Plus, my salary doesn't exactly make lake property affordable. But I'm saving my pennies, and someday I'll pick up a little fixer-upper." He grinned and then his demeanor turned serious. "I'm not really eloquent about these things, but there's something I have to address. But I don't want to make you uncomfortable if you're not ready to discuss it."

The hair on the back of Rain's neck stood a little in anticipation of what he might say next.

He surprised her by saying, "It sounds like not enough but . . . I'm sorry for your loss. Max . . . your mother told me. I'm a jerk for not reaching out sooner. I'm just not good at these things." He picked at the label on the bottle until he finally ripped it off clean. "I just thought you should know . . . I'm sorry for your loss."

Rain reached to squeeze his hand briefly and then let it go. "I appreciate that. And I've heard you've had a rough year, too. Abby? Julia told me."

"See, I knew I shouldn't have brought this up." He wiped his hand over his face and then took a sip of beer. "Just plain sucks. If it wasn't for her, maybe I would have a place on the lake by now."

There was a certain bitterness to his tone that Rain could relate to. "Let's not talk about it then."

This made him laugh aloud. "Boy, you're the opposite of Abby, she'd want to talk it to death, so thank you for that," Jace said with a smile and a sigh of relief.

"How about we talk about the case. I think we're both a little more comfortable with that line of conversation." Rain chuckled. "And that's what you stayed so late for anyway. So, I guess we'd better get to it, or neither one of us will get any sleep tonight. And I, for one, have had enough sleepless nights."

"Okay, but even though I'm still in uniform and we're getting ready to discuss a case, please know I'm officially off the clock." Jace pointed to the beer and then raised the amber bottle for another sip. "I'm crushing all the rules tonight," he said, wiping his lips with the back of his hand. "This is wrong on so many levels—" He winked. "Between you and me, this never happened," he added under his breath.

Rain wasn't sure if it was just drinking the alcohol in uniform he was referring to, or if there was a deeper meaning to his comment. She let it slide.

"Okay, I'm all ears. What have you uncovered? You mentioned something about your father being framed." Jace drained the beer and then reached for another in the cooler, causing ice to drip into his lap. He let out a squeal. "Ohh, that's cold!" He grinned, wiping the crushed ice off the bottle and then flicked the water droplets to land on the deck.

Rain hoped she had enough beer leftover from the barbeque to satisfy Jace's thirst and get him to loosen up. By the sound of his tone, and his loosening lip, her idea was already taking effect. She was a little afraid the officer would be mad that she hadn't shared more of her findings with him earlier, and somehow hampered the investigation by holding out.

"I'm not exactly sure where to begin." Rain kneaded her forehead with her fingers before dropping her hands to her lap. "Hey, before I get into it. Whatever came of your meeting with Frankie? Was the blood on his boat from beating carp like he claimed?"

"Yes, and that was not the murder weapon in his boat. We haven't found the murder weapon yet, and I suspect we won't. Whatever was used to kill Thornton Hughes is long gone or dumped in the lake somewhere. But the tests confirmed the blood on the billy club wasn't Thornton's, the blood indeed came from fish. Sorry, I know you were hoping for a slam dunk there."

Rain blew out a breath of frustration. "When you interviewed Frankie, did you ever find out what was going on between the two of them?"

"Apparently Thornton threatened to call the police on a few of Frankie's lake parties for noise pollution or something like that. Though, turns out they were random threats as there's no record of any of it back at the station. Sounds like they were just two guys who didn't get along."

"Oh."

"But why don't you stop beating around the bush and tell me why I'm here." Jace lifted the beer to his lips. "Besides this," he added before taking a long drink and then setting the beer down to rest on his leg.

"There's so much I need to tell you." Rain twisted the blanket in her hands and felt the comfort from the softness calm her somehow. She fingered the tightly woven fabric and wondered if the blanket was one her grandmother had knitted before her passing.

He must've sensed her tension because he asked, "You want one of these? It might help." Jace held the beer up, and Rain stopped him with a fluttered hand.

"No, I'm good. Thanks."

"How about startin' with what's pressing on your mind the most. You have my full attention."

"Okay, I guess we'll start by discussing my father's jacket." Rain breathed in and then cleared her throat. "I know it sounds like a longshot, but I think someone is trying to frame my father."

"How so?" Jace shifted in his chair to face her.

"Listen, Jace, I know the rumors that have been going around Lofty Pines. I realize, I recently arrived up north, but contrary to some belief, the speculations are not hidden from me. Already, I've caught wind of the chatter. I'm sure my dad has crossed your suspect list. Please don't try and protect me here . . . I'm aware of it. Is there a search for him or something? Tell me the truth, I can handle it."

"Rumors?" Jace leaned in closer and lowered his voice, even though no one was within earshot for miles.

"You're really going to make me spell it out for you? I'm sure you've heard the idle talk." Rain's tone was incredulous, and she wove her arms across her chest protectively.

Jace chuckled but then grew serious noting her tone. "First of all, I'm not at liberty to share with you who our suspects are. But you really think I'm going to arrest someone on a rumor?" He gripped the arm of the Adirondack chair tighter. "You've gotta give me a little more credit than that. Come on, Rain."

"So, have you heard?" She dropped her arms to her lap and clenched her hands into balled fists. "The talk around town about my mother and your murder victim?" Rain hated talking about this. Talking about her parents in this way, behind their back, and under murderous circumstances seemed incredibly disloyal somehow.

"Yes, I've heard. But, keep in mind . . ." Jace raised a finger to tap his ear, "I don't believe everything I hear! However, it's my job to follow wherever the evidence leads in this case. You have my word on that," he added firmly, his lips coming together in a grim line.

"Just so we're on the same page, *if* my father is on the suspect list, you need to take him off."

"Rain, it doesn't work that way. I can't take anyone off the suspect list, unless I have good reason to take them off."

"Hold on, I'm gonna give you a very strong reason why you should take him off. Let me try and spell everything out as clear as I can." Rain shifted forward in her seat, leaned her forearms on her knees, and turned to face Jace. "My father's

Chicago Cubs jacket is missing. I haven't been able to find it anywhere in this house." Rain nodded her head in the direction of the cabin behind them. "When I went to the hardware store, Hank mentioned he'd seen my father in town, wearing the jacket. Which is unequivocally impossible because my father is nowhere near Lofty Pines. He's in Japan. You mentioned the nylon, the piece of fabric you found left out by the road . . . Was the fabric blue by any chance?"

"Yeah, actually it was. To be precise, royal blue nylon." Jace sat straighter in his chair. "You're not exactly helping your father by sharing this with me." He smoothed his eyebrows with his fingers, his eyes downcast. Then a new light shone in his eyes as if he figured it out. "It's Chicago Cubs blue, isn't it?" he said knowingly.

Rain threw her hands up in the air. "Great. I still can't locate the jacket to prove that it's ripped. But if I could, you're saying your nylon sample could potentially be a match." Rain bit at her thumbnail and looked to the sky seeking answers. "Is that what you're saying?"

"Again, Rain, not helping. If anything, you're sealing your father's fate." He turned to face her squarely.

"No, no, no. Hear me out." Rain waved her hand erratically. "Someone stole *it*."

"Let me get this straight. You think someone used the outhouse key to go inside your cabin and steal your fathers' jacket to impersonate him? *Why?*" Jace set his beer aside the chair, leaned forward, and rested his chin on a cuffed fist. "Why would anyone do that?"

Rain could feel a lump forming in her throat. "Because up until today, I'm not gonna lie, the thought had crossed my mind. I mean, the thought that my own father could've had a serious beef with Thornton. If my father believed everyone else in Lofty Pines, and thought my mother was indeed having an affair with the guy! I get it, that's . . . well . . . the potential for . . . well it gives strong motive for murder. I understand that. I'm not stupid. I watch TV, I've read it in books . . ." her voice trailed off when she buried her face in her hands. "But I know my father, he wouldn't . . ." she finally said when her courage returned.

Jace seemingly took the information in like a sponge, reached for his beer, and then took a sip, considering. He wiped his hand across a weary face. "Yes, it does give him strong motive. I hadn't heard about the sightings of your father in town—until now. If you say that the nylon could match, it doesn't look good for Stuart at all. Is that what you want me to say? You want me to tell it to you straight—"

Rain interrupted him by holding up her palm. "Wait, Jace. Let me explain why I think someone is trying to frame my dad for this."

Jace took another sip of beer and said evenly, "I hope you have something really concrete here, Rain. 'Cause again, not helping your father here."

"I do."

"Then tell me."

"I know my mother wasn't having an affair with Thornton Hughes."

"And how exactly would you know this since you haven't been up north. When was the last time you spent any amount of time in the Northwoods? You have no clue what Willow—"

"Because he's my uncle," Rain blurted.

Jace shook his head, stunned, as if he'd just been hit upside the head with a football and feigned a concussion. "Excuse me? You must be joking." He removed his police hat and dropped it by the foot of the chair. He then raked one hand through his short hair, and barley shifted the blunt cut away from his head. If his hair was any longer, he really would look like Brad Pitt.

"I'm not. I have proof of it in the library if you want me to verify. Thornton was my mother's half-brother. I have the birth certificate to prove it. My grandfather fathered an illegitimate child in his younger years, and that child is Thornton Hughes."

Jace rubbed hard on his jaw. He gazed out at the lapping shore and then turned to Rain when she pressed. "Well?"

"No, that's okay, I'm just trying to take this new information in. I believe what you're saying, Rain, no need to verify by bringing out the paperwork just yet. And Willow? She knows this? She's aware that the deceased was her half-brother?"

"That I can neither confirm nor deny. As you know, my mother's out digging wells in Africa and was supposed to call me to share the best way to get hold of her this summer. I've yet to connect with her, but I'm not surprised. I've only been up here a few days and I'm sure she's just giving me time to get settled. I know my mother, and I'm sure she didn't want to call me right off the bat, because she knows I wouldn't initially be happy about reopening the library without her. She also knows I'd warm up to the idea over time. So no, as far as I know, she doesn't know about Thornton's murder. How could she? I can't even get hold of her, and I'm her daughter. I sent her a quick email to get in touch with me as soon as possible, but she's yet to respond. I didn't want to send this kind of news via the World Wide Web, so I kept it vague. I'm guessing she doesn't have service yet."

Jace scratched along his hairline and said, "the police station is only told to notify the next of kin. But we had no idea that the two were related so it's safe to assume none of the other officers or the chief attempted to phone your mom."

Rain held back from disclosing the part about Marge's sister. She didn't find that information pertinent to the case. Besides, she'd promised to hold the secret close to her heart. Jace was not a reader, so he probably wouldn't even make a connection from reading her grandfather's book anyway. It wasn't her place to disclose Maggie, she'd allow Marge to do that in her own time.

"Did you confirm that the blue necktie left inside my grandfather's book belonged to the victim?"

"Yeah, DNA results confirmed that the tie belonged to Thornton. I guess it's safe to assume that your mother lent him that book since he'd used his necktie as a bookmark, and it was found close to his body. It doesn't really prove anything; it only links him to the library or in this case— your mother."

"So, he'd come back to return the book to the library and wham-o! He gets bludgeoned to death. How awful. Clearly, my mother trusted him because no one, I mean, no one, outside our family has ever been told that the key was kept in the outhouse."

Jace tilted his head to one side to consider. "Huh? I wonder why Willow and Thornton didn't put a halt to the gossip then? Why would they allow it to continue? I mean, why would they let everyone around Lofty Pines think they were having an affair, if they weren't? They must've heard the talk themselves. You'd have to be a hermit not to."

"I'm not sure if it was because one of them wasn't ready to share the truth with the rest of the extended family? That part is still a bit unclear." Rain chewed at her nail. "That's the one thing I'm unsure of . . . why they would let the gossip fester. Honestly, maybe they just flat out didn't care what people thought. I'll certainly ask my mother the first chance I get."

Jace sat back in the chair and nursed his beer.

Rain looked to the sky, wishing for answers and not knowing yet quite where to find them. The sounds of cicadas and slow rolling waves along the shoreline filled the silence between them.

Jace broke the quiet when he said, "There are things at play here that you don't understand, and I can't share with you yet. Let's just leave it at that. Please understand, when the time is right, and I have substantial proof, and the case is wrapped up, I'll share it all with you. But again, please understand, I can't tell you everything right now. It would put the case in jeopardy."

"Yeah, I'd be lying if I said I was okay with it, I'm not—but I have to respect your work." Rain massaged her forehead and then decided to push forward with more questions anyway. Why not? What could she lose? "Can I ask about the money? The money that Julia found inside the milk carton. You haven't shared a word about that yet. I understand this is an ongoing investigation and you can't divulge much, but was Thornton rich? What else did you dig up from his background?"

"Rain. Don't. You know I can't share details of an ongoing investigation with you." Jace shook his head and Rain knew by the tone of his voice that there were things going on in the investigation that she was not yet privy to. She slumped back in the chair and returned her eyes to the sky.

"So, you still think my father did this? You think my father killed Thornton under the impression that my mother was having an affair with him? Is my father still on your suspect list after what I told you, Jace? Give it to me straight."

Jace paused longer than Rain liked before he answered.

"I don't think so. But I promise you this, I'll follow the traces of evidence wherever they lead."

That wasn't exactly the answer Rain was hoping for.

Chapter
Twenty-Six

The wail of a loon call sang out from the far side of the lake. Some found this echo haunting— as if the bird sounded desperate and foreboding. Rain had always found the sound hauntingly beautiful. The loon call reminded her of the Northwoods and the childhood memories back at her family's summer log cabin. The call typically happened at dusk, or early in the morning, as was the case that day. The lake was flat, as if she could step right onto it, and it would hold her bodyweight. And a slight haze hung over the water like a hovering ghost.

The sound of oncoming footsteps interrupted the loons and prompted Rain to raise her eyes from her grandfather's book. Julia's pink head shot up from the staircase, leading up to the wraparound deck. Her hair shimmered in the sunlight. Rain bookmarked the novel, and then set it beside the chair.

"You're certainly up early after a late night out. How was the bonfire after I left?"

"No kidding, a little too early for my liking, if you ask me. It was great fun! Kim says hello again, she felt bad you had to leave us last night, as did the rest of us. And after what I heard through the grapevine, I wish you would've stayed with us, too."

"Jace?"

"Uh-huh."

"Doughnuts again? You keep this up and I'm gonna need to join Weight Watchers by fall." Rain chuckled. She tented her eyes and watched Julia step onto the deck, balancing the bag of doughnut holes in one hand and The Brewin' Time cups in a disposable tray in the other. Her friend dropped the bag of doughnuts into her lap upon arrival, and then set the coffee down on the wide arm of her Adirondack chair.

"Yes, I found my brother camped out on my couch when we arrived home late last night." You're lucky I didn't come over and camp out here on this deck overnight and plunk the perp myself with one of Nick's hunting rifles." She reached into the bag of doughnut holes on Rain's lap, plucked one out, and popped the entire thing in her mouth. With a mouthful of powdered sugar, she added, "One evening I leave your side and all Havana breaks loose!"

"Yeah, pretty much." Rain reached into the bag and pulled out a powdered doughnut and took a nibble and then a sip of the coffee. "Oh Mylanta, these are sooo good. What do I owe you?"

"Oh *Mylanta*? I like it. I may have to use it. Hey, I guess, I'm really starting to rub off on you, aren't I?" Julia grinned.

Rain handed back the bag of doughnuts so not to be further tempted. She could already see that by summer's end she'd need to buy brand new jeans to fit her growing waistline. "Come on Julia, how much?" she pressed as she wiped away powder that had fallen from the doughnut bag and landed on her Harley Davidson T-shirt.

"You bought lunch at Portside, I think we're even. Let it go, will ya," Julia said in a teasing voice. "No worries, we'll do it again soon."

"Oh, we really should do that again soon, that was nice, I really like the ambiance over there. Or better yet, we should head over to Portside some Friday night for fish fry. That actually sounds better," Rain said smacking her lips. "Add that to our list of must-haves this summer." She grinned.

"Seriously, I'm starting to feel like a broken record asking, but are you okay?" Julia wiped powdered sugar from the side of her mouth and then licked her fingers clean.

"Yeah, I'm fine. The strange thing is that despite all this chaos in my life, it's actually starting to feel normal. Chaos seems to equal normal life for me. Am I making any sense? It's like I'm living in some weird twisted novel." Rain sighed and then turned her attention away from Julia to the waterfront when a soft breeze brushed across her skin. The morning sun danced atop the now rippling water. And calming laps serenaded, bringing serenity with each collapse onto shore. She felt the need to take a cleansing dip in the lake as soon as time permitted. The lake looked inviting.

"You wanna talk about it?"

"What? You mean the craziness called my life? Or the murder investigation?" Rain's eyes turned from the water back to her friend. "There are some missing pieces to our mystery that your brother won't fill me in on. Which is making this a little hard to solve."

"Like what?" Julia asked, shoving another doughnut hole into her mouth.

"Like the money you found in the milk carton. When I asked Jace about Thornton's finances, your brother clammed up. I still can't figure out why my uncle would be hiding gobs of money inside his refrigerator, it's very odd. A milk carton? Really? What do you make of that?"

"I don't make anything of that really, except that your uncle may have been dirty, stinkin' rich." Julia brushed the powdered sugar off her hands and onto her legs. "Jace is just doing his job and can't reveal too much, for fear it might compromise the case. You gotta give him a little leeway, Rain. He's not holding back to be difficult, I'm sure once this is all said and done, he'll open up like a flower."

"Oh? So, you're siding with your brother now?" Rain teased with a wry smile. "That's a 180-degree shift from the other night."

"Yes, agreed. The other night at the barbeque I pushed his buttons a little hard. But I was only trying to dig for intel, not unlike yourself. Truth is, my big brother loves me. Deep down he knows the barrage of questions come from good intentions—Jace knows we're just trying to make sense of all this."

"I think he's getting pretty sick of running to my aid. I'm starting to feel like a damsel in distress, and I don't like it." Rain smirked. "He must think I'm a weenie."

"On the contrary, my brother has mentioned on more than one occasion that he's glad to reconnect with you. He likes you, and he's happy you're back with us up here in the Northwoods. Along with the rest of the Lakers." She winked.

Rain wasn't sure how to take that comment. She had enjoyed reconnecting with Jace, too, but she wasn't sure if Julia was insinuating that there was more to it than that. Or that she inwardly hoped for more than that. She smoothed her teeth with her tongue, removing any residue of sugar and then shifted in the chair, tucking her legs beneath her. "One piece of the puzzle I toyed over well into the night and can't seem to let go of, is who might have been over here and attempted a break-in last night. And I think I may have an answer."

Julia sat up straighter in the chair, "Really? You think you know who tried to break in? How? Jace said the perpetrator was wearing dark clothing and that you said you couldn't see anything." Her head cocked to one side in confusion. "Did you hold something back?"

"No, not at all, at least not intentionally. I didn't think about this until long after Jace left. Truthfully, it crossed my mind while I tossed and turned in bed. Remember when we went over to Thornton's rental house to clean?"

Julia took a sip of her drink and then set it down on the arm of the Adirondack. She then made a sour face. "How could I forget cleaning? Best day of my life," she added sarcastically. "I'm never starting that kind of side business, by the way. I'm officially done." She rolled her eyes and clucked her tongue. "I hate cleaning. No, I take that back, I *loathe* it," she drawled.

"Maybe not?" Rain uttered while chewing the inside of her cheek.

"Oh, trust me." Julia shook her head. "I'm done, done! You can't pay me enough."

"Wait. Hang on a second . . . hear me out." Rain reached to console her friend, and Julia misinterpreted and stuck the bag of doughnuts back in her hand, which made Rain smile.

"No, I appreciate you bringing them, but I'm good on the doughnuts for now." Rain rejected the bag with an upheld palm. "No, I mean, when we were over there, Frankie mentioned that Thornton's friend had a foreign accent. Last night, Jace discovered the word that I heard the intruder yell might have been German. I think our guy that was here last night was a friend of Thornton's."

"Well, now that makes zero sense." Julia's face turned puzzled. "Why would a friend of Thornton's want to break into your house? Jace told me that he put the key back inside the outhouse? Why would he do that? That makes no sense at all."

"Yeah." Rain sat back in the chair and contemplated. "That's the part that I'm hung up on, too. So . . . I was thinking . . . maybe if we pretend we're going back to clean the house because we didn't get a chance to finish . . . Because we were interrupted by the police . . . We could approach Frankie and see if we can find out more about this foreign guy. We could pump him for more intel. Whatddaya say?"

"I say I have a better idea," Julia said intently as she drummed her fingers on the arm of the chair. She then turned to face the lake. "Where do guys go early in the morning when they own a Lund?" A smile formed on her lips and one eyebrow raised.

"They go fishing!" Rain exclaimed.

"Exactly. Let's go catch a big one." Julia grinned. "And by big one, obviously, I mean a big lead in this case. Let's find out more about our little German friend through Frankie. Maybe he'll know what kind of trouble Thornton was in that might have led to his demise. Who would know more than a friend, right?"

"Julia, you're brilliant!"

"Nah, don't give me that much credit, I'm just trying to get outta cleaning again. I'd much rather go fishing than cleaning." Julia looked at her nails. "I repeat. If you ask me to clean a McMansion again for scoop—it's not happening." She chuckled.

"No worries, I promise I won't use cleaning as our ruse in the future since you have such an aversion to it." Rain laughed and then switched gears. "Do you think we can borrow some of Nick's tackle to make it look legit? All my dad's stuff is buried in the boathouse, and I have no idea what kind of condition it's in. I haven't gone fishing in years. To be honest, I'm not even sure I ever put my own worm on a line." She grimaced. "My grandfather always did that for me."

"I gotcha covered," Julia said as she rolled up the dough-nut bag and then rose from the chair. We don't need to take a shower or get fancy or anything. Remember, we're pretend-ing to be fishing. No smelly perfume, lotion, or anything, it scares the fish and if Frankie catches the scent, he'll know we're bluffing. I'll meet you on the pontoon in say . . . fifteen minutes. Does that give you enough time to get ready?"

"Plenty," Rain said as she rose. "Bring the doughnuts, in case we're on stakeout and get hungry." She teased.

"Already planned on it." Julia's voice trailed behind her.

Her friend was barely out of earshot when Rain heard someone shuffle across the deck as she was just about to step inside the cabin.

"Rain?"

"Lyla, good morning." Rain secretly wondered what the woman was doing standing on her deck first thing in the morning. "Something I can help you with?"

"I went over to the library but it seems it's closed?" Lyla put her hands on her hips and waited expectantly with a frown.

"Oh, I see. Yes, I'm sorry but due to the circumstances I've been forced to postpone the opening, but we'll be open to the public just as soon as we can. Are you looking for a beach read? I'm sure I have one laying around the cabin that you could borrow?"

"No. I was actually looking for a book on numismatics. Do you know if you have anything like that on the shelf?"

"Gosh, I don't know. I'm a bit embarrassed to admit it, but I'm not familiar with the term?" Rain smiled.

"Oh, it's the study of currency. A numismatist is a person who collects coins and currency from other time periods." Lyla pushed back her shoulders proudly, protruding her ample chest as if showing she had one up on Rain due to her extensive . . . knowledge.

"Learn something new every day!" Rain chuckled. "I doubt we have anything like that in our little library, though. We mostly shelve works of fiction and a few memoirs and such. I highly doubt we have anything about currency collecting in our meager collection. Sorry I can't be of more help." Rain shrugged.

"Oh, that's okay. Brock sent me on another wild-goose chase. He just said it's not something he wants to google. He says the government is watching all the time." Lyla circled her fingers and put her hands in front of her eyes as if she was looking through pretend binoculars. "You know how those advertisements show up on your phone immediately after you google something? Brock absolutely hates that! I can't half blame him."

"Yeah, it is weird when that happens, I'll have to agree with that." Rain nodded.

"Anyhow, I guess, I'll be on my way then. Enjoy the day, it looks like it's going to be a magnificent one!"

"Yeah, you too," Rain said to Lyla's back as the woman had already turned from her and rushed away.

Rain stood dumfounded as she couldn't help but wonder why Brock was looking for a book on money and didn't want the trace of a google search. Especially when a dead man had been hiding some rare currency of his own inside a refrigerator. Something wasn't adding up. Or maybe it finally was.

*   *   *

The wind gusted up soon after the pontoon glided across the placid lake, causing Rain's dark hair to tangle across her face. She turned the vessel directly against the wind to allow her hair to fly freely again. Julia sat in the front seat of the pontoon with compact binoculars held up to her eyes in search of the Lund. Her friend turned toward the captain's chair.

"I can't see a thing; we're zipping along too fast. The new bumps aren't allowing me to focus," Julia shouted, dropping the field glasses to her lap.

"I'll slow it down once we get over to one of the common fishing areas and we get a visual of other boats out here. Right now, I'm not seeing much either."

Julia gave the thumbs up.

The lake was eerily desolate, despite perfect fishing weather. Usually, first dawn was peak fishing for most anglers, and different sections of hot spots around Pine Lake brought out a school of fisherman. Yet even at midmorning, the lake was void of them.

"Where is everybody this morning? I'm really shocked I'm not seeing anyone." Rain's eyes darted around Pine Lake, but no other boats were within sight. And they were clipping along at a nice pace.

"Oh rats, berries! I just thought of something," Julia shouted for Rain to hear over the groaning engine and splashing waves.

Rain lowered the throttle so she could hear Julia better. "What's that?" she cuffed a hand next to her ear to muffle the sound of whipping wind and waited.

"There's a fishing tournament over in Crivitz, and I can almost bet a bunch of guys went down there. It's a pretty big event they hold on one of the lakes every summer." Julia frowned. "I'm pretty sure this is the week they're having it. Maybe that explains why the lake is so lacking in fishing boats this morning?"

"That's not exactly the news I wanted to hear." Rain tightened her hands upon the steering wheel and brought her head to rest on it momentarily. When she lifted her head again, she asked, "What now? How are we gonna talk to Frankie and dig for more information about Thornton's friend, if Frankie's in Crivitz with the rest of the fisherman?"

"It's just a guess on my part. Why don't we take a spin over by Thornton's rental? If Frankie's boat is docked at his house, then maybe we'll get lucky and he didn't join the tournament this year. If it's gone, and we can't find the Lund somewhere on this lake, it would be safe to assume he's down there with everyone else."

Rain circled the steering wheel of the pontoon in the direction of Thornton's rental, and hugged the shoreline. She lowered the throttle to the lowest setting, so that she wouldn't cause a wake to form behind the boat. In order not to disturb anyone that had the privilege of a good night's sleep— unlike herself. She also didn't want to frighten the loons as she navigated around one swimming dangerously close to the boat. The bird dipped its head and then dove deep beneath the water and didn't pop its head again until far from the pontoon. The wind subsided, and Rain could tell by the warmth upon her shoulders, and the lake returning to a sheet of glass, that they were in for another hot day ahead.

"Back at the cabin, right after you left, Lyla stopped by for a quick visit." Rain said.

"Oh yeah? What did she want?"

"She was inquiring whether or not we had books in the library regarding currency."

Julia spun her seat around to face her. "You're kidding?"

"I'm not. She said Brock sent her over for it."

"*Really.* Is that so?"

"Yeah, really. What do you make of it?"

"I'm not sure, to be honest, I'd heard Brock was into coin collecting in his youth, but I didn't know he still had interest in that stuff. That is interesting."

"To say the least, the timing is interesting."

"Sure is."

"Speaking of interesting, have you thought about what you're going to say to Frankie? We should probably craft a plan here. You don't think it's possible that Frankie actually had something to do with Thornton's murder, do you? I mean, you're not still thinking the blood on his boat was Thornton's, are you? You mentioned something before that he too had a beef with the guy, or something to that affect. Maybe this isn't such a good idea after all. He might feel cornered." A look of concern swept across Julia's sunburned face.

"Truth is, Jace mentioned that the blood on the boat was indeed fish blood. And yes, Frankie certainly wasn't a fan of Thornton, but it sounds like my uncle burned quite a few bridges around Lofty Pines, the way Marge put it at the barbeque. It's a long shot, but we'll stick to the conversation being about Thornton's foreign friend. We'll keep the conversation light and away from any suspicions that might alert Frankie. Believe me, I don't want to spook the guy either. Maybe Frankie knows where the foreign guy works, though, or what bar he hangs out at. At the very least, he might know where we can find him so we can go talk to him. Maybe then I can find out what he was trying to accomplish by breaking into my house!"

"Jace is gonna kill us," Julia said with a smirk before spinning her chair back to face forward. She raised the compact binoculars to her eyes as soon as Thornton's rental came into distant view, then gasped.

"Did you find Frankie?"

"No, it's not Frankie because his Lund isn't docked there, and I remember what he looks like from Portside—this guy has a smaller build. Someone is snooping around Thornton's rental."

Rain looked on as a spectator as Julia kept the binoculars up to her eyes. "Who is it? Can you tell?"

"I don't know . . . it's not the homeowner either; I know Jeremey like the back of my hand." Julia dropped the binoculars to her lap and spun to face Rain. "Someone is definitely up to no good."

Chapter
Twenty-Seven

"Quick, let me see those." Rain cut the engine and moved to take the binoculars from Julia's hands. She then held them up to her own eyes.

"You want me to steer the boat?" Julia asked, jumping up from the seat, and stumbling past her. A sudden gust of wind picked up, and the waves overtook the pontoon, causing them to bobble idly in the water like a giant fishing bobber with a robust fish taking it down.

"Yeah, would you?" Rain reached to steady herself by grabbing hold of the back of one of the front pedestal seats and dropping the binoculars to her side. She waited until the boat stabilized, before plopping into the seat and raising the binoculars to her eyes again.

"See anything?" Julia asked.

Rain glanced over her shoulder to the captain's chair where Julia now stood and had taken over the controls. "I can't get a good read. I think it's a male, from the build alone. But he has his back turned to me. The guy doesn't look familiar, at least from the back. How many men do you know with mousy brown hair?"

"Uh-uh. Maybe like half the male population," Julia said with a chuckle.

"You've got that right."

"Bummer, I was hoping you'd be able to see who it was."

"Well, you definitely know a lot more about Lakers than I remember. You want to dock the boat and maybe we can check it out further? I'd like to take a closer look and see what this guy is up to," Rain suggested.

"Pretty brazen, breaking into a house first thing in the morning, don't you think? Why wouldn't he break in at night, after dark? Like the rest of the hooligans. You really think it's safe to confront the guy?"

"I'm not saying we should confront him." Rain looked through the binoculars, then turned to Julia again, and whispered. "He moved to the side of the house by a basement egress window. He just flipped the hood up on his sweatshirt to hide his face. And it looks like he has a pocketknife, and he's preparing to cut out a screen! Julia! We've gotta stop him somehow! Or at least find out what he's up to."

"I don't know if it's such a good idea for us to get any closer. What if it's the same guy that tried to break into your house last night! Is he wearing the same sweatshirt?"

Rain couldn't tell.

"And what if he stabs us with that knife!" Julia hissed. "I'd better call Jace. Where's your phone?"

Rain cringed sheepishly. "I didn't bring it." She held up one hand in defense, "I thought if we were pretend fishing . . . I wouldn't need it. I didn't see a use for it, until now. You?"

"Ahh, no. I didn't bring mine either. I guess we don't make the best amateur sleuths after all. What were we thinking not bringing our cell phones?" Julia said under her breath, through gritted teeth. She then threw up her hands in exasperation.

Rain rose the binoculars up again to watch the intruder, and then her arms shook in disbelief and excitement, "He got in! He got in! He's *inside* the house! What are we gonna do now? We have to find out what he's doing in there! What if he's removing substantial evidence!"

"He's probably burglarizing people's uninhabited houses around Pine Lake, like yours for example. Maybe he overheard somewhere, at a local pub or something, that a few rentals were still vacant. Maybe he thought he could score big on a few of those with no one around!" Julia suggested.

"Really?" Rain's tone went flat. "And I suppose he returns missing keys to outhouses too? Is that part of his MO? Should we call him the master key burglar?" She rolled her eyes and smiled. "I don't think so."

"Ahh, I guess you've got a point there." Julia twirled her hair between her fingers until a tight ringlet formed. "You really think this is the same guy who tried to break into your cabin last night?" Julia shifted the pontoon in order to back the boat up in reverse so they could continue to remain hidden behind the headland that jutted out into the water. The small peninsula gave them just enough room to maintain surveillance.

"What other conclusion would you make? Isn't it Jace who says he doesn't believe in coincidences? Plus, he just put the hood up on his sweatshirt. I can't say definitively if it's the *same* sweatshirt but that's beside the point. We gotta go over there and find out what the heck he's doing inside of Thornton's rental, otherwise we'll never get to the bottom of this."

"Excuse me?" Julia blinked rapidly. "You wanna do whaaaat?"

"What other choice do we have? We certainly can't see anything from here with all of these trees blocking our way." The boat continued to drift toward shore, causing the rental to fully disappear behind the headland of trees. "Here." Rain stood, and steadily guided her way back toward the controls. "Let me take over."

"Where on earth are you gonna park this thing?" Julia asked skeptically as she moved away from the captain's chair. "We can't park at Frankie's pier, and it's a little hard to hide a large pontoon. It's like trying to hide an elephant at the zoo."

"How about we anchor over there and wade in." Rain pointed out a shallow spot that would be tucked in and hidden from view from Thornton's rental. "We'll carry our shoes."

Rain hoped the obscure spot would enable them to inconspicuously sneak onto shore without being caught.

She maneuvered the boat to the neighboring location, then cut the engine to glide the rest of the way toward shore. Without a moment to waste, Rain moved to the front of the boat and carefully dropped anchor so as not to make a huge splashing noise. She guided the rope slowly through her hands until the anchor finally hit the bottom, then she gave a hard tug to make certain it was secure.

"Come on, hurry!" Rain summoned. She moved over to drop the ladder into the water and then held the top of the ladder to keep it stable while Julia descended into the lake.

Julia winced when her body hit the water. She gritted her teeth and danced up and down in thigh deep water while she waited. "The water's colder than a freezie pop!" She shook her hands frantically in the air as if it somehow helped control the urge to shriek.

Rain scrambled to join Julia in the lake. She, too, felt a rush of cold when her bare feet touched the sandy bottom. In an attempt not to scream out from the shock of icy water, she covered her mouth and then bit down on her bent index finger. So much for wanting a cleansing dip in the lake. That wouldn't happen anytime soon. The instant numbness of her legs made the walk difficult. Each step forward felt like wading through molten concrete. She looked over at Julia who was pushing closer to shore with one flip-flop dangling in each hand.

"Oh no!" Rain whispered.

Julia turned to question her. "It's too cold out here, eh? Did I mention the ice just came out of the lake in early

May?" She shook her head. "I can't *believe* we're doing this. What are we thinking?"

"No, it's not that. I forgot my shoes!" Rain looked back over her shoulder at the anchored boat, which had drifted away from them, and then decided to forge on ahead despite her lack of footwear. She carefully sidestepped a pile of zebra mussels, and a crayfish scrambled past her foot.

"Ouch! Rats!" Julia winced. "Owie!"

"What'd ya hit? Zebra mussel or crayfish?"

"I'm not sure, but I definitely stepped on something sharp," Julia hopped on one foot causing a rippling effect around her. She limped to shore and dropped onto the thick grass upon arrival. After she'd flipped her foot over for confirmation, and wiggled her toes for a few moments she said, "No blood no foul. I think I'll live."

Rain joined Julia on the shoreline, folded over, and rubbed at her calves vigorously in order to get the blood pumping again. "I forgot how long it takes for the lakes to warm up in the Northwoods. I don't think it'll be swimmable up here until late July!" She bounced up and down on her toes until she felt capable of walking again and blew out a few quick panting breaths, as if preparing for a marathon.

The two had landed on a neighboring rugged property that lacked any built structure. The vacant uncleared land held a small *For Sale by Owner* sign nailed to a nearby tree, close to the shore. Along with a *No Trespassing* sign on another. Rain hoped, for her sake, Julia didn't catch wind of the no trespassing one.

Rain then noticed the eagle's nest overhead and realized someone with vast wings had already taken up residence on the property. She'd heard that cardinals were the birds that often coincided with a loved one's death. She wondered instead if Max had chosen an eagle, since she'd seen so many eagles of late.

"Ready?" Julia asked, interrupting her reverie.

Rain nodded and then followed Julia toward the thick trees that blocked the two properties. After leaving the grassland, and crossing a dirt path, she looked to the pine-needled ground and sulked.

Noticing Rain's dilemma, Julia called her over with her hands and then crouched forward, waiting. "Come over here! Hop on my back."

"Seriously? You want to carry me piggyback?" Rain asked incredulously, tossing her head back with a slight laugh. "You must be joking; I think we're a little old for that."

"Do we have any other choice? You really want to walk over that?" Julia said as her observation dropped to regard Rain's feet which were now covered in gummy dirt. "Trust me, after having stepped on something sharp in the water, you don't want to do that."

Rain acquiesced and hopped unconvincingly onto her friend's back. Julia laced her arms through Rain's legs and readjusted her weight before carrying her across the needle-encrusted ground. When they arrived at a patch of turf, the familiar smell of Christmas candle filled her nostrils as Julia dropped Rain beside the real thing—a balsam fir.

"Nicely done, thank you." Rain smiled and patted Julia on the back.

Julia held up her arms, revealing her swollen biceps and said, "I guess all those field-day sporting events with the teenagers from school is finally paying off." She giggled. "Besides, you weigh less than half my students. I need to keep feeding you pastries and fatten you up a bit, lady."

Rain teasingly swatted one of her arms before Julia grew serious.

"Okay, we're here. Now what, Sherlock?"

The two peeked out from behind the branches.

Julia took a step back from the tree, squinted, and said, "I can't see a thing. He must still be inside the house. Can you see anything? And my hands are already sticky with sap." She sniffed at her fingers before attempting to move the branch away again that had been obstructing the view of the rental.

Rain smiled and reached into her shorts pocket to remove the compact binoculars. "I may have forgotten my shoes, but I didn't forget these babies." She clucked her tongue as she lifted the field glasses up to her eyes and refocused. There was no movement in front of the colonial, so she skirted her view. She focused in on an upturned canoe on the far side of the property but much closer to the house than where they were standing.

"I'm going over there by the canoe. I think it might help me get a better look-see." Rain pushed through the branches and disregarded Julia's attempt to make her change her mind by a grab at her shoulder. Instead, she abandoned the hideout behind the tree and galloped across the front yard as fast as she could. Pure adrenaline pumped through her veins, propelling her forward. She pumped until she reached her target and ducked behind the safety of the upturned canoe.

Rain crouched down until her labor breathing subsided, and then popped her head up to see Julia running toward her across the front yard. Her pink hair was like a beacon, shimmering in the sunlight. Rain hoped for their sakes the intruder was not looking out the window because her friend's hair was an absolute dead giveaway. When she arrived, Julia tripped, and landed face first to join her, skinning her knee in the process.

"Holy Hamburgers! What are you doing?" Julia hissed, gripping her own shirt at an attempt to slow her labored breathing. "You really think this is a wise choice? Have you fallen off your rocker?"

"Never mind me, look at your knee." Rain pointed to Julia's leg where it already began to drip blood. "You okay?" She winced just looking at the injury.

"Rain, you're gonna get us into big trouble here. Bigger than a skinned knee. If this is indeed the guy who killed Thornton, or tried to break into your house last night, what the chicken cluck are we doing?"

"I don't think he killed Thornton. Frankie mentioned these two guys were friends, if indeed this is the foreign guy he told me about." Rain frowned after flicking a finger in the direction of the house. "What I do know for sure, however, is this guy is breaking into houses looking for something important. I think it's up to us to find out what exactly he's up to. Maybe that, my friend, will break this case wide open, and I can clear my parents out of this mess once and for all. Now's the chance to tell me, are you in or out?"

"And how do you propose we do that?" Julia asked.

Rain tipped the canoe to reveal a wooden oar beneath it. Along with a host of bugs that scampered from the movement. She yanked the oar out and dragged it close to her side and then set the canoe carefully back down. She popped her head up and looked toward the rental to confirm there was no further movement from the perpetrator. "When I say go, we make a run for it."

Julia's eyes widened to twice their usual size.

Before Julia had an opportunity to change Rain's mind or hold her back, Rain whispered, "Go!" and clutched the oar in one hand and made a run for it. She sprinted toward the back patio and upon immediate arrival at the house, flattened her back as close as possible, pressing hard against the vinyl siding, keeping the oar in a death grip in one hand. She tipped the back of her head against the house while she caught her breath and watched as Julia rushed to join her. The two remained pinned flat against the house and waited for their panting breaths to subside before taking a quick peek inside the back door.

When they finally took that chance, Rain noticed the intruder had his head deep inside the refrigerator. The man stepped back from the refrigerator and closed the door. Rain held her breath while she watched, then gasped when he locked eyes on them.

Chapter
Twenty-Eight

"Son of a nutcracker! What are we going to do?" Julia squealed as she frantically flung her hands out nervously as if she was trying to fling large wet droplets from her hands. She danced wildly on two feet, her eyes the size of an owl's.

Rain didn't speak. She was too stunned.

"Well? Just don't stand there! He's coming!"

"I met him, at my house, and then at the bonfire." Rain whispered. "He was at Kim's house! At least when I was there. He was out on the pier. He must've left via wave runner!"

"What?" Julia hissed.

Rain raised the oar over her head and waited. "You try and distract the guy, and I'll whack him. Max always told me if I ever found myself under attack by a man, go for the eyes, or the jewels. Sensitive spots . . . you know the one." She nodded curtly and squared her shoulders.

Julia's eyes widened even more as they heard the back door slide open.

"Can I help you?" the intruder asked.

Rain lowered the oar but locked her knees tight and stood tall like a Redwood. "What are you doing?"

"Me?" He tapped a hand to his chest. "What are you two doing?" His eyes traveled between them and landed finally on Rain and the oar that she held with a death grip in her hand.

"Trying to understand why you're breaking and entering a friend's rental home? Care to explain?" Julia said, unexpectantly gaining composure.

The man's demeanor instantly changed. "You two shouldn't be here."

"No, you shouldn't," Rain said firmly.

The intruder rushed at Rain with outstretched arms as if he was going to disarm her. Even though she thought this was the man she'd met at Kim's, the man who'd introduced himself as Paul, she couldn't be hundred percent sure. It had been dark that night, and she hadn't gotten a good look at him. And the day he had stopped by the library, she was so in her own head, it could've been Godzilla who'd come to the door. After the volley in her head, it didn't matter. If it was them against him, she'd defend them to the end. As soon as he stepped foot on the patio, she hit the intruder over the head with a thud. He shook his head, stunned for a moment, but before she had a chance at a second crack, he reached to grab Julia by the arm, missed, and instead caught her pink hair at the last second and held it in a clenched fist.

"Let her go!" Rain seethed through gritted teeth as she watched the intruder cuff his arm around Julia's neck in a choke hold, and drag her backward, holding her close. He yanked her friend tighter to the threshold of the house, and Julia let out a squeal before he momentarily covered her mouth with his slender hand.

Rain lifted the oar to ready herself, in order to jab him hard in his privates, but she was too slow. The man, of equal height, flicked open a large switchblade, and held it against Julia's throat. Julia's eyes widened when she caught sight of it and he almost nicked her. Rain couldn't imagine how her friend must've felt as she watched in horror the sharpness of steel graze across her friend's neck.

"Drop the oar," he said.

Rain immediately caught the hint of a foreign accent. She hadn't caught it when they'd spoken before, but she knew when agitated, angry, or upset, people often fell back on their native tongue .

"No! Not until you let her go! *Depp*!" Rain yelled at him.

The man's eyes blazed. "Why did you call me an idiot?" he asked. "You're a depp!" he added in his native tongue and yanked Julia tighter to himself.

The man's answer confirmed what she'd already known, he'd broken into her house, too.

"You were Thornton's friend, right Paul? Frankie told me you two were friends." Rain lowered her voice and talked soothingly as if she was prompting a child. "We spoke the other night at Kim's, remember me? Out on the pier?"

Paul didn't reply; he just studied her as if he was trying to figure out what she'd do next.

"Let her go," Rain said, this time attempting to keep her voice steady and calm. "Let her go, and this will all be over."

The disgruntled man laughed at her. And then spit on the ground before dragging her friend fully inside the house. Julia let out a yelp, and then locked fearful eyes on Rain who followed them inside the rental, holding the oar steady in her hands. Her hands were white from the tight grip.

"I said let her go!" Rain demanded. "You're just making this worse on yourself. Just take whatever you were planning on stealing, get outta of this house, and get outta here before the police come."

Paul snickered. "The police are not coming," he said as he dragged Julia deeper into the living room. "Nobody is awake in this neighborhood besides you two fools!" he spat.

"Yes. Yes, they *are*. The police are on the way right now, we called them from the boat." She bluffed and noticed the fear flicker for a moment in the man's dark brown eyes. His tangled mousy-brown hair fell loose, almost to his shoulder, and Rain couldn't place how old Paul was, or if he was anywhere close to Thornton's age. She wondered how they knew each other—

What was the connection?

"What are you doing in here?" Rain finally voiced aloud. "I thought you were Thornton's friend. If that's true, why are you breaking into his rental?" She knew he had to be the friend Frankie had told her about, but she wanted

301

confirmation. She wanted to know his motive. "The money's gone. The police have it," Rain added, bobbing her head in the direction of the refrigerator.

"None of your business," Paul muttered. But Rain couldn't help but notice the flicker of surprise in his eyes. She could only conclude that the five-hundred-dollar bills were what he was after.

Rain moved closer, pointing the top of the oar fearlessly in Paul's direction, forcing him to drag Julia backward toward a tall shelf of books. She eyed Julia knowingly and said, "I knew it was *Always You*." Rain said, referring to her grandfather's book. She hoped for her sake, Julia understood the prompt. Julia nodded her head ever so slightly; Rain hadn't been sure.

"What are you talking about? *Always You*?" Paul uttered the title of her grandfather's book with such contempt, Rain wanted to poke him in the jewels instantaneously, but she refrained.

When Paul backed up into the bookshelf, he briefly turned to see what he had bumped into, and Rain screamed, "NOW!"

Julia snatched the thickest book she could find and clocked Paul on the head with it. Stunned, Paul teetered on his heel and accidently dropped the pocketknife. Rain rushed to grab the knife off the floor, and before Paul could beat Rain at the pass, Julia kicked him in the privates, sending Paul to crumble to his knees. The man cried out in agony.

Rain and Julia locked eyes in stunned silence.

When the intruder stabilized, he attempted a lunge in the direction of Rain. She stood tall and held the knife steady. "Look, buster. My husband cheated on me and I really haven't made peace with that yet. You ever hear of Lorena Bobbitt? That's exactly what I'm gonna do to you if you don't put your hands behind your back. Right. Flipping. Now!" She seethed through gritted teeth.

Julia let out a nervous giggle.

"Julia, go and fetch one of Thornton's neckties out of the closet, will ya? And make it a fancy one. We're gonna cuff this guy and send him to the slammer where he belongs," Rain said with satisfaction, holding her gait steady.

Julia scampered to her feet and ran out of the room. She quickly returned with a solid green necktie, along with a soft pink one, and held one in each of her hands like a couple of blue-ribbon awards. "I picked this one because it goes with my hair. Don't ya think?" She giggled nervously.

Rain beamed with pride at her friend but held the knife with a steady hand. She then turned her attention back onto the perpetrator.

"I don't know why, but I have a feeling you had something to do with my uncle's murder. There's something more here you wanted besides money. I may not know yet. But trust me, I will get to the bottom of this, I promise you that," Rain added with deep conviction and a tone unfamiliar to her own ears.

"Yeah, you pickled cucumber. We're gonna get to the bottom of this," Julia added punching her fists in the air like a boxer waiting for his opponent. The colorful neckties bouncing around in her balled fists.

Rain threatened the man further with blazing eyes and a twirl of the knife. "Turn around. Now!" She demanded.

After the man grudgingly complied with her request, Julia rushed over and wound the pink necktie taut to his wrists, and then Rain shoved him farther to the ground by pressing her hand hard on his shoulder. Julia then took her cue and wound his ankles with the green necktie, leaving Paul defenseless.

While Julia continued to bind up his ankles, Rain's eyes darted the room in search of a landline. She breathed a sigh of relief when she located one and immediately dialed 911.

*　*　*

The minute Jace entered the room, he rushed to Rain's side and removed the knife from her now trembling hand. She couldn't recall how long she'd stood there holding the knife in a defensive stance, while the perpetrator remained coiled, like the snake that he was, on the floor.

"Wyatt, cuff him and get him outta here," Jace directed with an extended finger and a curt nod at the young officer.

Jace then led Rain and Julia into the kitchen away from the criminal and the other officers who had come like a stampede of wild stallions to their aid.

"What in God's green earth are you two doing over here?" Jace's eyes traveled between Rain and Julia and then back again after they'd reached the center island inside the kitchen.

After a few silent moments and a shared glance, Julia said, "We came back to finish cleaning?" she asked hesitantly. A sheepish grin crossed her face, and Rain noticed how hard her friend worked to hold back the smile that was threatening to cross her face.

Jace shook his head. "Sorry Sis, not buying it. Try again." He rested his hands firmly on his police belt and waited. The vein in his temple pulsated and Rain thought, under different circumstances, he might've clocked his sister upside the head with his police baton. Jace then looked at Rain's feet.

"And where are your shoes, young lady?" He pointed to her feet and Rain curled her filthy toes in response.

"We came by boat!" Julia said quickly, as if that was a plausible excuse.

"Oh really? And where is it? Because one of the other officers circled the house before he joined us in here and told me there were no boats tied up to the dock. Not a pontoon," he directed to Rain. "Not a red speedboat," he transferred his eyes to his sister. "No boats anywhere in the vicinity." He circled his finger in the air dramatically. "Including the neighbor's pier, so where is the boat exactly? And whose boat did you bring over here?" Jace raised a brow and paused. His neck muscle protruded, and Rain wondered what she could possibly say that might ease the growing tension in the room.

Julia's eyes dropped downcast to the floor and she remained silent.

"Anchored out by the bend," Rain pointed in a direction none of them could see from their vantage point. "We brought my pontoon," she confessed finally.

"Ahh, I see." Jace nodded and then walked around the two of them as if he were an animal circling his prey. Rain and Julia remained huddled together in growing apprehension. "Let me get this straight. You hide the boat out yonder," he flicked a finger lakeside. "You come over here without shoes." His eyes traveled back to Rain's feet. "Maybe it's me, but something tells me you two were not over here first thing in the morning— before breakfast I might add, to *clean*." He clicked his tongue, and then his expression hardened. "Call me crazy, but something tells me, ladies, that what you are saying, simply doesn't add up." He threw his hands up in disbelief before he laced his hands across his chest and glared at them through disbelieving eyes.

"Actually, we ate. Doughnuts. We ate doughnuts. There's more in the boat if you want some." Julia's eyes wandered back to the floor.

"I, mean, I . . ." Rain stuttered and then closed her lips in a grim line.

"Exactly," Jace interrupted. "You two . . ." Jace wagged a finger between them. "You two," he said again, this time with growing agitation, "should've never been here. So, which one of you is going to tell me the real reason that led you here?"

"Frankie was the original reason," Rain said softly and then her shoulders sank.

"The neighbor?" Jace's brows knit together and then Julia pipped up.

"Yeah! Rain forgot to tell you, but when we were over here cleaning, you know, the day we called you about the money . . . the money that we found in the fridge?" All three sets of eyes landed on the refrigerator and then back to Julia. "Anyhow . . . Rain had a chat with Frankie that morning, and he told her that Thornton hung out with some foreign guy . . ."

"And you came back here to question him?" Jace interrupted and then dropped his arms to his side and held his hands tight to his legs in balled fists. "About some foreign guy?" He lasered in on Rain. "The foreign guy that you and I talked about? You actually thought it would be a good idea to go and find him yourself? After he attempted to break into your cabin? Are you nuts, Rain?"

Rain reached out to touch his arm, "Actually, I was only trying to get you to see that my father had nothing to do with this. How would you feel if the tables were turned and people suspected your sister?" Her eyes traveled to Julia. "Wouldn't you want to clear her name and protect her? Wouldn't you do anything to protect your family?" Rain straightened her shoulders and stood tall with new resolve.

Julia piped up, "Hey, don't put me in the middle of this!"

"I'm sorry," Rain said to Julia. "I'm just trying to make him understand." She lifted a palm in her brother's direction.

Jace's eyes softened, though, so she continued. "I'm only trying to get to the truth here. I'm sorry if I acted hastily and dragged Julia, too, into this. It's just . . ."

Jace stopped her with a lift of his palm. "I get it. I do." His tone softened. "I just wish you two had called me. Why didn't you? You both put yourselves in grave danger, and that's genuinely concerning to me. I should throw you both in jail just to teach you both a lesson."

Rain and Julia looked at each other and said in unison, "He'd never do that." Causing the three to lose tension between them as a smile crossed Jace's lips, and he shook his head as if he knew he'd lost the battle.

"Seriously, what am I going to do with you two?" He smirked.

"Look, neither of us could've imagined it would get this far. We were honestly just attempting to dig for intel. That's all." Julia swiped her hands out like she was calling safe at a baseball game.

"Again. Not your job," Jace said calmly.

"Despite all the danger we put ourselves in, did we solve the case?" Rain asked hesitantly. "Did we provide any help at all?"

Jace attempted to hold back a smile, "As much as I hate to admit this, if it hadn't been for you two catching Paul in the act of burglary, we'd have nothing to hold him on. We're still in the process of collecting evidence, but we didn't have enough to present it to the District Attorney yet. So yeah, I guess you helped solved the crime. Let me wrap up this investigation, but then I think we'll need to regroup."

"Can I ask you something? Do you know anything about Brock and his interest in coins and currency? Does he have anything to do with all of this?"

Jace only acknowledged her comment with a smile.

"You know the motive behind this crime, don't you, Jace?" Rain asked.

"Yes, Rain, I most certainly do."

Chapter
Twenty-Nine

A n entire week passed before Rain was able to reopen the
Lakeside Library to the citizens of Lofty Pines. Both
she and her new coworkers, Julia and Marge, had decided
the three would come together to prepare for the pre-initial
grand reopening a few hours before the first patrons were
due to arrive. Julia was working diligently on cataloging
the last of the new novels. Marge was meticulously dusting
every inch of the library with a feather duster. And Rain
was shelving books, when the door opened, and officer Jace
Lowe appeared, filling the space with his commanding
stance.

"Good morning, ladies." He tipped his official police hat
to the three. "How we all doin' today?" he asked, rocking
back and forth on his heels. A welcoming smile raised to his
lips.

"Good morning, Officer Lowe," the three women said
in unison, and then collective laughter flooded the library,
filling the room with new life.

"May I?" Jace said, removing his hat and stepping deeper into the room. "I'd like to have a word with you ladies if you can indulge me a few moments of your time. I have something important to discuss, and I think each one of you will want to hear what I have to say." He cleared his throat. "It's pretty important. And I'm guessing I owe it to you since you helped crack the case wide open."

The sincerity in his voice instantly grabbed their full attention and they all dropped their collective duties to go and meet with the officer.

"I'm guessing this is about the case? Did you officially charge Paul? Rain clutched her heart, waiting.

Jace held up a palm to stop her. "I think we're gonna need to back up a bit. There are some unconnected dots that I need to fill in for you so that you can completely understand the full picture."

Rain felt confused. After not hearing from the police department, she'd imagined everything had been pretty cut and dry. Instead of barraging Jace with a million questions that were instantly forming in her mind, though, she waited patiently for him to continue.

"The man that was murdered, out by your outhouse, was not who you think he was," Jace said.

"What?" Julia asked, her tone bewildered. Which Rain imagined, pretty much summed up the astonishment of all of them, including herself.

"Of course he was!" Rain said finally with conviction. "We have the proof!"

Jace shook his head. "I'm sorry, Rain, that's where you're mistaken."

Marge clutched the sleeves of her blouse and raised her hands to her heart. "The man that died wasn't my nephew then. Did I hear you correctly, Officer Lowe?" she asked. "But that doesn't make sense, because Rain told me how my sister's baby didn't die. And she found the birth certificate of my nephew Thornton to prove it!" She tapped her foot impatiently on the floor, making a clicking sound.

The ladies shared another look of confusion before Marge added, "Wait! Luis wrote about the baby. It was written in the book." Marge left the group and quickly returned with the copy of *Always You* in her hand. She handed it to Jace. It's all right there," she said, lifting her chin. "Here, read it for yourself. I'm not sure if Rain told you my secret yet, but I'm ninety-nine percent positive my sister Maggie was the muse in the novel. It's all right there in plain ink." She tapped the top of the book, clicking hard with her polished fingernail as the officer held the copy of *Always You* in his hand.

Jace held up a hand of defense. "I'm not saying that there wasn't a baby, or that the baby didn't survive. What I'm saying is, the man who was murdered out by the outhouse was not Thornton Hughes." Jace handed Rain the copy of her grandfather's book, and she held it protectively to her chest.

Julia and Rain shared another puzzled glance before he continued.

"The man who was bludgeoned to death was not your uncle. It was a man who had stolen your uncle's identity.

The murder victim was a thief and a conman. He'd been doing time in a federal prison, was released on good behavior, and was using Thornton Hughes's identity to start over. The man that was killed was not any relation to either of you. The man who was murdered by the outhouse was Neil Abbotsford."

"Neil Abbotsford? But how?" Rain asked, still stunned from the news. "How do you know this for sure?"

"After looking into his wonky financials, we put the man's DNA in CODIS, which is the national criminal database, and we got a hit. I'm not going to explain the nuts and bolts of everything, but something about the way Neil handled his bank accounts and credit cards tipped us off. The guy was convicted of fraud in the early nineties and was released early for good behavior. But, apparently, for Neil, old habits die hard. So, in answer to your question, we found out by good ole' fashioned policework." He winked.

Rain shook her head, unable to comprehend what she was hearing. "What about my mother? Are you saying the man she was getting to know, was nothing but a fraud?"

"That's exactly what I'm saying. We believe Neil was trying to get close to Willow to solidify the stolen identity. He was attempting in every aspect to *become* Thornton Hughes. Because he couldn't very well use his own identity. The guy had priors!" Jace threw a hand in the air before resting his hands comfortably back on his hips. "Neil used the identity to reinvent himself in order to become an upstanding citizen in the community. Someone who was tight with your mother and the Lakers, who could then wheel and deal in the Real Estate market. By impersonating Thornton, Neil thought he could cash in the bills to a local collector with no chance of ever getting caught. However, there were a few wrinkles in his plan. We discovered the real Thornton Hughes had already filed an Illinois police report of a burglary that had happened at his parents' home located on the Wisconsin/Illinois state line. That's when the unsealed adoption records were stolen. Neil took those records and decided to seek out Thornton's biological ties and immerse himself into the family. We believe, once this was accomplished, his cohort, Paul, had plans to kill the real Thornton. It was only a matter of days, possibly hours. Thankfully though, that plan was stopped in its tracks." Jace waved a finger between Rain and Julia. "And really, kudos to you two gals, because if it wasn't for you catching Paul in the act of burglary, we might've lost him with nothing concrete to hold him on. It gave us the time we needed this week to get our evidence points in line for the DA and build a solid case."

Rain and Julia exchanged a quick smile.

"And your actions may very well have saved Thornton Hughes's life." he added grimly.

"So, this was all for money." Marge said with a sad shake of her head. "What a terrible shame."

"Yes, the report suggested that the money found in the refrigerator, belonged to Thornton's adoptive parents." Jace nodded.

"So, the money was stolen? That's why Neil hid the treasury bills in the refrigerator?" Julia asked.

"Yes, the money was stolen. We traced the serial numbers and that's how we found the real Thornton and the report he'd filed out of Illinois. Neil hid the money inside the refrigerator because he didn't want the owners of the rental to find it. They knew they needed to trade the bills in to a collector before the money was spent, otherwise it would trace back to them," Jace answered.

"Wait." Rain held up a hand to interrupt them. "I'm still a bit confused about the money . . ."

Jace continued, "Thornton's adoptive parents owned the bills as part of their treasury collection. And Thornton had been willed them upon his adoptive father's recent death. That's how the thieves worked; they followed the obituaries in the newspapers to find their next victims. When they realized how rare some of the five-hundred-dollar bills were, they realized they wouldn't be able to cash in without getting caught. One five-hundred-dollar bill from 1928 is worth over ten thousand dollars alone! The collection added up to well over $250,000. Anyhow, it was then they decided to completely steal his identity, right down to playing the part of a family member. When they studied Thornton's past, they realized he'd been adopted through unsealed records, and continued the charade. The real Thornton shared with the police department that he never looked for his biological parents as he felt his adoptive parents were so good to him, he didn't want to hurt their feelings. We believe Neil would've stopped at nothing to play the part of your uncle—Willow's brother. Once everyone in town was spreading gossip about an affair between the two of them, it made it even easier for Neil and Paul to use your parents as a ruse. Paul perpetuated that idea of an affair and used it to his advantage as a perfect alibi, allowing your father to hopefully take the hit."

Julia interrupted with an upturned palm. "Wait. You said *them*. And brought Paul into the mix."

"Yes. Neil and Paul were in this together. The two met in the Illinois State Federal Penitentiary."

"So, the German friend, Paul, wanted to frame my father for Neil's death behind the outhouse? And create the perfect alibi for himself? Then why did he kill his partner? Why did this Neil character have to die if they were working this burglary plan together?"

"The motive comes down to plain ole' greed. What Neil didn't realize is that Paul was not only convicted of fraud back in the day, there were allegations he'd also committed murder, but the DA couldn't get those charges to stick. The state lost out on a technicality. We also have a hunch that Neil wasn't quite ready to add murder to his rap sheet. The two argued about whether or not the real Thornton should die. Unfortunately for Neil, he picked the wrong partner to collaborate with. Paul got greedy, it's as simple as that. We don't think that he ever had any intention of sharing those bills. Although, he, too, wasn't the smartest tool in the shed because little did he know that Thornton's adoptive parents had the serial numbers of those bills insured. So, he'd have been caught anyway if he spent even one five-hundred-dollar bill. They both thought if they found a collector to buy the bills and then hide the money in real estate dealings, such as the new condo complex, no one would catch on to their scheme."

"So, is that where Brock fits in to all of this?" Rain asked.

"Yes, Neil had heard that Brock was a coin collector and gave him one of the rare five-hundred-dollar bills—a rare 1928 worth over ten grand, to see if he could find a buyer for the entire collection. He'd promised Brock if he found a buyer, he'd give him more than fair deal on one of the new condos he was planning to develop. Brock still had the rare bill in his possession after Neil's death, but hung onto it for fear it would implicate him in the crime."

"I could see how that would put him in a sticky situation." Julia agreed. "I'm surprised Neil didn't use Brock as the scapegoat instead of Rain's father to take the hit for all of this."

"Yeah, me too." Jace said.

"So, Paul tried to frame my father by stealing the jacket? That was his plan? And he would've gotten away with it!" Rain said, her tone rising with each additional word.

"That's right." Jace nodded. "With all the gossip around town, it made it easy for them to go along with it. We found your father's Chicago Cubs jacket at the location Paul was staying, a rental in the next town over. Thornton, aka Neil, was the one who tipped him off about the fact that no one would be caught DEAD wearing Chicago gear in Wisconsin—except your father."

Rain interrupted. "Paul said he was renting a cottage about a mile from my house. Guess I shouldn't be surprised that he lied about that, too."

"I'm not surprised he lied to you. Most criminals return to the scene of the crime to cover their tracks. He probably wanted to prompt you to see if you'd seen the murder. He didn't know Willow's daughter was expected at the cabin," Jace answered. "Or he was attempting to return the jacket, but you were home and thwarted that plan, too."

Rain chewed on her lip, "It's still unclear to me. How did he even know about the jacket?"

Jace continued, "Your mother was the one who gave the idea to Thornton's imposter and shared how it was the joke around town that your father wears a billboard for the Cubs, so he stole it one night after spending time with your mother and then gave it to Paul. Neil was attempting to link your father to the case, making himself virtually invisible as a suspect. His main goal was to frame your father for the murder. Unfortunately, they fought over the money, and Neil took the blunt force trauma to the head, but Paul kept the alibi," Jace added shifting his weight and then leaning against a bookcase for support. "He thought by implicating someone else, there would be no other suspects and the case would close."

"So that's why Paul was attempting to return the jacket and put the key back inside the outhouse," Rain said allowing the thoughts to flow.

"The perfect crime," Julia uttered.

"Not exactly perfect," Jace said. "We would've easily been able to corroborate Rain's father being in Japan. A simple plane ticket would've verified the truth if it had come to it."

"Does my mother know?" Rain asked.

"That we're not entirely sure of yet. We're getting our information from Paul, which is spotty at best. We haven't been able to get hold of Willow yet either. So, I'm pretty sure all of these new revelations will come as a surprise to her as well," Jace said, slipping his hat back on his head and adjusting it.

"Back the train up. Tell me more about this guy you arrested for the crime. This cohort guy, Paul. Might I add, the guy Rain almost castrated?" Julia giggled. "Well actually, I kinda did the deed with my foot too. That had to hurt." She grimaced. "Anyhow, who is he? Is his real name Paul?"

"His name is Everett Kahn."

Julia giggled and shared what was on her mind, "Khan? Any relation to Chaka Khan?"

"I don't know what I'm going to do with you, sis." Jace wagged a finger at Julia. "This isn't funny business." But he, too, couldn't seem to contain his smile.

"I know, I know." Julia waved her brother off with a fluttered hand. "I'm just trying to lighten the mood. We've had a bit of a crazy start for Rain's inauguration back up here in the Northwoods. A little unfair for a reunion, don't you think?" She grinned. "I'm just trying to help ease the tension, cut me some slack, will ya?"

"Speaking of reunions . . ." Jace let the comment linger while he lifted away from the bookcase and straightened his back, to seemingly ease a kink that needed readjusting.

"Then if Neil is not Thornton, where's the real Thornton Hughes? Where is my nephew?" Marge prompted. "Apparently you've spoken with him and he has his money and his ID back?" she leaned in expectantly.

"That's exactly what I was about to tell you. I have some even better news that will lighten the mood and make Rain feel a little more welcome to the Northwoods. At least I think so." Jace nodded.

The three women leaned in closer to the officer with expectation.

"Yes, Marjorie it's true your sister Maggie had a baby. And that baby survived. He's out on the deck lakeside, waiting to meet his aunt." His eyes then trailed to Rain. "And his niece."

Rain gasped. "What? You're kidding?"

"That's right. The real Thornton Hughes is here. And he's anxious to meet you both," Jace said with a trickle of pride in his voice.

*   *   *

The real Thornton Hughes walked across the deck to greet them. A spitting image of her grandfather, it was utterly uncanny, Rain thought, as she took in the sight of her uncle for the first time. He was tall like Luis. Same bulbous nose, same kind eyes, same wild hair, though devoid of the white strands she remembered in her grandfather's mane.

Thornton greeted his aunt first. "It's lovely to meet you," he said extending a hand to her. Marge's eyes misted as she took in the sight of him. "It's lovely to meet you, too, dear. I see my Maggie in you." She smiled weakly before extending her hand to have Rain join in closer to them.

"Hi, I'm Rain," she said. "It's a real pleasure to have this opportunity. Thank you for coming. I can't imagine what the last few weeks have been like for you." She still couldn't believe the real Thornton, her grandfather's child, was standing right in front of them.

"Actually, I'm the one who's sorry for what you had to go through on my behalf and what has brought us here today. However, I must admit, it's been a lifetime of wondering and questioning for me to locate my bloodline. I never felt I should, as I was loyal to my adoptive parents' wishes. They'd been so very good to me. I was told early on that my biological father searched to find my mother to learn the truth, as he never really believed that she'd died while giving birth. When my father found out about me, he was filled with shame and remorse. My adoptive parents encouraged me not to contact him, because they told me that he'd never told his current wife about his past . . . or me, for that matter . . . I also learned my biological grandfather strongly disapproved of my parents' relationship and if we reconnected it just would bring more harm than good . . . but I'm happy to finally hear the other side of the story regarding my birth. So, thank you," Thornton said with obvious deep gratitude. "I'm hoping you'll be able to fill in a few gaps."

When Thornton smiled it was like looking directly into the eyes of her grandfather, Luis. She was saddened that her grandfather had felt so much shame that he'd hidden the birth certificate from everyone in his family and selfishly held his own grief. Rain plucked the book from beneath her arm and handed it to him. Her eyes filled as she handed him the copy of *Always You*. "A story about your biological parents. I think you should have this. I'm sure it'll fill in a few of those gaps you were referring to." She presented the novel as if she was handing over something sacred. And she was, the story of his biological parents—their true love story. "Your father wrote this, he's the author."

"Thank you," he said, and his eyes danced with elation just as her grandfather Luis's had. The mannerisms so similar, it instantly transported Rain back to her youth. It was like looking back in time.

Rain couldn't help but smile inwardly with pride. She wondered if it reflected on her face, too.

Rex came and jumped on Thornton's leg excitedly. As if he was reconnecting with an old master.

"Rex! Rexy! Stop that!" Marge scolded. The older woman then turned to her nephew and said, "I'm so sorry for my dog's behavior."

"It's all right," Thornton said calmly as he knelt graciously to pet the pup.

"He gets a little overexcited sometimes, I think he just needs a run out on the grass." Marge said apologetically.

"Shall we?" Thornton said, tapping his leg and leading the dog down the deck stairs and onto the grass. Marge followed, but Rain stayed behind to give them a moment alone to converse, and to get to know each other.

Rain leaned her arms atop the deck railing and watched from a distance as Thornton and Marge reconnected. The waves curled onto shore rhythmically, like breaths of time, breathing in and out—in and out.

Rain realized then that she'd finally honored her grandfather's writing, as she watched the two bridge the gap of lost years between them. Marge's introduction to her sister Maggie's son, and a man seeking the truth of his ancestry. She couldn't erase the shame of her great- grandfather, Lorenzo, for keeping them apart this long, but somehow, finding the truth, and uncovering the real story, made it all better somehow.

As she looked around and felt her heritage wrap around her like a giant hug, it was if she'd never left the Northwoods, never been with Max, and felt as if she was now living, a different chapter, in a completely different novel.

Rain realized, after carrying the torch, that she was now the writer of her own unwritten story. Sometimes within a storyline the details could easily be overlooked, or exaggerated, or are nowhere near the truth. She still had the chance to change the narrative of her story and move forward. And many blank pages begged to be written as she looked over her shoulder and noticed Jace sending her a wide, satisfied grin. And Julia wiping a tear from her eye as she, too, watched everything unfold.

One thing Rain felt, deep within her gut, and she was sure of it . . . *she had found home.*

Recipes

Rain's Pesto Chicken Marinade for the perfect summer barbeque

4–6 chicken breast fillets, pounded thin

1 cup loosely packed Fresh basil (Rain suggests if you have access to a local farmers market, that's a great place to find some!)

1 tbsp chopped fresh oregano (ditto on the farmers market!)

4 garlic cloves

½ cup parmesan cheese

¼ cup lemon juice

1 tbsp Dijon mustard

¼ cup olive oil

*skip the pine nuts (can't find them at the local market in the Northwoods of WI anyway)

Fresh pasta noodles or serve with roasted vegetables on the grill

Directions:

1. Pound the chicken with a mallet within ½ inch thickness (then set aside)

2. Place the basil, chopped oregano, garlic, parmesan, lemon juice, and Dijon in the food processor, and process until combined.

3. Gradually add the olive oil, with the processer running, until smooth.

4. Reserve ½ cup pesto

5. Coat the chicken fillets with the remaining pesto and marinate at least an hour or overnight if time permits. (If marinating overnight, be sure the chicken is in a sealed tight container—freezer bag or plastic wrap—so that basil doesn't turn brown.)

6. Place chicken on a disposable pan and cook under a medium grill for 5 minutes on each side or until cooked through, brushing with any remaining marinade during the cooking process.* Can throw on the grates at the end to sear lines.

7. Serve over buttered noodles with remaining pesto or with roasted root vegetables or roasted Yukon gold potatoes.

Acknowledgments

Enormous gratitude to Sandy for treating my career as sacred as her own. Equal gratitude to my editor and her eagle eye. I grow more as a writer with each additional book, and it's all because of you, Faith. And everyone at TEAM Crooked Lane Books. Thanks to Jesse Reisch for the fabulous cover design. Thanks to Linda for being a cheerleader and confidant. Thanks to Heather for first draft read and enormous support. Mark, thanks for readjusting our Covid-19 life to making the writing of this manuscript possible, despite the logistical challenges . . . And all the discussion walks that were *priceless*! Most of all, thanks to YOU readers. For allowing me into your home, your life, and your time, to take you on what I hope is a journey of escape to the Northwoods.